# SECRETIVE ROYAL

CLUB ROYAL, BOOK TWO

ELOUISE EAST

# CONTENTS

# DEDICATION

*To Emma,*
*For believing in me and helping me keep the magic alive when I*
*falter*

# SUTCLIFFE ROYAL FAMILY

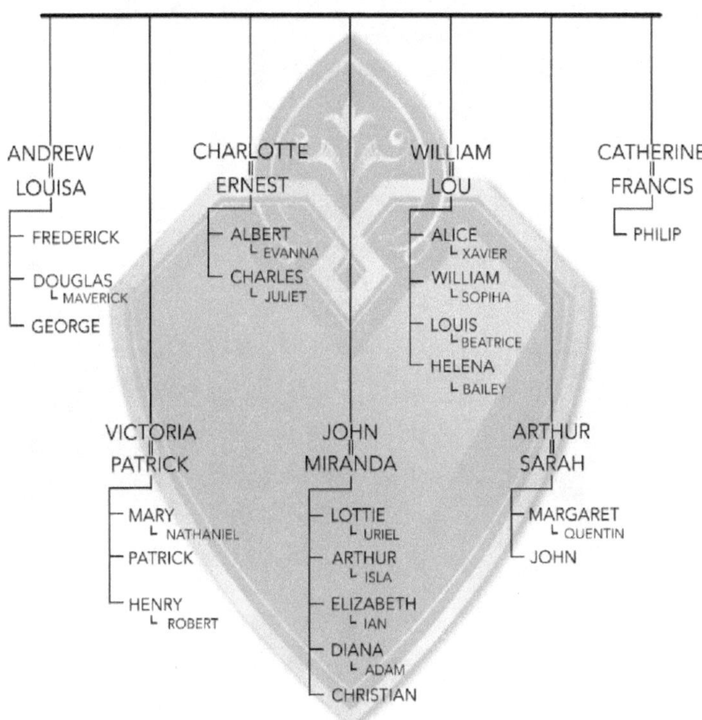

LIST OF CHARACTERS
(ALPHABETICAL ORDER)

Albert, cousin, Charlotte and Ernest's child
Alice, cousin, William and Lou's child
Andrew, King of England, Henry's uncle
Arthur, cousin, John and Miranda's child
Charles, cousin, Charlotte and Ernest's child
Charlotte, Henry's aunt
Christian, cousin, John and Miranda's child
Clarice, Club Royal's receptionist
Damon, Frederick's best friend
Douglas, cousin, Mav's boyfriend, Andrew
    and Louisa's child
Elton, owner of The Den, friends with
    Robert
Ernest, Charlotte's husband
Finn, Robert's friend and employee
Frederick, cousin, heir to the throne,
    Andrew and Louisa's child

George, cousin, Andrew and Louisa's child

Hadley, Robert's sister

**Henry, sixth in line to the throne**

Kean, Henry's childhood friend

Liam, pup named Barney from The Den

Lou, William's wife

Louisa, Queen Consort, Henry's aunt

Maverick, social media manager, Douglas's
   boyfriend

Naomi, Robert's friend and employee

Oliver, Club Royal bartender

Ophelia, Robert's sister

Patrick, Henry's brother

**Robert, florist**

Simon, Kean's late brother

Talon, bad guy from Rogue Royal

Vincent, sleazy bad guy

William, Henry's uncle

Winnie, Robert's mother

Xan, submissive at Club Royal

Zachary, Robert's father

# SECRETIVE ROYAL

# HENRY

Henry Sutcliffe followed his best friend down the hallway to a quieter room, one with large windows, so they didn't have to peer over several people's shoulders to see the fireworks. He'd almost cancelled his appearance at the New Year's party because the thought of being around a lot of people sent his stomach fluttering and his hands trembling. The only reason he turned up at all was that Kean Seymour had persuaded him to come.

A pink glow lit up the room before it darkened once more, and a loud bang sounded. They wandered closer to the window until the night sky filled Henry's vision. Bundled up in coats, scarves and hats, some guests chanced the winter weather in the garden, but he was content staying in the warmth.

"They've put on a splendid display so far," Kean said before sipping his bourbon.

Henry nodded. "They have. I must admit to expecting lower quality. Shame on me, I suppose."

"You can't always trust the Hightons to do things properly." Kean chuckled.

They stood in silence as more fireworks exploded in the sky, and the slight scent of smoke filled the air even though no windows were open. The silence was something Henry appreciated about Kean. He didn't push for conversation. After knowing Henry for over ten years, he understood Henry was a thinker, not a conversationalist.

"Do you need another drink?" Kean asked.

"No, I'm good." He had barely started the one Kean had originally given him upon entering the house.

He heard Kean moving about behind him, glasses clinking as he refilled his tumbler, then he returned to Henry's side. He glanced at him and frowned when Kean threw the drink back all in one go and grimaced.

"Looks like you're trying for Dutch courage, Kean. Which girl are you aiming to get into bed tonight?"

Henry stared at him, which was not a hardship as he was gorgeous. He blinked rapidly and returned his gaze to the display outside the window. Thoughts like those were going to get him into a world of trouble, and he pushed it down, reminding himself he was straight and single and happy to be both.

"None."

It took a moment before Henry figured out Kean was answering his question. He opened his mouth to answer, but Kean stepped closer, coming to stand in front of him. A muscle clenched in Kean's jaw as he stared at Henry.

"Twelve years of wanting this but not knowing if you were of the same mind has driven me insane. I have nothing to lose now."

Henry frowned, not understanding until Kean leaned forward and kissed him.

Startled, Henry pulled away. "What?"

His heart raced, and he panted, the noise sounding loud in the quietness. What the hell was going on? Kean knew he was straight. Why was he kissing him?

Kean stepped forward again, but Henry retreated. They did the same dance until Henry stopped against a wall. Kean rested his hands on either side of Henry's head, the two inches height difference appearing like more.

"What are you doing?" Henry asked.

"Taking what we need," Kean murmured, lowering his lips back to Henry's.

Kean's words circled in Henry's head, and he didn't realise he was kissing Kean back until the man groaned. Henry paused, breath stuttering, but Kean kissed him again. All thought fled except for the feeling of…he had no idea what he was feeling, but everything he had suppressed for the last twenty years exploded out of him like the fireworks in the distance. He gripped the back of Kean's jacket, holding him tightly, not wanting this to end. Trembling started in his whole body, and he locked his legs to keep from falling.

He knew it was wrong. He knew he shouldn't be doing this, but he couldn't stop.

Bourbon and some sort of spicy mixture were what Kean tasted like, and Henry knew he could become addicted to it. Kean's tongue massaged his own as the kiss gentled, but when it let the voices surface in Henry's brain, he felt desperate and held Kean harder.

"Henry?"

Like a bucket of cold water, his cousin's voice had him pushing Kean away and wiping his mouth, closing his eyes in mortification.

"Henry, it's okay," Kean said.

Henry held up his palm, not wanting Kean any closer. He couldn't be what Kean wanted. Henry's life was not a fairy tale, no matter what the public's perception was of royalty. He inhaled, steeling himself against what he knew he would see when he spoke his next words. He stared straight at Kean.

"Never do that again."

He clenched his jaw against the pain that swam across Kean's face, but Kean nodded sharply once. Henry pushed away from the wall, steadying himself with a hand before stalking to the door where his cousin Frederick—the heir to the throne—currently stood.

"Henry—"

"This never happened," he said for Frederick's and Kean's ears only and stormed out of the room and house.

*Eleven months later*

"Henry dear, would you be so kind as to help Douglas and Maverick with organising and setting up the children's event?" His mother, Princess Victoria Elizabeth

Sutcliffe, smiled at him from her perch on her favourite chair in one of the informal living rooms of Bagshot Park. She wore her long, black hair in a clip attached at her nape and a pristine royal blue dress and jacket as if she planned to go out for the afternoon.

"Of course, Mother. I don't have any plans for today. You're looking lovely. Are you going somewhere?"

Henry sat in a chair opposite her and crossed his legs, linking his fingers and resting his elbow on the arm. He had his mother's looks. No one would ever doubt he was hers, and she had the looks of the royal line. Their features still ran strongly through both the male and female descendants.

"I'm going to meet Andrew and William for a late lunch."

The easy-going way she spoke of a king and a prince would shock the public, but they were, after all, her brothers. Henry smiled at the thought of her calling them by their titles all the time.

"I'll let you finish getting ready." He stood and leaned over to kiss her cheek while Victoria patted his cheek and smiled.

"Thank you, sweetheart. Will we see you for dinner today? Charlotte and Ernest are coming. Albert and Charles might be there, too."

Henry's heart dropped, and he licked his lips and cleared his throat. "I think I'll spend some time with Douglas and Maverick. I've not seen them for a while."

"All right. Have a good time."

He bid goodbye and left the room, leaning back against

the door with a heavy exhale. Under no circumstances would he purposefully put himself in a room with *that* part of the royal family. He'd seen, on more than one occasion, how unkind and manipulative they could be, and he would avoid them at all costs. Uncle Ernest and Cousin Albert weren't too bad, but Aunt Charlotte and Cousin Charles were horrible people. He put Uncle Ernest and Albert into the same box as the other two because they never spoke out against them. Even if they didn't believe in the rants about homosexuality being an abomination, they never said a word.

He strode to his wing of the house, glancing at his watch. The hallways of the main house were not as regal as some properties within the royal family, but they were as tall. Sometimes, it felt as though Henry was an ant bumbling along the shiny floor with how high the ceilings were. His wing, though, was his pride and joy, and no one would ever take that away from him. It was far too big for him with sixteen rooms, but he hoped one day to fill them with his own family.

The thought soured his mood. He needed to stop thinking about a family because he could not have one. Not without too many lies and indiscretions between him and his potential wife. It was the reason he didn't have many sexual relations with people at the club or anywhere else.

Henry shook his head and grabbed what he needed from his rooms. He required little security despite being sixth in line to the throne, so he only took a bodyguard with him when he was attending royal functions, which meant he didn't have to wait to leave. As the drizzle came down, he listened to the radio. What would they ask him to do when he got to Windsor Castle? He'd heard about the event his cousin Douglas had set up for the children in the area. A large Christmas party with bouncy castles and lots of other entertainment and activities to keep the children amused for hours. Luckily, the rooms at Windsor Castle were large enough to have the bouncy castles indoors; there was no chance of the rain cancelling the event.

When he arrived twenty minutes later, he asked where to find Douglas and was sent toward one of the large ballrooms. He smiled at the flurry of activity and chatter of conversation that filled the air when he entered the room. There were people all over the place, scurrying back and forth, catching and fetching things.

"Henry! I wasn't expecting to see you here?"

His cousin hugged him with a back slap, and Henry noticed Douglas's boyfriend beside him. The strength Douglas must possess to take what he wanted and forget about everyone else stunned Henry. Douglas didn't have a care in the world, or at least, it didn't seem like it. Was he even aware of what was said behind his back by some of the family?

He smiled. "I was told you needed some extra hands, and I had some time."

"Great, thanks. Mav, what needs doing?"

Maverick checked the clipboard he had close by and ran a finger down the list. "The flowers?" He raised an eyebrow at Henry. "Would you mind?"

Henry relaxed. This was something he could do. "That's cool. I help Mother in her garden. Flowers don't bother me. What exactly needs to be done?"

Maverick glanced around the room. "Robert!" He waved his hand to get the man to come over. When he did, he introduced him. "Robert, Henry can help with the flowers if that's okay with you?"

Robert was a slim, toned man with short, curly hair, a barely-there moustache and chin beard. He accessorised his look with jewellery and makeup and caught Henry's eye. And not for a good reason.

"Of course. Follow me, Your Highness. I'll show you the plans." Robert pivoted and sauntered back the way he'd come.

Henry didn't follow, staring after him while his stomach fluttered and churned, not knowing if he wanted to vomit. There was no way he could work with that man.

"Everything okay, Henry?" Douglas asked.

Henry started and glanced at them, his cheeks pinking. "Yes, sorry. Off in my own little world. I'll…"

He pointed with his thumb in Robert's direction. His body had other ideas than walking away because he followed in Robert's wake. This wasn't good. This wasn't good at all.

Robert stopped by a table filled with carnations, daisies, chrysanthemums, peonies and freesias. When Henry stepped closer, Robert pointed at a piece of paper. "We have certain flowers in groups depending on colours because they will be part of some games, and the colour code must be spot on. The flowers on this table are not to be used for decoration. We will weave them into crowns for the visiting children. Does the plan make sense?"

Robert held out the paper, and Henry held it up, his eyes glazing over instead of focusing. The scent of flowers overwhelmed the air, but there was still a thread of something else that caught and held his attention. It was as distracting as the man's voice. From Robert's appearance, he wouldn't have expected such a deep baritone to come from his mouth. It was extremely stereotypical of him, but he couldn't help it.

"Does it make sense?" Robert's tone held a bite of dominance, and Henry clenched his whole body to stop any reaction from occurring.

"Yes, it does. Where would you like me to start?" His voice was a little higher than normal, but if he ignored it, maybe Robert would, too.

"Start with these." The man leaned into his personal space and pointed at the far corner of the room.

"Okay." It was far away from this man, so he was happy with that.

"Please remember the colour code. It's important."

Henry nodded. "I can use any flowers on these tables except the table we are currently at, is that right?"

Robert nodded. "Yes."

"Okay."

Henry inhaled deeply and strode to a table closest to the corner he was starting with. He couldn't resist taking one more sniff of whatever cologne Robert was wearing. Shaking his head, he pushed aside any thoughts other than what he needed to do and focused on the colour scheme. This corner was pink, and he found the table filled with pinks of different shades.

His mother loved gardening and had taken it up before she'd met and married his father, then continued it as a hobby. When he was old enough, he began helping her until it became "their" thing. Now, whenever he found her in the garden, he would drop to his knees to help her weed or do things she wasn't as easily able to do at sixty-three—not that she'd ever let anyone say that to her face. Henry had learnt over the years that he needed to approach such things with caution, and instead of asking if he could do it for her, just take over.

He snorted at the idea. Victoria had also taught him how best to arrange a bouquet. She believed that if someone was presenting a bouquet to someone else, they should also know what to do with it. Because of that, he knew the longer stems needed to go to the back, the shorter to the front and the incremental lengths in the middle, creating a type of fan effect. The freesias were good filler flowers for any gaps that were too obvious, add in a little greenery, and it looked great. He tweaked a few things and jumped when someone spoke to him.

"Have you trained?"

Henry glanced to the side. Robert stood with one arm across his chest, his opposite elbow resting on it and his chin on his fingers. The green of his eyes took on an almost iridescent shine with the spotlights on him as they were. His moustache and beard did nothing to hide the shape of his face or the plumpness of his lips, and Henry found himself fascinated once more.

"Prince Henry?"

He blinked. "Sorry?"

Robert tilted his head at him and quirked the side of his mouth. "Have you had training?" He waved towards the flowers. "In flower arranging?"

"Oh, not officially, no. My mother has a large garden that we both spend a lot of time in. She taught me everything I know."

"She's an amazing teacher. Beautiful work." Robert nodded once and pointed to the next corner. "Reds next."

"Yes, sir."

Henry's breath caught at the sight of Robert's eyes narrowing. Robert's back straightened, and his jaw firmed before he lifted his chin to indicate the other corner of the room. Henry swallowed hard and turned away, barely breathing as he followed the silent instructions. Despite the five-inch difference in height, Robert's mannerisms gave him the ability to appear larger than Henry, to be capable of dominating him, and Henry wanted nothing more than to submit.

Something he had only ever done once.

His hands shook as he gathered the flowers he needed for the red corner, and he tried to breathe through it. He'd kept everything inside for many years now. No one was going to make him break. He was sure he just needed to hold on a little tighter for a little longer.

A look over his shoulder—he was *not* checking to see where Robert was—found his gaze caught on a large red rose. He put down the flowers he held and wandered across the room to grab it. When he returned to his table, he found a small knife—his preferred tool—and sliced the thorns off, putting them into the bins provided so that no one hurt themselves on them when clearing up. The rose slipped in, right in the centre of the bouquet, surrounded by the other flowers. He finished up with a few smaller buds to break it up and stood back, staring at it.

Once satisfied, he moved onto the blue corner. Lost in the rhythm of flowers, like he was whenever he was in his mother's garden, he felt free in a way he had felt nowhere else but there. By the time he'd finished the yellow corner, his body had relaxed. He looked around to see where everyone was, but there were fewer people than when he'd arrived. His mouth dropped open when he checked his watch because several hours had passed.

"You were completely in the zone," Robert said, sidling up beside him with a small smile. "You've done a good job. Thank you."

"You're welcome. I enjoyed it."

"You'll have to come work in my shop for a few weeks. You'll soon change your mind when you eat, sleep and breathe flowers." Robert snorted.

"Sounds like heaven to me," he said.

He caught Robert's eye and couldn't look away. When he shivered, he broke away, inhaling shakily. "I, uh, have to go."

Walking away was the hardest and easiest thing he'd ever had to do.

## 2

# ROBERT

"Naomi, I need you in here!"

Robert Martin inhaled, the mix of flower scents tickling his nose. The final flower arrangements for the children's party needed to be finished in an hour, and he was running out of time. Prince Douglas and his boyfriend, Maverick, had done a fantastic job with the children's events, but they had insisted on flower-woven crowns for each child. On any day, this would have been a big ask, but when the royal family requested it, it was more so. His hands never trembled, though. He would get this job finished if it was the last thing he did. He *wanted* this contract, and it appeared he would get it.

That was until Prince Henry arrived. What he could do with flowers made Robert second-guess why they had chosen him for the job. Surely, they could ask the prince to do it? Not that he wanted to do himself out of a job, but the royal family seemed more likely to trust an insider instead of an outsider.

Whatever happened, Robert needed to forget about the prince and concentrate on his work, but he found his thoughts circling back to those long, slim fingers as they created masterpieces. And he wasn't exaggerating, either. What Prince Henry had created had taken Robert years to learn, but maybe it was the same with him. If his mother had taught him, they had probably been working together for years.

"What do you need?"

Robert faced one of his best friends. "Get to it." He nodded at the crowns. "They're damn fiddly, it's taking me longer than I thought."

"Right-o."

He'd met Naomi at college. They'd found a mutual love of floristry and ended up taking the same courses at university. Once Robert had finished his degree, he started working full-time with his granddad. After two years of working with him, Robert took over his business —the man was more than happy to retire at sixty-eight— and he hired Naomi and Finn to help him.

Naomi was a free spirit in that she didn't do anything anyone expected her to do. She lived her life as she wanted to and didn't apologise for it. Robert tried to take a petal off her flower and do the same, but it was difficult when too many people had hurt him. As for Finn, well, he'd turned up for the interview at the flower shop, and the rest was history. They hit it off immediately, and the three of them became inseparable.

"Hold still, Robbie. You have something near your eye, and if you touch it, you'll smudge yourself." Naomi leaned closer, her fingertip brushing against the skin beneath his eye twice before she deemed him eyelash-free.

"Thanks."

Robert took a minute to survey the large ballroom. Despite the number of flowers in the room, it was not overwhelming, probably because of the size of the place. The four bouquets Prince Henry had created sat in the four corners, several small designs sat in the centres of the tables, tall lilies and bamboo leaves were lining the walls just inside the entrance, and single flowers of varying types hung alongside the twinkling lights that dangled around the perimeter of the room. And that was just in this room. Two other rooms had a similar treatment, although fewer flowers, as those rooms housed the bouncy castles.

His phone buzzed, and he pulled it out of his pocket. It was the half-hour reminder.

"Where's Finn?"

Naomi shook her head. "I don't know."

"All right. Keep doing this; I need to find him."

Robert checked around the room but couldn't see Finn anywhere. If the man had gone off to get laid when he should be working, Robert would kick his ass. It wouldn't be the first time, but it might be the last.

He bumped into Finn as he rounded a corner, knocking their heads together.

"Ouch!" Finn said, rubbing his nose.

Robert ignored the pain in his forehead. "I need your help. The crowns need finishing."

"Sure."

He side-eyed Finn. "Where were you?"

Finn grinned. "Not doing what you think I was doing, that's for sure. Not for want of trying, though." He winked.

"Hmm."

They worked together to get the final crowns finished with barely a minute to spare.

"Those look amazing!"

Robert smiled at Prince Douglas. "I'm glad you like them, Your Highness. Your idea was just charming. The children will love them, I'm sure."

Prince Douglas rested his hands on his hips and studied the room. "I think we're as ready as we're going to get."

Maverick stepped up beside the prince, resting a hand on his shoulder. "It's going to be great. Stop worrying." Maverick caught Robert's eye. "He doesn't want to let them down."

"You don't need to worry about that. This is like a kid's dream. I'll get everything tidied away, and we'll be out of your hair so you can finish preparing."

Prince Douglas held out his hand. "Thank you for taking on this job, Robert. I appreciate your hard work. I'll be in touch about the contract as soon as I've recovered from this event." He laughed.

Robert chuckled. "I can imagine that will take a few days. It's fine, Your Highness. Take your time."

He didn't want Prince Douglas to take his time, but he said the words, anyway. He wanted this contract. He didn't need it because his business was doing well, but Robert wanted more. If he couldn't have a family of his own, he wanted a business he could throw his heart into so he wasn't wasting away in a house all by himself.

They cleaned up the mess, throwing everything into the large bins provided, then collected the items they were taking back with them, climbed into the large van and drove back to the shop.

As Finn parked in front of the shop, Robert smiled up at Floresco. The shop had been in the same location since his great-grandfather first opened it in 1959. Handed down father to son until Robert's father said he wasn't interested. Therefore, Granddad had to wait until Robert was old enough to take over.

The Latin name always made Robert smile. Floresco meant to flourish, to thrive, to blossom, and he loved that it could mean flowers or people or a business. Robert thought of it in a business sense, and it helped him focus on his goals and forget about what couldn't change.

"Right, let's get our equipment back into the shop, and you two losers can get lost."

"Hey!" Finn said, pouting and trying to give Robert puppy dog eyes.

Robert shook his head and rolled his eyes, ignoring him. It took them less than twenty minutes before his two best friends hugged him goodbye and climbed into a car. Finn and Naomi shared a two-bedroom flat in the centre of Windsor, while Robert lived above the shop. He locked the doors to the shop, set the alarm and climbed the steps to his place.

He yawned. It was only two in the afternoon, but he was ready to sleep. It could have something to do with being at Windsor Castle since six that morning. The children's event was due to start at four o'clock and last for several hours. He would've loved to see the children's faces when they saw the rooms. They were in for such a surprise.

He jumped into the shower, relaxing under the spray while trying to stay awake, then decided to hell with it and dried himself off, cleansed and moisturised his face and climbed into bed. He'll give himself three hours, and with that thought, he fell asleep.

His alarm pulled him back to the land of the living, and he groaned. It hadn't been his smartest decision to go to sleep, but he'd needed it because he was going out that evening. His warm cocoon called his name, but he wrapped his dressing gown around him and padded to the kitchen.

He dialled his phone. "Hi, Mrs Li. My usual order, please. Thank you."

While he waited for his takeaway to be delivered, he made a coffee to wake him up a bit. Finn and Naomi were meeting him at The Den—an unoriginal name for a BDSM club, but one that resonated with Robert for some reason—later that evening. He wished Finn and Naomi would get their heads out of their arses and try a relationship. They'd been tiptoeing around each other for years.

Should he push them? He was on the edge of doing it to give himself some peace.

A knock sounded, and he smiled at the delivery guy and paid cash before shutting the door again and inhaling the scent of Chinese food. It wasn't the healthiest, but he ate takeaway probably three times a week and made his own versions of Chinese food for the other four days. He needed to learn to cook true Chinese instead of the knock-off versions he already knew, but he never had time.

Once he'd eaten, he showered again and dressed in his leather suit. This suit was his favourite of all his leather-wear, but it was a bitch to clean. It was a full-length suit; therefore, it covered him from his ankles to his neck to his wrists, and there was a patch on his front and back stating "Handler" with a cute paw print underneath. His calf-length boots and leather belt accessorised the outfit. He stood in front of the mirror in the bathroom and applied some dark green eyeshadow, black eyeliner and black mascara, along with a hint of gloss on his lips. There would be no jewellery to add because he didn't wear jewellery when he went to The Den. It was always busy, and the jewellery could get caught on something, scratch someone or be pulled out, and none of those results were worth it.

When he was ready, he called for a taxi and texted Naomi to tell her he was leaving. They were already on their way, so he'd meet them at the bar.

The Den sat on the outskirts of Slough and, from the outside, could seem a little seedy-looking. The neon flashing name would've been better served as a solid, non-flashing design, but to each their own.

Robert thanked the driver and headed inside, signing in at the reception desk in the foyer before wading through the crowds and into the main bar area, heading towards the bar. He had no hope of seeing anyone over the heads of the people crowding around. He started at one end of the bar and weaved through the masses until he found his best friends, already sharing a drink.

"Hey, you made it!" Finn said, passing over an unopened bottle of water.

"Yeah." He frowned at the sheer number of people squashed in the space. "Have they not opened upstairs yet?"

Naomi shook her head. "No, although it should be any time now. Hopefully, half of this lot will move up there once it has."

The Den had two floors. The main floor, which they were on now, was a basic club with dancing, a DJ and smaller sectioned-off areas for the voyeuristic and exhibitionists. The upper floor was where the more diverse club members went. It held everything else from age play to bondage play to pet play, which was where he was heading. Naomi and Finn were more into bondage play—another reason they'd be a perfect fit for each other—and when all three of them went upstairs, they split up knowing that if one of them left, they'd send a message to the other two. Therefore, no one stayed behind alone without meaning to be. It was a safety net they had never needed and, hopefully, never would.

Robert drifted around the area, nodding his head in greeting at those he knew, smiling at the boys, girls and pets he saw. A group of three handlers sat on two sofas bracketing the top part of a pet play area. The club spread a large area of soft mats out, and Robert counted seven pups playing. It was not unusual to have more pups than handlers, and it made his job a little easier.

He was a handler to those pups who didn't have one. Most of the time, he would only be their handler for the night, but because of the lack of handlers, he often took care of a pup more than once. It was a shame that some pups weren't able to find permanent handlers, but there was a shortage of them in the community.

He took a seat on the end of one sofa, greeting those who were sitting, resting one arm across his knees and letting his other arm hang forward, so the pups could sniff at him if they wanted to.

He was patient and received a reward when the first pup came across, gave a small sniff and pulled back, before moving in for another one. Robert didn't move, allowing the pup to explore him. When a ball came bounding past the pup, Robert lost the pup's interest as he scampered across the mat, chasing after it with the other pups.

Robert didn't mind. When something caught a pup's attention, it was difficult to regain their attention without training, and some of these pups didn't have training.

He waited patiently, occasionally sipping his water, until one pup—whose name was Dodo—nudged his hand. Robert glanced at the pup's neck, seeing no collar to identify him as being owned, which he knew anyway but wanted to check, and murmured, "Do you want some scritches, pup?"

A short, sharp bark and a wagging tail was his answer, and Robert turned his hand to smooth over the pup's brown head before scratching beneath the pup's jawline.

"Would you like a handler tonight, pup?" Another bark. "We need to have a chat first, okay?

He had played with Dodo before, and the pup knew those words were his cue to sit beside Robert and go over what they expect to get from their night. Although they had played before, Robert still asked the same questions to ensure nothing had changed before he allowed Dodo to get back into his pupspace. As Dodo went for the ball Robert had thrown for him, he caught the attention of a server and requested a drink for the pup. He would be thirsty because Robert hadn't seen him drink anything since he'd sat.

The server returned with the water and Dodo's choice of snack and left again. "Dodo! Here, boy."

Dodo came scampering over and stopped in front of Robert with his head tilted.

"Good boy. Have a drink."

Robert placed the straw in the pup's mouth and allowed him whatever amount he wanted. When Dodo pushed it away with his nose, Robert placed the bowl of small snack pieces on the floor between his feet. It would stop any of the other pups from trying to get at it. While Dodo ate, Robert stroked over his head and back in soothing motions.

A loud couple of barks and a small yip sounded through the air, gaining their attention. One handler had brought out some squeaky toys. Dodo's tail wagged, and Robert could feel the tension in him, but he held still despite his legs twitching to join in. Dodo whined and nudged a hand at Robert's leg until Robert smiled and patted his head.

"Good boy, Dodo. Go on, pup."

Dodo shot off, chasing after the squeaking toys and rolling over the other pups. He had never understood why he needed to be a handler, but as serenity washed over him, he didn't care why; he only cared that he was home amongst everyone there. One day, he'd love to have a family of his own, but the pups from his past had never seen past his looks. They'd said he was too small, too slender, too feminine to be a handler full-time. He couldn't deal with another refusal or break up, and he'd chosen to focus on what he could do for the community and helping those pups who did not have handlers was the second-best option.

Robert spent a good four hours playing, caring for and praising Dodo before he had to say goodnight to the exhausted pup. He helped Dodo come out of his pupspace and tended to his needs before they parted ways. Every pup was different, the same as every submissive was different in what they needed from their Master or handler. Dodo had needed to feel Robert wrapped around him to tether him as he returned to his human mindset, so Robert had held him, murmured to him and made sure he drank plenty before leaving.

As he descended the stairs, he texted Finn and Naomi, who had both already left messages saying they were leaving, to tell them he was on his way home, and he'd see them on Monday morning.

He climbed into the taxi, staring out at the bright lights winking in and out of existence in the dark sky. The relaxed feeling from playing with pups never lasted long, and soon Robert was back to his usual self, full of self-doubt and painful memories. This was his life now, and he'd better get used to it.

## 3

# HENRY

Several days later, Henry still couldn't stop thinking about Robert. He'd hardly spent any time with the man, but there was something about him that kept Henry's attention even as he strolled around the pet play area at Club Royal—the BDSM club owned and managed by the royal family. The story goes that the club had begun as a secret kink by one of his predecessors, who had a hidden room he solely used for his own plea-sures. When his son lost control, the king had introduced him to it, hoping to curb the sowing of his seeds. More and more family members found out about the kink and became members of the first unofficial get-together. The royal family inducted members into it to bring the family "closer and teach them the control and humility needed to be a royal public figure."

In more recent years, the club allowed a safe place for them to play away from the prying eyes of the media.

There were members of the public who had memberships, but every person completed frequent non-disclosure agreements, and the royal family came down hard on those who broke them. Despite the rumours abounding in the media, no one confirmed anything, and therefore, no one knew for definite if it existed, except for the people who frequented the club.

When Henry had first been told about the club, he'd been in his mid-teens and was unsure what to think. He wasn't a Dominant; he knew that from the beginning, but every royal family member trained as a Dom and learnt everything there was to know about the different kinks because the club catered to everyone and everything. The rules that related to Club Royal had no bearing on any other club. Club Royal's rules were just that…Club Royal's rules. They did things differently than other clubs.

Although Henry didn't feel like a Dominant, he could pretend with the best of them, and he would allow no one to get hurt because of his own feelings. When the time came for his shifts at the club, he made sure he acted the part.

A pup came scrambling up to him, and he smiled, lifting his gaze to the pup's handler and receiving a nod of permission. Henry crouched down, holding his hand out to the pup and allowing him to sniff him until the pup nudged his head under Henry's hand. Chuckling, Henry began petting the pup. The gorgeous black and white hood felt soft under his hands, and he scratched under the pup's ear, laughing as a tremble ran through the little guy.

"Good boy. Are you being a good boy for your handler today, pup? I bet you are," he crooned.

The pup answered in a soft bark and a tail wag before going in a circle a few times and trotting off again. Henry rested his arm on his knee, watching the pups interact on the soft mats provided by the club. This. This was what he wanted. To let go of the burdens of the human mind and be free to play and frolic with other pups. He didn't want to be a handler; he wanted to be a pup, but he couldn't be one. They would see it as too submissive for a member of the royal family.

His mood souring, he rose, concentrating on the excitement he could hear from the mosh. The unhelpful thoughts receded as he focused on the here and now. He crossed over to his perch by the main entrance of the area and leaned against the wall. If he couldn't join in, he could at least make sure everyone had fun.

"Master Henry."

He glanced to the side at his name and smiled at his cousin Christian. Prince Christian was four years younger than he was, but he was as close to him as his own brother and cousins Douglas and Frederick. The five of them—six if you included George on the odd occasion he joined them—spent a lot of time together growing up, and it had changed little as they'd grown older. The club helped them to stay close, but it was away from the confines of the club that Henry could be more himself, even though he was still lying to everyone around him, except Frederick because he knew what had happened.

"Master Christian. I didn't realise you were working tonight."

"I'm taking over for Master Alice. Their family needed them."

Henry frowned. "I hope everyone is well?"

"I believe so, but I don't have the details. I'm taking the floor, but I wanted to check in with everyone before I started."

It was something they all did to ensure they received the most up-to-date information about the happenings of the club. Sometimes, things got missed, so each Master checked in with the other five at the beginning of their shift.

"Nothing's happened anywhere that I'm aware of. In here, all is calm." He chuckled at the sight of four pups tangled in a heap on the mat. "Or as calm as it can be."

Christian squeezed his shoulder and grinned. "I think this area is the most relaxing in the whole place."

"I think you're right."

"I'll catch you later."

Christian placed his forefinger under Henry's chin and slid it forward in a move the six of them did with each other—a reminder to keep their chin up no matter what life threw their way. Henry reciprocated, and Christian left, allowing Henry to wallow in the happiness surrounding him.

Whenever he was in the pet play area, his shift seemed to go a lot quicker than the other times. He wandered to the gender-neutral changing rooms, then veered right to the "Monitors Only" room, setting his thumb against the fingerprint sensor before it allowed him access. Because of their status, the club gave them a separate changing area for security reasons. No one wanted to take the chance that someone would put something in their locker or do something to their belongings. Henry didn't mind the space. As soon as the door closed behind him, his shoulders relaxed even more.

An introvert at heart, Henry tried his hardest to be social when expectations made him, but he'd prefer to be at home, locked away in a room, reading or doing puzzles or playing board games. The latter, for obvious reasons, wasn't always possible alone. Only when his group got together did he feel as calm as when he was alone.

The door clicked open, and he glanced over his shoulder.

"Henry!"

George came barrelling into the room and threw his arms around Henry's shoulders, knocking them both back into the lockers. Henry pushed him away and rubbed the back of his head, a mock frown on his face.

"How come you're always energetic at the end of a shift? I feel like I could sleep for a week."

George lifted his fists and bounced and weaved around in front of Henry, reminding him of a bouncy puppy. "What can I say? I have energy to burn! I'm going out for a drink now. Do you fancy coming?"

Henry's worst nightmare. "Nah, I'm good. I'll head home and get some of that weeks' worth of sleep I need."

George pouted, "Why? I never see you anymore."

Henry laughed. "That's because you're always off gallivanting everywhere. Most normal people go to bed when they're tired, not off somewhere else."

"We're not normal, so that's okay!"

"You're not normal, you mean." Henry ducked back out of the way when George came for him. They tussled for a minute before George backed off.

"Let's set up a time to meet. All six of us. We've not done that for a while," George said.

The door clicked open again.

"I'm in," Henry said.

"In for what?" Freddie, his cousin, asked.

"A night in for the Scandalous Six!" George announced, jumping in the air. "It's going to be great."

Freddie shook his head. "How old are you?" He didn't wait for an answer. "I'm sure we can arrange one. I'll check with Douglas. With him having Maverick now, he might want him to join us."

"I'm happy with that," George said, finally opening his locker and getting changed.

Henry focused on pulling on his clothes while the conversation behind him continued. This was what he enjoyed as much as solitude, the unguarded, relaxed behaviour of his family. The door opened again, and the mood dropped to a more sedate level when Arthur wandered in.

"Evening, Arthur. How is everything?" Freddie asked, ever the peacekeeper.

"Frederick." He nodded towards him and George. "Good, thanks. I don't know if you heard about Isla being pregnant again."

"I hadn't heard! Congratulations to you and your wife! Do you have a due date?"

Henry had to admit, Freddie was good at feigning interest in what Arthur said. Henry could be pleasant, but he could not interact with more than a few words, worried he'd say something that would set off a chain of events he'd not be able to pause.

"Yes, April twentieth."

"That's fantastic. I'm happy for you. What does Evie think of having a new brother or sister?"

Arthur laughed. "She's six. She's already into babies and pretending to be a mum. You can probably imagine what she's like."

Freddie joined in the laughter, and Henry smiled. Arthur often behaved unkindly towards people, but Henry always thought if Arthur had been born to different parents, he would be a nice man.

Henry slid his watch into place, palmed his phone and closed his locker. "I'll see you all soon." Before he could exit, Freddie caught hold of him and said, "Goodbye." The emotion in Frederick's eyes when Henry peered at him overwhelmed him, but he knew what Freddie wasn't saying—he had Freddie's support should he need it. Henry nodded in acknowledgement and trudged to his car. He had a forty-five-minute drive ahead of him before he could lock himself away.

"Henry!"

He pressed the lift button and faced George, reacting on instinct when something came speeding towards him and lifted his hands to catch whatever it was. The wrapper crinkled as he spread it to see what it was. A fudge variety pack. He glanced up at George with a smile.

"Thought you might like some!"

George ducked back into the changing rooms, and Henry got on the lift, still smiling. He waved goodbye to Clarice, the club's receptionist, and sighed when the doors closed. No more having to pretend for the night. He could let go.

The fudge was half gone by the time he reached home. It was bad for his teeth, but he didn't care. Fudge was his favourite treat, and everyone knew it. He slid the half-empty bag into his pocket and yawned on his way to his wing of the house. There was no one around because of the late hour.

When his door closed, he rested against it and exhaled in a rush. Several deep breaths later, he wandered to his bedroom, shedding his clothes along the way and throwing them into the washing basket outside his door. No one entered his bedroom, not even the cleaning staff. He kept his room tidy enough not to warrant it—he even changed his own sheets. No one came into his sanctuary. It comprised his bedroom, his bathroom and a large closet. Staff could access the closet from the living area, but there was a lock on the door to his bedroom, and while the staff could put his clothes away for him, they couldn't gain access to his bedroom. He took his privacy seriously.

He locked his bedroom door behind him and strode for the bathroom, silence consuming him. It was heaven.

His bathroom was bigger than he needed, but he

wouldn't complain. It had an open plan shower in the corner of the room, a large claw-footed bathtub to one side, two sinks and several cupboards and drawers. Once again, this room had a door from the living room but locked from Henry's bedroom.

He'd planned to have a shower and climb into bed, but he was enjoying the solace, so he started the taps on the bath, checked the lock for the main room was in place and re-entered his bedroom to find the book he was currently reading. He made no attempt to hide his love of romance novels, and he grabbed it from his bedside table. The front cover was of a man with his shirt half-open, and the story followed his career as an FBI agent who fell in love with his female colleague. His hand twitched as he stared at it, and in the end, need overrode sanity.

He put the book back and dropped to his knees, reaching beneath the bed for the box he hid under there. He sat back on his heels and, with a shaking hand, lifted the lid. His breath caught as soon as the books came into view. Similar covers to what he had on his bedside table, but the content was slightly different. Instead of male and female main characters, both characters in these books were male.

He licked his lips and chose a book, closing the lid and shoving the box back from where it came. The cover beckoned, and he smoothed a hand across the shiny surface. He stared at the cover while he made his way back to the bath, placing the book on the shelf next to where he would be before slipping out of his underwear and into the steaming hot water.

This was one secret he would never tell.

He got comfortable, dried off his hands and dived into the book. When he shivered, he checked the time and realised he'd been reading for nearly an hour. No wonder he was cold. He climbed out of the bath and set it to drain, then stood under the shower to warm up. Once finished, he dried and pulled on some clean underwear before sliding into bed.

Within seconds, he got up and raced to the bathroom, grabbing the book from the shelf. He dropped to his knees beside the bed and placed it back into the box. Henry returned the box to its hiding place and sat, puffing. He shook his head. That was a close call. If he'd fallen asleep with the book still in the bathroom...he didn't want to think about the repercussions.

Shaking, he tucked himself into bed again and closed his eyes, tears leaking from the corners.

"I need to order some flowers to send to Arthur and Isla," his mother said the following day.

"You have an entire garden full of flowers, my dear. Why do you need to buy some?" his father, Patrick Senior, asked.

After crawling out of bed at eleven o'clock, Henry met his mother and father for lunch. His brother, Patrick Junior, had already left for a royal event, and Mary, his sister, was off with her husband and four children at the park, his mother told him.

Victoria's words registered finally, and Henry lifted his head. "I can get some for you, Mother."

She raised her eyebrows. "Are you sure, sweetheart? I can get one of the staff members to do it."

"I don't mind at all. I don't have any plans today."

His mother smiled at him and patted his cheek. "That would be lovely. Thank you, darling. See, honey. Henry understands. The flowers in my garden are for us to look at. If I used my flowers to give to others, I'd have none left. That might make me selfish, but I love my flowers."

Henry stared at his plate as his stomach completed several somersaults. Why had he offered to get the flowers? *Don't be stupid, Henry. You know exactly why?* He took a bite and chewed, tasting nothing; his mind was already on his destination. A stalker he was not, but he had driven past the flower shop several times in passing over the last few days. Not that he'd seen anyone.

The meal finished, and he told Victoria he would fetch the flowers now and bring them back so someone could deliver them. Henry dashed through the hallways to his rooms, changed his shirt and tried to tame his hair. The sides were easy enough because he shaved them, but the top was longer and had an annoying curl in the front if he didn't glue it down. When it finally did as Henry told it to, he locked his room and headed to his car.

The journey wouldn't take him over twenty minutes, but that would be twenty minutes of wondering what the hell he was doing. It was a bad idea to have come here without security, but he couldn't change it now. He parked on the street, sliding a beanie onto his head to hide his features, hopefully. The hair taming he had done was pointless, but he figured it would be worth it as long as they did not throw him out of the shop.

Floresco had an old-fashioned look about it from the brickwork, but the window displays and signage showed how fun and current it was. He stepped inside, a ding of a bell sounding in the back somewhere, and inhaled, closing his eyes.

"Can I help you?"

A woman he recognised from the children's event stood at the counter, her head tilted, eyes squinting.

"Yes. I'd like a bouquet."

"Okay." She glanced over her shoulder. "Do you know what flowers you would like in it?"

"It's to congratulate someone on their pregnancy. Nothing too overwhelming, though they are past their first trimester, so that might not matter now."

"Let me see what I have in the back. Bear with me."

The woman disappeared, and Henry pulled his shaky hands from his pockets. The layout of the shop was of similar design to many. Shelves and shelves with buckets and buckets of flowers on display in every shape and colour he could imagine. On the wall hung paintings of flowers in various locations. In the glass by the counter, there were accessories to go with bouquets and various other trinkets for sale.

Henry crouched to see what was there and had his nose close to the glass display when someone called his name.

"Prince Henry, to what do I owe the pleasure?"

He rose to stand, threading his fingers together to minimise the trembling. "I'd like a pregnancy bouquet, please." He kept his voice steady, though his whole body shook as he locked gazes with Robert.

Robert lifted his chin and narrowed his eyes. "Don't you usually have other people do your errands for you?" Despite his words, he rounded the counter and headed for some purple chrysanthemums.

"We do, but my mother asked me to do this personally." Not quite the truth, but no one will tell. "It's for a family member."

"Fair enough. How many flowers would you like?"

Henry didn't have a clue. "However many you think would be appropriate."

Robert glanced at him again, then bustled around the shop, gathering flowers. Henry watched him, fascinated by the way he moved. He wore a bright blue silk shirt with a black bow at the neck, tight black jeans and black boots with a small heel. A gentle clinking sounded as he moved, coming from the many coloured bangles on his wrists, and he had long earrings that reached his shoulders. All of that was fascinating, but it was his face that had captured Henry's interest again. Flawless skin, rosy cheeks, a deep purple eyeshadow and glossy lips made a face that was born to break hearts.

Henry blinked when he realised Robert had said something. "Sorry. I missed that."

## 4

## ROBERT

obert touched the corner of his mouth with his tongue, wanting to see what the prince would do. "I said, are these okay?"

Henry tore his gaze away to view the bouquet. "It's perfect."

It was, in Robert's opinion. In shades of purple, pink and blue, it looked exquisite.

"Would you like us to deliver?" he asked. Not that he thought Henry would take him up on the offer.

Henry frowned. "No, I can do that. Thank you." He paid and stared at Robert before grabbing the bouquet and heading to the door.

"Let me get the door for you." Robert was reluctant to let the man leave. There was something about him that… He shook his head.

Robert skimmed past him and inhaled the scent of something rich, nothing to do with flowers. Henry manoeuvred the enormous bouquet out of the door and thanked Robert. As he laid the flowers on his back seat, Robert watched—he couldn't help it. Closing the door, Henry glanced back at the shop, waved and climbed into his car. Robert waited until the car disappeared before returning inside.

"Why was Prince Henry visiting your humble business?" Naomi asked when the door closed behind him.

Robert wanted the answer to that question as well. "No idea why he chose us unless it was to see how well we did what they asked of us outside of the royal contract."

Deep inside, he kept the idea that Prince Henry was there to see him close. At the event last weekend, Robert had seen interest in the prince's eyes but had ignored it, convincing himself he didn't care. But seeing him again had dissuaded him of the notion. He *did* care whether Prince Henry liked him because despite being in his presence for only a short amount of time, the man had left his mark. It took a lot for someone to gain Robert's attention. He was demisexual and didn't feel sexual attraction to anyone he found attractive; he needed an emotional bond before the sexual attraction kicked in. It didn't stop him from wanting to get to know the man, though. There was something about him that called to Robert, and it was unsettling.

"It didn't seem like it to me. Maybe he's sweet on you."

Robert rolled his eyes and went back to his work. Currently, he was creating some Christmas bouquets and other related Christmas designs to photograph and add to their website. He would also put them in the window of his shop. With the countdown to the big day started, he wanted to get as much advertising as possible. It was party season, too, so anyone who had a date might want flowers to give.

The designs took his attention for most of the afternoon, giving Naomi and Finn a breather from his hovering.

"Robert, how are things going?"

He swung around at his grandfather's voice and smiled, walking into the old man's arms for a lengthy hug.

"Everything is going well, Granddad. I've not heard about the royal contract yet, but hopefully soon."

"Pfft." Joseph Martin waved a weathered hand. "They're stupid if they don't give it to you. I can see you've turned your attention to other things in the meantime. That's good." His grandfather was nearing eighty-three and was still as spritely as ever. No one dared tell him to slow down, not even his doctor, especially since his grandfather had lost his wife eight years ago. It was as if he needed to keep busy, which Robert could understand.

"Yes. Christmas waits for no one. What do you think?" He stood beside the spray of greenery dotted with several shades of red flowers and interspersed with small white buds, which he had intended to mimic snowflakes.

"It makes a wonderful display piece. Are you creating smaller versions as well or anything to match it for those who want a unified design throughout their home?"

Robert nodded. "Here." He reached under the counter and pulled out a box of smaller place settings and larger centrepieces. "This is what I have." They were a similar design to the larger bouquet but on a smaller scale.

"Nice. I see you have it covered." Joseph patted him on the shoulder as they strolled to the front of the shop. "Now, what are these two miscreants up to?" He chuckled at Robert's best friends.

"No telling. I feign ignorance at their antics."

Robert snorted and carried the bouquet to the empty window display. He placed it in the far back corner, so it wouldn't stop potential customers from seeing inside the shop. After several more trips, he had all the designs he needed. He secured the larger table centrepiece in the opposite corner for the same reason he did the gigantic bouquet. In the centre, he put a plain white dinner plate with a knife and fork nearest the window, a red napkin twisted into a rose on top, then the smaller flower designs in front of it. He dropped a few fake rose petals over the white sheet, added some fairy lights and glittery baubles, and it looked great.

Needing to see it from the front, he exited the shop and stood with his arms crossed over his chest. The larger bouquet needed moving slightly, but the rest looked good. He needed to remember to put the prices in front of the items. Despite the advertising trick of not having prices on things to entice customers to enter the shop and ask about it, and potentially buy something, Robert hated doing that. He, himself, hated it when he couldn't see a price on something he saw and often refused to check it out inside. So, he didn't do it at his shop; everything in the window had prices.

"Good job, Robert," his grandfather said.

"Thanks."

"Right, I'm off to the supermarket. I'll see you later." Joseph waved a hand above his head as he walked away.

"Bye, Granddad."

Robert returned to the shop, finished the display and retreated to the back room again. His phone buzzed, and he grinned when he saw messages from the group chat he had with his sisters.

*OPHELIA: What on earth is happening? Mama has sent like a hundred messages this morning. Has something blown up I don't know about?*

*HADLEY: No, only your phone apparently. I've not heard anything from her. What did you do?*

*OPHELIA: I didn't do anything! At least, not that she should know about.*

*HADLEY: Bet one of the old biddies saw something and reported back.*

*OPHELIA: Nah, unless they were at Myriad last night, lol.*

*HADLEY: Why were you at Myriad? I thought you hadn't received your confirmation yet?*

*OPHELIA: I received it yesterday! I told you. Or at least, I think I did. I can't remember who I texted and who I didn't, now. Anyway, I got it yesterday, and I visited last night. It is amazing. I can't obviously tell you much about it because of all the NDAs and secrecy and stuff, but it's worth it if you like the kinks I do.*

*HADLEY: I'm surprised you didn't try for a membership at Club Royal.*

*OPHELIA: I did, but I heard nothing back. I would've loved to have confirmed whether the royal family really ran it.*

*ROBERT: And that's probably why you haven't heard from them. You've not exactly been quiet about your views on who runs the place.*

*OPHELIA: That is true. You should root for me, though.*

*ROBERT: Why?*

*OPHELIA: Because then I could put in a kind word about you.*

*ROBERT: I'm doing fine on my own, thanks.*

*HADLEY: Did you get the job????*

*OPHELIA: You got it? Are you working for the royals?*

*ROBERT: I've not heard yet. It looks promising, but the longer they go without saying yes or no makes the chances slimmer.*

*HADLEY: You'll get it, I'm sure. Erika just reminded me to ask if you'd both like to come for dinner tonight?*

*OPHELIA: I can't tonight. I've already made plans but give me a bit more notice, and I'll be there next time. Promise.*

*ROBERT: Sorry, Hads, I can't make it either.*

*HADLEY: You boring old farts. I'll pick a date two months in advance. Will that suit you?*

Robert laughed, putting his phone back in his pocket. Hadley didn't mind. She knew they had more of a social life than she did because Hadley preferred to stay in with her girlfriend instead of going out. Guilt consumed him, though, because he had lied. He had no plans at all, but he needed a night in to himself. Too much had been happening over the past few weeks: getting ready for the royal children's event, setting up for Christmas, finishing up everything for a wedding that had taken place on Friday of last week. It had been a busy few weeks, and he was looking forward to a quiet night in.

"Boss, it's time to wrap up. Do you need either of us tonight?" Finn asked, leaning against the doorframe.

"No, you're free agents. Everything's finished, and we have nothing on the agenda until next Thursday unless the royal contract comes through." Robert finished tidying away the bits and pieces he'd used over the course of the afternoon. "Can you give the floor a quick sweep before you leave, though, please?"

"Sure thing."

Finn left, and Robert finished up, locking everything away that needed to be, including the money from the till. After saying goodbye to his friends, he locked the front door and weaved his way around the flowers to the back door to ensure that, too, was locked. Then he made his way up the stairs to his apartment. As soon as the door closed behind him, he relaxed as if a weight had been lifted. Silence reigned, and he closed his eyes and focused on his breathing. He wasn't prone to anxiety attacks, but he found, as the day wore on, he became wound tighter and tighter and had taken to doing some breathing exercises to get rid of the tension.

As his breathing slowed, his brain calmed, and his thoughts turned to Prince Henry. Robert didn't know a huge amount about him. He had never followed the media circus surrounding them, but he found himself intrigued. Wandering through his apartment to the bathroom, he undressed and stepped under the shower spray, thinking about what his story might be. He'd seen some reports about Prince Douglas's antics—they were hard to miss even when avoiding TV and radio broadcasts—but Prince Henry...he didn't remember ever seeing anything about him.

By the time he'd washed and dried himself, he was feeling more human. He shuffled to the kitchen, wearing his silky negligee covered by a large, fluffy dressing gown. Most people would think it defeated the object of wearing the negligee, but Robert loved the feel of both fabrics. In his book, it was a win-win situation. And besides, no one saw him, so it didn't matter.

Instead of his usual Chinese, he cooked chicken tagliatelle. An easy recipe his mother had taught him when he was a teenager. His mind returned to Prince Henry again while his hands were busy following their instinctual movements. When his food was ready, with another portion cooling for another day, he carried it to the sofa and curled up in the corner. Resting the plate on the arm, he pulled out his phone and searched for the prince's name. Surprisingly, there wasn't a tremendous amount of information about him. There was the usual, "He is sixth in line to the throne," and mentions of who his immediate family was, but there was nothing personal, unlike other royal members.

He spooned a forkful of food into his mouth and

clicked images. His screen filled with images that didn't do the man justice. Most showed his serious face at events like hospital openings or royal parties, but Robert found a few with six stunning men, lounging around, laughing or smiling with each other. He pulled one up and zoomed closer. Prince Henry's face filled the small screen, and Robert couldn't help but smile at the relaxed, open expression. The man was obviously surrounded by people he loved. He mentally made a note of those men: Princes Frederick, Douglas, George, Patrick and Christian, according to the comment under the photo.

Saving the image to his phone, he put it aside, flicked the TV to his current favourite film, *A Dog's Journey*, and finished his meal. Despite the film having a sad storyline, the underlying meaning called to Robert's heart. Who would've guessed the resident aloof, distant guy most people met actually had a heart?

He shook his head and returned his plate to the kitchen, rinsing it before putting it in the dishwasher, and strode for his bedroom. It was early, but he wanted to get some rest. Before he could, he needed to follow the routine he'd enjoyed for the last however many years since he'd been single. He removed his makeup, cleansed his face, cleaned his teeth and moisturised.

His dressing gown dropped to the floor with a shrug of his shoulders, and Robert stood in his silk negligee. He liked how he looked in it, but it was the sensation of the soft, smooth fabric rubbing against his skin that sparked the beginning of his arousal. Wandering back to his bedroom, he climbed into bed after throwing the covers back. He spread himself out, resting his head on the pillow, and closed his eyes. His hands smoothed over skin and silk while he imagined himself with an indeterminable man. His perfect man, if he wanted to be specific.

Being demisexual made relationships difficult occasionally because he needed to have an emotional bond with someone before he could feel sexual attraction to them, but he'd found over the years that he could satisfy his needs by creating the perfect man in his mind. This perfect man had everything Robert could ever want in a partner, and the sexual attraction he felt for this fictional character was more than he'd felt for his past partners, which said a lot about his choices.

The vision of the faceless man swam before him, and his breath hitched. He cocked his leg to the side, sliding a hand under his balls and hefting their weight. The gentle tug ignited a fire in his groin. Sliding his other hand to the base of his shaft, he encircled it with his thumb and forefinger.

As he imagined what the man would do, he reached a hand towards his bedside table, where a dildo and some lube waited. Without opening his eyes, he squirted some lube onto one set of fingers and the other hand, then stroked his cock and pressed against his pucker. When the first finger sank inside, he bit his lip, muting his groan. Working himself open took several long minutes, but by the time he was ready for the dildo, sweat covered him, and he trembled with need.

He coated the seven-inch, lilac, silicone boyfriend and rested it against his hole. Bringing his knees higher, he bore down and pushed the dildo home in one thrust. His mouth opened as a long, drawn-out moan left him. He stroked his cock in time with the thrusts and knew his man would get him there.

"Ah," he panted, licking his lips. "Fuck." Sharp, shallow breaths escaped as he tried to keep his climax from barrelling over him just yet. He wanted this, but he wanted it to last.

Robert circled his hips, allowing the plastic shaft to nudge his prostate, but not enough to send him over the edge. He squeezed his eyes tighter, listening to the words his man would speak, the words of love, tenderness and want. His hand tightened around his cock when he couldn't hold back any longer, and he slid his fingertips to the sensitive nerves located under the head of his dick. As his man pounded into him in his mind, he followed directions with his dildo while his fingers flicked and grazed and tapped against the nerves with enough familiarity that Robert's orgasm crashed over him within seconds.

His stomach clenched as his muscles contracted until his movements became sporadic and shaky, then stopped. He collapsed against his sheets and allowed his breathing to return to normal.

The forgotten dildo slid from his ass with barely a wince from him, as exhausted as he was. He'd clean everything up once he'd basked in the feeling for a while longer. By the time he set everything to rights, Robert felt sleep encroaching, and he climbed into bed, switched off the lights and lay in darkness, waiting for slumber.

The looming obscurity lay just out of reach, and

images of Prince Henry crowded in. Robert wished he knew what it was about the man that made Robert's insides take note. He hardly knew him. Why would he be interested? Maybe he saw something in Prince Henry that called to him. But why?

It was a question he had no answer to, so he pushed it aside. Instead, he focused on the prince's face, the one from the photograph of him with his cousins, so carefree. Why did Prince Henry seem like he had the weight of the world on his shoulders in every picture but that one?

## 5

# HENRY

*L*aughter rang through the living room of the future king, and the thought of what the public would say should they see what the six of them were like behind doors had Henry laughing harder. All the poise and strait-laced demeanours were thrown out of the window once they added alcohol to the mix.

Henry's laughter dialled down to a chuckle, and he drank some more. Despite being close to his brother and cousins, this didn't happen often. Their schedules clashed more than collided, but when they could get together, it was worth the wait.

Christian cleared his throat and glanced at Henry. "So…I saw Kean the other day. He said he'd not spoken to you since New Year. Why'd you fall out?" Christian gulped his beer and sat back on the sofa. "You were thick as thieves for years. I can't remember a time when you weren't together as we grew up."

Henry ignored the question, a wave of soberness overtaking him. He hadn't spoken to Kean since that day, no matter how many text messages and voicemails the man left. Taking a sip of his bourbon, Henry peered at Freddie, who gave a small nod of encouragement.

Henry rubbed a hand over his mouth, trying to gather his thoughts. He wasn't sure what to say. "Kean kissed me," he blurted out, without thinking about the repercussions.

A chorus of "What?" and "Go Henry!" sounded through the room, and Henry shushed them all. How could he get them to understand what he felt without giving away his true identity?

"He took something I didn't want to give, and I don't talk to him anymore." It was a blatant lie, but he couldn't admit the truth.

"Henry…" Freddie said. "We're with friends. Family. Talk to us."

Henry's heart raced. He stood, placing his glass on the table, and strode to the window, looking out at the dark sky. His stomach churned. He knew he was in good company, but still, he hesitated. Douglas was gay, and he either didn't know or didn't care that they talked about him behind his back, and George was bisexual and appeared happy. As for Freddie, Patrick and Christian, they all played with women, and Henry had heard nothing different about their orientation, but they didn't hate Douglas and George. Why did he think they would be any different to him?

"I'm gay," he whispered, unsure whether he wanted them to hear.

"That's okay," Douglas said, coming to a stand several feet away as if he knew he couldn't touch Henry or he'd break apart.

Henry gave a small huff and raised his eyebrows at Douglas. "Is it, though?" He turned back to the window and shook his head. "To have people gunning for you because you're gay is okay, is it? To have slurs and… threats of retaliation said behind your back is okay? To be beaten because you told the wrong person you're gay…is okay? Because that is what it's like when you're not around, Douglas. I don't know if you hear it and ignore it or if you don't hear it at all, but too many people in our family are homophobes. Too many people 'take care' of those who are not heterosexual. I don't know if I have the strength to go through that," he finished on a mumble.

There was silence for a minute, then Douglas said, "I've heard the words, Henry. I've heard everything and more. The problem I have is that I refuse to live my life according to other people's opinions. If I did that, I'd be living a lie and a lonely one at that. I can't…no, I refuse to switch it off because someone has an issue with it."

"We all know Aunt Charlotte has a problem with homosexuality," Freddie said. "Most people in the club don't care one way or the other. Aunt Charlotte has not grown with the times, unlike our father or Uncle William. I bet even your mother wouldn't say a word against the new world. You don't need to worry when you have many people at your back, Henry."

Henry inhaled deeply. "That's not all, though." He licked his lips and crossed his arms over his chest, facing his family. "I'm a submissive, and I want…to be a pup," he finished quickly, dropping his gaze to the floor.

"So am I."

Henry's gaze snapped to George's face. "What?"

"I'm a submissive. Always have been, always will be."

Freddie clasped his hand to the back of George's neck and shook him a little. "Why didn't you tell us?"

George shrugged. "It doesn't really change things. We," he flicked a finger between him and Henry, "still have to 'pretend' to be Dominants. Father wouldn't accept us any other way, would he?"

Freddie removed his hand and linked his fingers together between his knees, sighing. "Probably not. He's not opposed to anyone choosing any gender to have a relationship with, but for the club, the rules state we should be Dominants."

"Do you think he would change that rule if we spoke to him about it?" Douglas asked, sitting back on the sofa and reaching for his drink.

"I really don't know." Freddie sat upright. "But I'm going to damn well ask."

"No!" Everyone turned to stare at him. "I don't want to be the cause of someone getting hurt or upset."

"It's not just you, remember, Henry." George wandered over to him, resting a hand on his shoulder. "If we can get the rules changed, it will help many people. People we don't even know about."

Henry swallowed hard. He understood what they were

trying to say, but he didn't know if he could even come out if they changed the rules. "Don't do this for me, Freddie. Please. I don't know if I'll ever come out, not with what I've seen and heard. I can't…" His breath hitched, and he faced the window again, George's hand dropping off.

"That's okay, Henry. You don't need to do anything you're not ready for. No one will push you for more than you can do. You know that, right? We're all here for you. Especially me."

It was the first words his brother had spoken since Henry had thrown out his secret, and Henry closed his eyes and blew out a breath. He hadn't thought Patrick would stand by him, though why he wasn't sure.

"Now, come and tell us about being a pup," Christian said. "I'd love to hear more because those pups sure are cute."

Henry snorted, the weight on his chest lifting a little. He sat beside his brother, who shoved a full glass into his hand and squeezed his shoulder before grabbing his own drink.

"I don't really know what to say about it." Henry shrugged. "I love the pups. They're free, without a care in the world, and I love the idea of that. Being able to play and lose myself in the world, free of burden, free of expectations of anything but my handler…" He paused, trying to gather his thoughts.

"Freedom," George said.

Henry nodded. "But I can't. The first person to see me as a pup, and despite the NDAs, I'd be front-page news."

"We hide you," Christian said.

"What do you mean?" Henry frowned.

Christian sat forward, resting his bottle on the table. "You can get a hood to cover most of your face. If you are worried about any identifiable markings on your body, get a full bodysuit. No one will know it's you. You could wear it going in and out, so there is no chance of you being identified."

"But he doesn't have a handler," Douglas said. "Who would keep an eye on him?"

"I will." Patrick sat forward.

"No!" Henry held up a hand. "I'm sorry, but I can't have my brother seeing me like that. Not yet."

Patrick's face fell, but he nodded. Henry knew he'd hurt him, but he couldn't let his brother see him. It had nothing to do with submissives being less than Dominants because Henry knew as much as everyone else did that it wasn't true. It scared Henry that he'd try being a pup but wouldn't like it. Then everything they had done to help him would be for nothing. He didn't want to waste their time.

"I'll do it," Christian said. "I love those pups as much as you do, and I know how to be a handler. I have some extra…training that will help me, too."

"If you're going to be his handler, it will need to be at the club. You can't go somewhere else." Freddie sipped his beer.

Henry's breathing increased. "I don't know if I could go to the club. What if something happens and I'm found out?"

"It would be much worse if that happened at an outside club," Freddie said. "We have a better chance of containing it if you're at the club."

Henry dropped his head into his shaky hands. He couldn't do it. "It's a good idea, but I can't. Thanks for your help, though." He downed his bourbon and stood to get another.

"I know someone," George said. "He doesn't have a pup of his own but often helps when pups don't have handlers with them. He's a good guy, and I'm sure he will sign an NDA, too. We could even keep Henry's identity from him. He won't know anything other than he's a new pup."

Henry stared at George, biting his lip. The idea had merit, but he understood Frederick's concern for anonymity. He focused on Freddie and raised his eyebrows.

Freddie worked his jaw back and forth as he twirled the bottle on his knee. "I don't know if this is a good idea, but I will support you if you want to do it. I would prefer it if you did it at the club, but I understand why you don't want to. Is there another club he could use?"

George nodded. "The one the handler uses regularly is not as secure as ours, but there is another one I know he's a member of. Henry would need to apply and wait for the owners' agreement before attending. That sometimes takes weeks."

Henry didn't think he could wait weeks now that the idea had rooted in his head. "I'll go to the other club. It's a chance, I know, but if George trusts this guy, I'm sure he'll do everything he can to help."

"What's the name of the other club?" Freddie asked.

"The Den is the less secure one; the more secure one, Myriad," George said.

"What do you think, Henry?" Freddie leaned forward, staring him down. "This is your choice at the end of the day."

Henry's heart pounded at the thought of being able to be a pup. "I want to do this. I *need* to do this."

Freddie nodded. "George, set it up, but I want you, Henry, to message us when you get there and when you get out, and, of course, if there are any problems. Douglas, we need to find someone who will visit the club on the same night, so we have someone in the building with him. It might mitigate the potential damage if he's outed."

Most people would hate being spoken about as if they weren't in the room, but Henry didn't mind. He knew these five people had his back. Why he'd been hesitant to explain his situation to them before now was something he'd always regret. He should've known they'd support him, no matter what. Henry closed his eyes, a small smile curving the corners of his mouth while his body relaxed fully for the first time in what felt like years.

"You never fully answered about what happened with Kean," Christian said.

Henry blinked at him and sighed. "He kissed me on New Year's Eve. It seemed like he'd wanted to for a while."

"And you didn't?"

"I'd never let myself think of anyone like that, not even when I was alone. When he kissed me, I was shocked." Henry's cheeks heated, and he dashed a hand at them. "I fell into the bubble he wound around me until Freddie came in."

Freddie rubbed the back of his neck. "Yeah, sorry about that."

Henry gave a brief smile. "It was a good thing. I wasn't ready. I don't know if I'm ready now. Anyway, I pushed Kean away. He knew something about me I didn't want anyone to know. I locked him out."

"Why not me?"

Henry glanced at Freddie. "Because I can't shut you out when you're family. I had to trust that you would have my back, as you always have. Despite knowing Kean for years, I couldn't chance us getting any closer. I knew Kean would push and push if we remained friends, and it would destroy us. At least this way, Kean is okay."

No one said anything for a few minutes until Christian cracked a joke. Henry let the flow of conversation lull him to a state of calm. His gaze locked onto Patrick's. In his brother's eyes, hurt flashed, and Henry knew he would need to mend the tears he'd made in their relationship. He never wanted to hide from Patrick, but he didn't know how to explain who he was when there were many oppositions to his dream lifestyle. He would apologise later, in private.

Food was delivered, and Henry turned his nose up at the five cheeseburgers that surrounded him. He hated them with a passion and instead had a chicken wrap. The rest of the evening returned to the carefree atmosphere it had been before Christian had first asked about Kean.

When it was time to go home, he weaved his way to

where his driver was waiting and climbed into the back-seat. He wasn't drunk enough to not know what he was doing but pleasantly buzzed. All the others had chosen to stay overnight, but Henry had plans with his parents in the morning and went home. He might regret it when he woke the following morning, but it was too late now.

An electrical sensation flowed through him when he thought about the plans they'd made for him. To try out being a pup was a dream come true for him when he'd only ever done it in the privacy of his bedroom. What he hadn't told his co-schemers was that he already owned the outfit he needed. He'd bought it and had it delivered to an anonymous post office box about eighteen months ago, but he'd never worn it outside as it left nothing to the imagination with how tight it was.

He locked all the doors behind him after thanking his driver and wandered to his bedroom. The cleaning staff had been in, he could tell, and he held his breath until he unlocked his bedroom door and saw nothing had been disturbed. He might appear a little obsessive about it, but he truly needed this tiny piece of privacy where no one could get to him.

Undressing, he threw the clothes into the washing basket in the bathroom and brushed his teeth. While doing the menial task, he stared at his reflection. His eyes were glassy and his cheeks rosy, but he was relaxed. There were no stress lines on his face, only the normal lines getting older entailed. He wished this reflection would stare back at him every day, but it didn't.

He finished up and headed to his bed, flicking the

covers back. The sheets were cool, and he dragged his covers over him and tucked them around his naked body, hoping they would warm up quickly.

As usual, it took him a while to relax enough to sleep even with the amount of alcohol in his system, and images bombarded him. He smiled as he remembered the way the pups rolled and tumbled together, chased after a ball, squeaked a toy and more. He hadn't had the luxury of experiencing it as a pup yet, so he could only imagine what it was like, but hopefully, he would soon get to see. It was like his dreams were coming true. As soon as he thought that, the images were replaced with those of his nightmares. The scenes of men being beaten and whipped for announcing they were gay, of his aunt watching from the sidelines with disgust on her face and hateful words spouting from her mouth. Henry tried to wipe away the images, but more and more came. Words said in revulsion and loathing, vile threats whispered amongst the crowds, terrible accusations thrown at innocent people. Henry had seen and heard it all, and terror paralyzed him. Not only for his future should his truth get out but for his cousins Douglas and George, who were known for being gay and bisexual, for his cousin Helena who had taken a female partner, and for his cousin Alice who had defied royalty and come out as non-binary. How they had the strength to go up against the crown was beyond him.

They had more strength and integrity than anyone Henry had ever known.

One day, Henry hoped he'd have the strength to join them openly, but for now, the nightmares of what awaited him were too much. He would stay in the shadows and hide, listening for anything that could harm his family.

Hopefully, Henry could help to keep them safe. Even if it killed him inside to pretend he wasn't like them.

Henry rolled onto his back, staring into the darkness at where the ceiling would be. It was four o'clock in the morning, but he wouldn't sleep now. His body could rest, though, while his mind worked through the problems they all faced.

He was a nothing, a nobody within the vast branches of the royal family, and there was little he could do to stop it.

6

---

GEORGE

George had seen the distress in Henry's eyes when he'd told them he was a submissive and could do no more than admit to his own. It wasn't fair to either of them that they needed to be one way or another, but it was how it was. Despite Freddie's beliefs he could speak to their father and potentially change the rules, George didn't think it would change. The royal family needed to be seen as strong, and as far as the club was concerned, that meant they needed to be dominant.

How his father believed that crap when he advocated that submissives were strong by giving up their control, was beyond him.

He strode towards his room and locked the door behind him. Pulling his phone from his pocket, he dialled a man he knew of but had never spoken to—no one needed to know about his extra-curricular activities. He stood before the windows, watching over the goings-on in the town beyond the walls, and waited for the call to connect.

"Elton Franks."

"Elton, it's Georgie Cliff," he said, using the name he often did when he wanted to be inconspicuous.

"I didn't expect to hear from you, Georgie. What can I do for you?"

George inhaled, glad, for a change, that his reputation preceded him, even though Elton only knew his alias because Elton made a point to know everyone who frequented his club. "I have someone who wants to experience being a pup but doesn't have a handler. Do you still have that one who helps those pups who need to let loose?"

"I do. Who is it for?"

"A celebrity who wants to remain anonymous. They will have a hood on at all times as they do not want to be recognised."

Elton was quiet, and George wasn't sure if he would agree. The man was a stickler for rules but would do whatever was necessary for the benefit of the club.

"I can ask the question. Anything I need to know?"

"Other than he's new to being a pup, but not to the lifestyle, and wants the handler to remain as anonymous as he will be, nothing. You will both need to sign NDAs, and there will be two security guards in the building but not in the pup area."

"I don't see that being a problem as long as...the handler agrees. Can I call you back when I've spoken to him?"

George closed his eyes. "Of course."

"I might not be able to reach him until tonight."

"There's no rush, Elton. This needs to be done correctly, and if it takes a few days or weeks, we'll deal with it."

"Understood."

They spoke for a few more minutes, then George hung up. He'd done his part. Now, they needed to wait and see what the handler's answer would be.

Several hours later, Elton returned his call.

"The handler has agreed but has requested Saturday if possible."

"Okay, let me check their itinerary, and I'll get back to you."

George knew it would be too late to call Henry that evening, so he called him first thing in the morning.

"I can't do Saturday because of the charity event," Henry said.

"Shit, yeah. I forgot about that. What about Sunday?"

"Sunday is good for me."

"Okay, leave it with me."

George blew out a breath once he'd finished the call with Henry. This back and forth made his head spin. He was about to call Elton when his mother requested his help. Help that took all day. It was the weekend by the time George could call Elton back.

George shook his head, although Elton couldn't see him. "Unfortunately, the pup can't make it today. Could we do tomorrow instead?"

"I'll double-check, but that shouldn't be a problem."

"If he agrees, send me a message, and I'll get the lawyer to drop by at eight o'clock tonight with the NDAs. He'll also be able to answer *some* questions you might have."

"Will do."

George dropped his head back against the chair, staring at the ceiling. Hopefully, this would be good for Henry. He didn't know the handler personally, but from what he *had* heard, the man was amazing.

Elton called back and confirmed, and George returned Mr Kiln's call and requested he visit the club. Mr Kiln was a nice man that he'd found when he'd needed some specialised NDAs for his own use. He knew Henry was in excellent hands. When it was all completed, George dropped into bed and slept.

## 7

## ROBERT

"I'm glad I bumped into you, Robert. I've had someone request your services."

Robert frowned across at the owner of The Den and crossed his arms over his chest, the leather he wore creaking in argument. "What do you mean?"

"I had an interesting phone call earlier today," Elton said as he reclined in a chair that appeared too delicate for his frame. "Someone with enough clout to ensure I and everyone involved signed an NDA before getting any information."

"A celebrity? What would they want with me?"

Elton linked his fingers over his stomach. "They want your special skills as a handler."

Robert rolled his eyes. "Let me guess. They want me to babysit a celebrity while they play dress-up?"

"Not quite. From what I can gather—remember, I've not signed the NDA yet—someone is already in the lifestyle but does not have a handler. They want to be free to be a pup with no one connecting them to who they are in real life."

Robert perched on the edge of the seat opposite Elton. "Why me?"

Elton spread his hands wide. "I'm assuming your reputation precedes you. You're single, and you're an amazing handler. Word gets out."

"Have they given you any rules or any other information?"

"Only that the person will enter in full pup gear, covered up, and we are not to try to figure out who it is. There will be security in the building, but not where the person will be as they do not want to be seen like that."

"They're ashamed of their needs? Why would I want to be part of that?"

Elton leaned forward, the chair protesting his movements. "I wouldn't be sure they're ashamed. It could be that they are too high ranking for it to be good for their career. I really don't know. I wanted to get your permission before I signed anything. If you decide to do this, we'll get more information about them, although we won't know who it is for definite, only a rough idea."

Robert sat back, crossing his legs. This was a bad idea, but something pulled at him. He could never put this on his resume, of course, but to know he'd helped someone be who they wanted to be when it wasn't possible in their daily life was like a fish going after the food on a hook, even knowing it might catch them.

"All right. I'd prefer it to be on a Saturday night, if

possible, but it's not essential." He stood. "You have my number. Ring me if they decide to go ahead."

"Will do."

Robert left the office, yawning behind his hand as he exited the building. He'd been ready to leave when Elton had caught him. Now, although he felt tired, his brain brought up questions faster than he could think of answers to them. He didn't know what to think about it. He could understand why someone wanted to hide something that could affect their career, but wasn't there somewhere more secure they could do it, instead of risking being found out should the wrong person get involved?

It wasn't his concern; it was the security team's job to handle any issues, but Robert would get upset if something happened on his watch. Plus, despite Elton saying the pup had training, he didn't have Robert's training, so they would at least need a brief conversation before anything happened.

Pushing the strange request aside, he drove home, going through his to-do list for the following day. There was another wedding scheduled for that weekend, and they would provide the flowers for a Christmas party on the twenty-third. Naomi and Finn had taken point on that job, and Robert only had to concentrate on the wedding. Although he'd said Saturday would work best for the celebrity, he hoped it wasn't this weekend because the week usually exhausted him by the end of the day. Thinking about it, it probably wouldn't happen before Christmas or even New Year because those days fall on weekends that year.

He climbed into bed, trying to forget about the request, but sleep eluded him for a long time.

"No, I asked for pink roses, not white. They are two different colours! How can you say this order is right? Mother!"

The bride-to-be threw her hands up in the air and turned to her mother, chuntering about crappy service and stupid staff. In all his years of owning a flower shop, Robert could honestly say he'd met a dozen bridezillas, but this one took the trophy. He calmly reached for his folder, glad to have every piece of paper the bride had filled out regarding this order. Pulling out six sheets, he stepped forward once more.

"Miss Carden, if you look at these order forms you filled in, you see that in your original order, you requested pink roses. A week later, you came to us and requested the change to white lilies. Several days later, another change, requesting pink roses once more. I have three other dated and signed—by you—order forms where you've changed your mind. The latest order was for white roses, requested last week, and we advised this would be the last change you could make because we were placing the order that day. As you can see on the order form, we noted this was the last order, and it was signed, by you, on the date you ordered them. Unfortunately, it is too late to change now, but luckily, white roses go with everything, and I know they will look amazing on the tables. Your bouquet looks fantastic."

The bride crossed her arms over her face and listened while her mother spoke to her in hushed tones. Robert didn't listen; he didn't care what they were saying because the order was in black and white and paid for. If the bride decided she wasn't happy, she could try to find someone else to do the decorations in the next five hours because Robert would take the offending flowers with him. He had grown a backbone since becoming the owner of the business and realising people tried to take advantage.

The mother of the bride wandered closer. "Thank you, Mr Martin. I appreciate everything you have done for us. We will happily accept the white roses, as that was what Isabella requested. I'm sorry for the confusion." She gave a pointed look, and Robert understood the undertones.

"That's not a problem. I understand emotions are running high on such a special day. We will continue our work, and it will be one less thing the bride needs to worry about."

"Thank you."

Robert turned to the people he had hired to help with the flowers and gathered them, explaining the plan. Their job was to decorate the tables with the centrepieces and to slot in a single rose into the back ribbon sash of each chair. Robert's role was to ensure the flowers on the top table and on the perimeter of the room were all in order. It wouldn't take more than an hour and a half as long as no one else argued about what it should look like.

His phone rang as he worked, and he clicked the button on the side of his earpiece.

"Hello?"

"Robert, it's Elton."

"Hey, how're things?"

"Good, thanks. Look, I've heard from them about the request. They'd like to do it tomorrow night, if possible? I know you said today, but the pup couldn't make it."

Robert sighed, moving a flower into position. "Yeah, that's fine. Just means I won't get as much sleep before work on Monday, but I can deal with that."

"Are you sure?"

"Yeah, it's fine."

Elton chuckled. "In that case, I need you to drop by tonight at eight o'clock to sign the NDA. The security team will be here to witness you sign it. They're going all out on this one. I'd love to know who it is."

"Yeah, me, too. Okay, I'll be there."

He moved onto the next display, energy already waning, and it was only two in the afternoon. They worked diligently, and Robert found the mother of the bride to let her know before he left. He made her sign the form to say the job was complete and sent the helpers home with a heartfelt thank you. Climbing into his car, he headed for the shop, hoping Naomi and Finn hadn't burnt the place down in his absence.

He guided his car down a narrow alley to the tiny car park behind the building and let himself in the back entrance, carrying the remains of the unused flowers. He dropped everything onto the workbench, inhaled the scent of home deeply, then shut the door and drifted down the hallway towards the main shop.

"Boss!"

Finn's overexcited voice pierced his eardrums in the small space, and he winced. "Yes?" He glowered at Finn with narrowed eyes.

"Sorry." Finn lowered his head. "Prince Henry is here again," he whispered.

Robert raised his eyebrows. "Really? They're pushing the boat out trying to ensure we are a good fit; I'll give them that," he mumbled, resuming his trek.

Naomi stood next to the tall prince, gesticulating with her hands and almost knocking over the flowers. Prince Henry had a polite smile on his face, but Robert could tell he was uncomfortable.

"Naomi?" Robert waited until he had her attention. "I think Finn needs your help in the back."

"I was just helping—"

"It's okay. I can take over here. Please help Finn." He nodded with a smile.

Naomi's smile dimmed a little, and Robert would apologise for it later, but at the moment, he couldn't risk anything. Naomi was fabulous with a lot of things, but she was extremely starstruck when it came to celebrities and the royal family. Her chin dropped, and he caught her arm as she slipped past him. She lifted her gaze to his, and he smiled, pressing a kiss to her cheek and whispering, "I saw him first," and gave a wink. She flushed and batted his shoulder before skipping off. A good thing he knew how to cheer her up. He'd still apologise later.

"Good afternoon, Your Highness. How can I help you today?"

Prince Henry stood taller and held his hands behind his back, his long coat opening and giving a glimpse of a black suit. He had yet to meet Robert's gaze, which he found interesting.

"I was in the area and…wanted to pick some flowers for my mother."

Robert rolled his lips inwards, hiding his smile at the obvious lie. "Fabulous. What would you like?"

The prince's eyes widened, and he glanced around. "Those!" He pointed at the purple carnations.

"Okay." Robert humoured him and chose a small bunch, taking them over to the counter to wrap.

"How is business?" Prince Henry asked.

"It's going well, Prince Henry. Thank you for asking."

"Henry, please."

Robert paused and tilted his head, studying his companion. "In private, yes, Your…Henry." He bit his bottom lip and watched Henry's gaze drop and a flush colour his cheeks. "In public, no, Prince Henry."

"Understood."

Robert resumed wrapping the flowers, and Henry paid. Robert held out the flowers without a word, and Henry grabbed them, their hands touching for a brief, tingling second. Neither had lowered their gazes, and Robert saw when Henry's breath hitched, and his eyes widened.

"Have a good day…Henry," Robert said with a small smile.

Henry lowered his head in a slight bow. "A good day to you, Robert."

He watched as the prince left the shop and disappeared. Blowing out a breath, he returned to the back of the shop, holding his hands out to Naomi. "I'm sorry, Naomi. I'm a sucker for a pretty face, but I should've let you finish your conversation."

Naomi waved him away. "Nah, it's fine. I was just babbling anyway. You know how I get. He was probably happy to be rid of me. Anyway, what's going on with you two?"

Robert shook his head. "Absolutely, nothing. Though, wouldn't that be a dream come true? My own fairy tale prince." He chuckled.

"It might happen. Don't cross anything off your wish list," Finn said.

"True. Tell you what, I'll keep it on my wish list, but I won't hold my breath. How about that?"

"Sounds good to me."

They snorted, and Robert got them back to work. They still had a couple of hours left until the shop closed, and there was work to do.

By the time Naomi and Finn left after closing time, Robert was ready for bed. He had no idea why he was tired lately, but he figured it was probably the stress of waiting to hear from the royal contact about the florist position. He showered and re-dressed, then grabbed something to eat before wasting time watching TV until it was time to go to The Den and meet Elton.

The owner met him in the foyer and escorted him to the office.

"They're not here yet. Do you want a drink?" Elton asked.

"Sure, though make sure it's water or juice because I'm driving."

"Sure thing."

Robert sat in the visitor chair and got comfortable. "Have they given you any more information yet?"

Elton shook his head as he handed Robert a glass of chilled water. "No, they said they'd explain everything in more detail once they had the signed NDAs. I'm as in the dark as you are at this point."

"Interesting." Robert shrugged. "I don't know if I should feel complimented or worried that I was requested for this. I'd love to know who put me on their radar."

"I have no id—" A knock sounded. "Come in." A man entered, striding straight for Elton and leaning down to whisper in his ear. "Okay, send them in. Thank you."

The man nodded and re-opened the door, indicating for the people waiting to come inside. Elton and Robert stood as three men entered, all looking like they belonged in a Special Ops mission, though with suits.

"Mr Franks, nice to meet you. I'm Ian Kiln, the lawyer representing my client."

"Nice to meet you, Mr Kiln. Please call me Elton. This is Robert Martin, the man you requested."

"Nice to meet you, Mr Martin. I've heard a lot about your skills. I'm hoping we can work together to make sure this is a beneficial agreement."

Robert raised his eyebrows. "Nice to meet you. I will admit to being a little out of my depth here, Mr Kiln."

"Please, call me Ian, both of you. I can understand that. These two men behind me will be the ones escorting my client tomorrow night. I thought it wise you meet them beforehand so you will know them on sight, and I will explain why in a moment."

"Take a seat. I'll have some more chairs brought up."

"That won't be necessary, Mr Franks. We're happy to stand," the tallest of the two said.

"Okay. Let's get down to business. I'm sure you don't want to spend your Saturday evening filling out paperwork." Ian settled himself on the other visitor chair and pulled out some paperwork. "This is the non-disclosure agreement we are requesting you to sign. Please read it carefully because it will be legally binding. If there is anything you don't understand, ask me, and I will explain. Sorry to be a hard-ass, but if something happens and you say you didn't realise it was in the contract, you will be taken to court because not understanding is not an excuse."

Robert raised his eyebrows. "Sir, yes, sir," he mumbled, earning a chuckle from around the room.

He took the paperwork and began reading. It seemed standard in most ways. No cameras or photographic equipment of any kind, no trying to find out who the person is, no asking questions that don't pertain to the role they are playing, no intercourse, and so on. After he'd read it, he only had one question.

"I'm happy with everything, but I have a question."

Ian waved. "Go ahead."

"Why do I need to wear a mask? It's not *my* identity that needs to be hidden."

Ian leaned back in his chair and crossed his ankle over his knee. "That was put in at the request of my client. He has asked that his handler remain anonymous because he doesn't want to potentially pass you on the street and know who you are. He said he would feel self-conscious even if you had no idea. This was the only compromise he could think of to ease his concerns. Is it a problem?"

Robert considered his options. He hated wearing face masks; they felt too constraining for him, but maybe he could find one that was less restrictive.

"It's not a deal-breaker, but I will need to buy one, which I will do tomorrow."

"We will pay for that and any other expenses you incur. You will also receive a wage for your time."

Ian pulled out a piece of paper and passed it to Robert. He opened it, and his mind went blank. There was a hell of a lot of zeros on that paper, but he couldn't accept it.

"Thank you for the offer, but I decline."

Ian raised his eyebrows. "You won't do it?"

"Oh, no, I'll be the handler, but I refuse to be paid for it." Robert felt a little sleazy doing that.

Ian frowned. "May I ask why?"

"Because to me, it's not a job, it's a lifestyle. It's what I do every time I'm here anyway. I wouldn't feel right taking money when I don't take money from anyone else. Expenses, I'm happy for you to pay for, although I doubt there will be many, however, my time, no."

Ian studied him for a long minute, then nodded. "Understood."

Robert borrowed a pen from Elton, and they both signed the agreements. Once they had done and Ian had tucked them away somewhere, the man explained a few more details, but not many.

"My client will be called Dusty from this point forward. This is his pup name. He has experience with the lifestyle. Although he has never been a pup himself, he has always been a handler. He knows the rules of the lifestyle and also understands there will be a need to speak with him before the play begins. If you have any rules or questions you need answers to beforehand, please let me know by emailing me here as soon as possible." Ian handed him another slip of paper. "I will reply within the hour with the response. Tomorrow night, Dusty would prefer to have no human voice from the moment he arrives. Will that be a problem?"

Robert shook his head. "On the understanding that if something happens, I may need him to answer, but I will email you a phrase I will say if that is the case."

"Agreed."

"In which case, I think we are all set. Do you have any questions?"

"No."

"I look forward to hearing from you. Have a good evening, gentlemen."

Ian and the two security guards exited the room, and Robert stared at Elton. "This should be interesting."

8

HENRY

$\mathcal{A}$t the time Henry knew Mr Kiln would be meeting with the handler, he paced his living room while George watched him. George had already talked him down from cancelling the whole thing probably ten times in the last few days.

"You're going to wear a hole in the carpet," George said, appearing relaxed and calm.

Henry supposed it didn't matter to George because he wasn't the one who was putting his life in the hands of someone he didn't know. He scraped his fingers through his hair, no doubt making a mess of it. He linked his fingers behind his neck and squeezed his elbows closed, hiding his face. What had he done? When George had first brought up the idea, Henry had thought it was a great way to experience being a pup, but the closer the time came, the more Henry regretted his decision to set the wheels in motion. He closed his eyes and inhaled, trying to banish the images bombarding him.

Hands pushed against his elbows, and he released his hold on them. "Everything will be fine. Mr Kiln is a brilliant lawyer, and nothing fazes him. He'll cover every scenario and ensure that the handler is who I think he is. I've never seen the guy in action myself, but I've heard a lot about him." George didn't blink as he spoke, and Henry knew he believed every word.

"I trust you, George. It's difficult to allow myself to be the person I've been hiding for many years."

"Why did you hide?"

Henry averted his gaze, instead staring out of the window to his side. There was no way he could explain what he'd seen, what had made him frightened of being his whole self, why he wished fervently that his cousins stayed out of harm's way and didn't receive any of the treatment he'd witnessed others endure.

"It's okay. You don't need to tell me. I wish you had told me you were submissive. We could've had this experience out of the way by now." George grinned.

"Ha, ha." Henry rolled his eyes.

George's phone beeped, and he checked it, wandering to the door. "Mr Kiln is here. I'll get him."

George disappeared for several minutes, leaving Henry alone with enough time to panic again. What was he doing? His stomach rolled and pitched, and a wave of nausea flowed over him. He breathed through his nose and sat in an armchair, resting his head in his hands. This was a disaster in the making. How had he even agreed to this?

The door opened, and he glanced up. The lawyer stepped closer with a gentle smile on his face.

"Prince Henry, nice to see you again."

"You too. Please, have a seat." Henry swallowed hard to get the words free.

Mr Kiln sat in the seat closest to Henry and pulled out some papers. "Mr…your handler has agreed to the terms set out in the NDA and contract, although he refused the monetary benefits except for expenses incurred on the day."

Henry frowned. "Why? We should pay him for his time." He glanced at George in question but received a shrug in reply.

"He refused on the grounds that he accepted no payment from any other pups he helped, so why should he from you?"

"It's different. I'm asking more from him. He should receive payment."

Mr Kiln held out his hands. "The only way he would sign was if he was not paid. If you feel strongly, maybe you could donate the money to a charity." It wasn't the lawyer's fault.

"Thank you, Mr Kiln. I appreciate you doing this for me. Were there any other issues?"

"No. He was happy with the terms. A little confused by the mask request, but still happy to oblige."

Henry nodded slowly, staring at the paperwork he

would not look at because he didn't want to know the name of the man he would play with. It sounded terrible when he said it aloud, but he knew himself, and if he saw the man on the street, he wouldn't be able to resist speaking to him. If he knew his name, he wouldn't be able to stop himself from researching him. It was better for everyone involved if Henry didn't know who was helping him.

"Is everything set for tomorrow?" George asked.

"Yes. I agreed with the owner that you will arrive in full pup gear with a hoodie hiding your appearance, and you will meet your handler in the owner's office. From there, your handler will take charge. I expect to have a list of questions or rules for you later this evening. I will forward them on when I receive them."

"Thank you, Mr Kiln. We appreciate your confidentiality."

Henry said nothing, staring at the floor.

"That's good. All sorted for tomorrow."

George's voice startled Henry, and he realised the lawyer had gone. He'd have to apologise to the man when he saw him next. It was rude of him not to say goodbye.

"This is it." He cleared his throat. "Am I doing the right thing, George?"

George knelt at his feet and clasped his hands over Henry's. "You are. I still can't believe how you've kept this buried for so long. You need this, and you deserve this. Let yourself believe that at least."

Henry exhaled and nodded. "I won't cancel. I promise.

It's hard to…allow myself this, but I will do it. I must. I need to find out."

It was barely an hour later when the email came from the lawyer. Henry brought it up on his laptop for them both to see.

*Do you have a preference for what you are called, e.g., good boy, or does it have to be Dusty alone?*

*What do you prefer for snacks and drinks?*

*Is there anything you would prefer not to happen? For example, playing with other pups, being petted.*

*How long would you like the session to last?*

*Are there any body language cues I need to watch for?*

<u>*Rules for Dusty*</u>

*In an emergency, I will insist you use your human voice.*

*Be positive and engaging with those around you, but be respectful of other people's boundaries.*

*Sexual intercourse is off the table.*

*I will watch your body language for clues to how you are feeling.*

*If you are uncertain at any point, move in front of me and rest your chin on my knee. If this happens, we may need to have a vocal conversation.*

Henry blew out a breath as he read. He could answer most without problems, but the body language question was tricky. He'd never had to think about that before, and he couldn't answer it. He'd read and watched videos about using his tail as a clue for his emotional state, but when he was in pupspace, he didn't know if he used his tail to signal his feelings.

"Are you okay?" George asked.

Henry wrinkled his nose. "Yeah. It's just becoming real. I've not had to think about these things when it's been me alone."

"But just think how much fun you'll have playing with the other pups." George grinned.

From what he'd seen on videos, Henry could imagine, and a smile broke out. "I hope so."

And he did. He hoped with everything in him that this was what he wanted because otherwise, he'd wasted too much time.

Henry took a shower, dried off and wrapped a towel around his waist. His pup suit was waiting for him on his bed, and his stomach churned as he stood beside it. George had offered to help him with it, but Henry had learnt to do it himself. The supple leather looked huge as it laid flat and had a quilted effect with many buckles. Beside it was a bodysuit, which he needed to wear underneath the leather to stop it from chafing and sticking to his skin. Other people might wear it differently, but he'd found this was the best choice for him.

Dropping the towel, he dragged the bodysuit on,

adjusting himself as he needed. For him, being a pup wasn't about sex. It was about letting go of everything that weighed heavily on his shoulders. It was about being free.

Once he had positioned the bodysuit comfortably, he lifted the leather pup suit. The first time he'd tried it on, it had surprised him how light it was because it didn't look like it would be. He stepped into the legs and slid his arms into place. Reaching behind him, he clasped the zipper and pulled it up as far as he could, then held the long piece of rope tied to it and switched his hands over his shoulders to pull it further. He kept the rope in front of him and contorted himself to fasten the buckles. It was difficult, that was for sure, but he had refused to allow anyone to see him like this; therefore, he had figured out a way to do it without help.

The clink of the buckles had his nerve endings firing up. He associated the sound with his pup now and could feel the beginnings of the mental change happening. Usually, he would sink as fast and as far as he could because he would remain in his room, but he couldn't this time, as a car journey stood between him and his pup being freed.

Henry put a hoodie over the top of his suit and joggers over his legs and slipped his feet into trainers. When he'd been researching, he'd decided not to go with the strait-jacket-type of suit, where his entire legs were encased in a bent position. It felt too vulnerable to him. Instead, he chose a full-length, black leather suit with detachable gloves, feet and mask. Without those on, he could pass as pretending to go for a motorcycle ride. Those items he put into a black bag to carry with him.

His phone buzzed, and he saw that the security guys had arrived. He'd play while two men stayed in the building with him, though not in the same room. They would give his handler a button to press should there be any problems, and the men would know to get to him. He messaged George, telling him he was on his way and headed for the front door. He kept his breathing deep and even, but his legs and hands were trembling.

"This is what I want. I can do this," he murmured to himself.

He smiled at the men, one of them opening the back-door for him to slide into the car. Henry lifted his hood over his head, hiding his face.

"Please tell me when we are five minutes away," he asked the men.

"Yes, sir."

*GEORGE: You'll be fine. You'll enjoy it. I know you will. Let me know when you're leaving, and I'll meet you at your house.*

*HENRY: If I can forget that I'm not supposed to do this, I will enjoy it. I'll message later.*

He pocketed the phone and watched the scenery lit by streetlights. The car ride wouldn't be long, but enough time for Henry to freak out. He couldn't believe he was doing it. After many years of telling himself he couldn't risk it, he was laying everything on the line to experience this. He hoped it didn't blow up in his face.

Henry felt selfish, in a way. He enjoyed being a handler, helping the pups, teaching others to be handlers and seeing a relationship develop between a handler and their pup. But he wanted to experience the other side of things. He knew he'd like it because he'd tested the waters alone in his bedroom, but he couldn't go deep enough into his puppy self to find the freedom he craved because there was only him around when he did it, and he had to be careful.

"Five minutes away, sir."

His stomach rolled, and he squashed the nervousness as much as he could. Pushing his hood back, he retrieved his mask from the bag, sliding over his face and attaching it into place. He removed his hoodie, trainers and joggers, then slid the feet of the suit on. They had harder soles for when he needed to walk but were flexible enough to not be a hindrance in pup form. The last item was his gloves. He could've chosen a boxing glove style, but he wanted a bit more flexibility with his hand movements. Once he was ready, he closed his eyes and waited for the car to stop.

When it came to a halt, the back door opened, and Henry climbed out. He could see easily through the mask and didn't need to be guided. One man walked in front of him, one man behind. As soon as they reached the entrance, the guy at the door let them in. They didn't wait and instead turned right and strode down a hallway. The security guy knocked and was told to enter.

Henry saw a sturdy, military-looking man sitting in a rickety chair behind an old wooden desk and a smaller framed man sitting in front of it. Both rose when the three of them entered.

"I'm glad you could be here," the man behind the desk said. "Your handler will take you from here."

One of his security men held out an orange button. "If you need us at any point, press that, and we will come to you. You don't need to search for us. If it's an emergency, press it twice in succession. It holds a locator, so we'll know your position."

"Thank you."

His handler's voice was deeper than he'd expected, but it was soothing. The hood gave a certain amount of sensory deprivation, and it distorted noises, especially voices. It made it easier to ignore some things. He focused on the man, seeing a full leather suit, similar to his own, with a separate hood made from a thin material that moved with his words. His features were indistinguishable, which Henry had wanted, but something about him made him wish he'd not made the request.

"Dusty, we will walk to the pup area because the floors are not clean down here. Once I tell you, I want you to present and walk to the pup area by my side. Do you understand?"

The soft, melodic tones of his handler met his ears, and he blinked and nodded.

"Before we go, can I please tie this to the back of your suit? It allows others to see you are with me, and they won't try to claim you themselves." Again he nodded, and his handler tied a blue ribbon to him. "Please follow me."

Henry turned when his handler moved out of his line of sight and followed him through the crowds. Being jostled while in his suit made it next to impossible to keep up with him, but his handler reached back and grabbed his wrist, pulling him closer. His handler let go, and they ascended some stairs into a quieter area. Henry's ears pricked when he heard barking and yipping from somewhere in front of them.

His handler stopped. "Okay, present."

Henry took a deep breath and dropped to his knees, resting back on his heels and resting his hands between his spread knees.

A hand cupped the top of his head briefly. "Good boy. All fours, and let's meet some pups." His handler's voice had become more playful instead of gruff, and Henry instinctively reacted. He walked forward on his hands and knees, keeping his head lifted so he didn't bump into anyone. He needn't have worried because most people moved out of his way to give him room when he came close.

"Come on, Dusty! Come on, boy!"

He yipped and paused. He had thought it would take some time to acclimatise to being around other pups, but the relaxed tone of his handler's voice helped him stay calm. He moved closer to his handler when he saw the number of pups on the mats spread out along the floor. The comforting hand rested against his head, and Henry leaned against his handler's hip while he watched the pups rough and tumble around.

He was startled when something nudged his shoulder, and he jerked around and came face-to-face with a black and white pup with a wagging tail. The pup lowered his front and wagged his tail, then jumped a step closer before stepping back again. Henry grinned at the antics. Leaning forward, he nosed at the pup and yipped at him. The pup turned in a circle and scrambled away, then came back again, barking at him.

"Go on, Dusty. Go play. I'll be right here."

Dusty tilted his head, yipped and bounded off to follow the pup. The pup waited for him on the mats with his chest lowered and tail wagging. When Dusty reached him, he reached out a paw and batted at his nose, causing the pup to bark and jump forward. Dusty yipped and ran in a circle before being bowled over. He quickly found his feet and twisted around to face the pup who'd barrelled into him. It was a small brown pup who lifted its head and dashed away.

Within seconds, the first pup was back, and Dusty lost himself in the rough and tumble amongst the eight other pups.

"Dusty!"

The voice permeated his play, and he yipped, extricating himself from the pile of pups. He raced over to his handler, panting and barking.

"There you are. Good boy, Dusty. Here's a drink for you."

His handler placed a straw at his mouth, and he drank

his fill, resting against his handler. After, his gaze tracked the other pups, watching what they were doing. He wasn't sure where to look because everything was fascinating.

"Are you having a rest, Dusty?"

A hand petted his head and neck, and he tilted his head, leaning against his handler's leg.

9

ROBERT

The pup had dropped into pupspace quicker than Robert had expected him to, thanks to the mischievous black and white pup called Nomad. He'd seen the pup many times and often sat talking with its handler about the lifestyle. Tonight, though, his attention was on his pup. When he'd first seen the tall, fully leather-clad man, it had surprised him how much of a pull he'd felt towards him. He assumed it was something to do with the need to take care of him as a pup, to ensure his experience was a good one.

There wasn't much for him to do apart from making sure Dusty kept hydrated and fed and that no one bothered him, but Dusty seemed to enjoy himself thoroughly.

Robert scratched at his mask, wishing he could remove it. He hated the feeling of being constricted, and although the mask was made from soft fabric, it stopped him from being able to see around them properly. When a voice piped up near him, he had to turn further to see them.

"He's a fine piece of leather. Who does he belong with?"

Robert narrowed his eyes at the person who had sat next to him. Vincent Dwyer was a well-known business owner in Slough and had many ventures, including, some would say, a drug business. No one had ever found out the truth of that rumour, but Robert wouldn't put it past the man. He was as sleazy as they come, and Robert knew more than one submissive had fought their way out of his grasp.

Gritting his teeth, Robert said, "Which one?"

"The newbie. Full, black leather. I'd love to get my hands on him." Vincent's eyes gleamed, and Robert didn't like the conclusions he came to from his expression.

"That won't happen. He's with me."

Vincent glanced at him and raised his eyebrows. "Is that so?"

Unfortunately, at that moment, Dusty scampered over. He leaned against Robert's thigh, puffing. Robert rested a hand on the top of his head, ignoring the bully beside him.

"How are you feeling, boy? Let's get you a drink."

"Here, have this one."

Robert didn't trust Vincent as far as he could throw him. He snatched his own bottle and held it up. "I have mine, thanks, though." He refocused on Dusty. "Here we go."

He held the straw to Dusty's mouth, allowing him to

drink his fill. Once finished, the pup leaned against him again, his head laid on his thigh.

"Aren't you going to introduce me?"

Robert exhaled, and he touched Dusty's shoulder, squeezing gently and hopefully conveying his need for them to be careful. This man was too powerful to piss off, despite what Robert wanted to say.

"You know the rules, Vincent. The pups choose who they want to approach." And he had never been more thankful for that rule.

Vincent smirked and held out his hand towards Dusty. The pup tilted his head, made a soft, confused noise and moved closer to Robert.

"He's shy. Maybe next time."

Vincent glowered at them but said nothing as he removed his hand. Robert tried not to smile but remembered he had a mask on which hid his expressions and grinned. Absent-mindedly, he scratched the back of Dusty's neck, touching the blue ribbon, and watched as Vincent retreated to the bar. When he left, Robert leaned down to Dusty.

"He's not a man to take no for an answer, Dusty. Be careful of him," Robert whispered.

Dusty yipped in acknowledgement.

"Time for a snack, don't you think?"

Robert changed the subject, not wanting Dusty to worry on that front too much. He dropped some fudge pieces into a bowl and set it on the floor. Dusty instantly pounced on it, and Robert laughed. It had surprised him when his questions had come back with thorough answers instead of the one or two words he'd been expecting. Finding out the pup loved fudge had made him chuckle because he knew someone else who had a fudge addiction—Naomi. Whenever there was a craft show in the area, she would go because often there were people who sold fudge. Naomi had once told him that her favourite place to shop for it was in Edinburgh. There was a lovely small business that made a vast variety of flavours, and she had found nowhere better. As it had been short notice, Robert had asked Naomi for some of her stash, and he'd agreed to make it up to her when the next show came to town.

Robert smiled as he watched Dusty devour the fudge. When he cleaned the bowl, Robert asked, "Is it time for a bathroom break?"

Dusty sat back on his heels and tilted his head before giving a soft whine, which he took to mean yes.

"Come on. Let's get you sorted, and you can get back to playing."

Dusty stayed by his side until they reached the bathroom.

"I would suggest standing for this. As you can expect, hygiene in a bathroom is not a top priority." Dusty whined again. "I know, but you'll be back in pupspace soon, I promise."

Dusty hesitated but climbed to his feet, standing upright.

"Good boy. Come on."

They entered the room, and Robert stood with his back to the urinals to give Dusty some privacy. He heard Dusty relieve himself as the door opened, and Robert straightened as Vincent came in, one of his goonies behind him.

"Ah, this is a surprise," Vincent said, his eyes sparking with something Robert didn't like. "Will you introduce me now?"

Robert sighed, not knowing how to get them out of this. "At least allow the pup to finish first."

Vincent held up his hands. "By all means."

Dusty stood ramrod straight and fiddled with his suit, then whirled around and stalked to the sinks. He washed his hands, and Robert found the first show of skin to be teasing. When he finished, Dusty strapped on his gloves and stepped to Robert's side. If that didn't show unwillingness, nothing did.

"Dusty, this is Vincent Dwyer. Vincent, this is Dusty, my pup."

"Nice to meet you, Dusty."

Dusty didn't reply, and Vincent glanced at Robert, who shrugged. "He's voice off tonight."

"Mute? Interesting."

"No, not mute, just made a choice to stay in pup form tonight."

"You've not taught him well if he ignores introductions." Vincent took a step closer.

Robert shook his head. "I've taught him to be true to who he is. If he doesn't want to communicate, that's his choice."

"I think I'd like to see what Dusty looks like under the mask." Vincent drifted closer. "Take off the mask, pup."

Vincent's voice was hard, but Robert stood his ground, stepping in front of Dusty. "No, Vincent. That's not your call."

Vincent lowered his head, locking eyes with Robert. "Everything that happens in this town is my call."

Robert swallowed hard but refused to back down. He'd promised his pup he wouldn't allow anything to happen to him. A hand slid into his pocket, and Robert stayed still, keeping Vincent's focus on him and not what his pup was doing. Dusty's hand found the security button and pressed it twice, from what Robert could tell, then the hand slid free.

"You have no control over me, though, Vincent."

"But I have the final say if you're allowed back in this club. I'm sure if I speak to Elton and express my concerns, he will back me up."

Robert knew he would because Elton would have no choice. If Vincent made Elton's life difficult, he'd prefer to close the club than become a puppet, and that wouldn't be fair on the patrons of the business.

"Possibly, but at the moment, this pup is *my* business."

"You—"

The door behind Vincent and his goon flew open, Dusty's two security men stepped inside.

"What's the problem here?" The man who'd given him the button spoke in a firm voice.

Vincent smiled at them. "There's no problem at all. We're just having a friendly conversation."

"Please take your *friendly conversation* elsewhere."

Vincent held out his hands. "I was just trying to get to know Dusty here."

The security guard moved closer. "Dusty is not your concern. He belongs to his handler. Stay away."

Vincent narrowed his eyes and transferred his glare to Robert. He knew this wouldn't be the last he'd heard from Vincent, and he wasn't at all looking forward to their next meeting. The bully elbowed his way out of the door and disappeared.

"Thank you."

"Would you like us to stay on this level with you in case he comes back?"

Robert glanced at Dusty, who shook his head. "No, we'll be good."

The security guards glanced at each other and exited the bathroom. They reminded Robert of the FBI agents he'd seen in movies, all movements matching as if it had been rehearsed millions of times. He turned to Dusty.

"Are you okay?" Dusty whined and nudged his head into Robert's shoulder. "I'm sorry that happened. He's not a nice man, but also not one we want to piss off too much. Let's forget about him. Are you ready to play some more?"

At Dusty's small bark, they left the bathroom, and Dusty dropped to his knees again. Robert swore he heard the pup sigh as if he was more content on his knees than he was upright. It could be true. Many people liked becoming pups to lift the burden on their shoulders in real life or to escape from reality. He could imagine Dusty being similar.

They wandered back to their seat, and Nomad yipped

and barked at Dusty until he joined them again. Robert kept an eye out for Vincent but saw nothing of him. He hoped it meant he'd gone home. Checking the clock, he realised they'd been there for over four hours. It was after midnight, and Dusty was still going strong with Nomad by his side. If Robert was to get any sleep that night, he needed to calm things down now so Dusty could come out of pupspace slowly.

"Dusty! Come here, boy!" Dusty dashed across the mats, bumping into Robert's knees. "Slow down, boy. Time for a drink." He held the straw to his mouth again and waited for Dusty to drink his fill. "It's time to wrap this up for tonight." Dusty whined, his tail wagging as he fidgeted. "I know, Dusty, but we can't stay like this forever." Robert scratched the top of his head. "Come and sit beside me to cool down."

Instead of resting against him as he had done all night, Dusty curled up next to Robert's feet, his head resting on his front paws. Robert leaned forward and smoothed a hand down the pup's back several times. Dusty's body relaxed, and Robert sensed he'd fallen asleep. Despite the late hour, Robert didn't dare disturb him and allowed him to doze. While he did, Robert catalogued every inch of the pup's body, reminding himself of what it was like to have someone to take care of every day. He believed they'd meshed well in the dynamic, but he doubted Dusty would ever do this with him again, and the idea made him sad. He brushed aside the thought. There was nothing he could do about it.

After half an hour, his strokes became firmer to gently

bring Dusty out of his slumber. The pup stretched and rubbed at his face with his paws. Robert saw the moment Dusty realised he was still in pup form and grasped the back of his neck.

"You're okay. I'm still here. Time to go, though."

Dusty climbed to a kneeling position, gave a yip and rested his head on Robert's knee.

Robert chuckled. "I had fun, too. Let's get you downstairs." Dusty rose to stand, and Robert steadied him with a hand on his arm. "Careful now."

They made their way through the reduced crowd to the stairs and descended them, meeting the security guards at the bar.

"All done."

"Thank you for this. I know he appreciates it."

Robert nodded at the finality of the statement. Turning to Dusty, he said, "I enjoyed tonight. I hope it was what you were looking for. Take care, okay?"

Dusty laid his head on Robert's shoulder for a moment, then lifted it again. Robert smiled, though he knew Dusty couldn't see it.

"I'll leave him in your care now. Thank you for your help earlier."

"You're welcome."

After one last glance at Dusty and a whispered, "Goodbye," he left, ripping the mask off as soon as he reached fresh air. Not wanting to hang around and watch as Dusty left, he climbed into his car and drove home.

The emptiness of his house drove home how alone he was. Despite all his reassurances—to others and himself—

he didn't like it. He wanted someone to share his life with, someone to care for, someone to support him in return, no matter what he looked like. Stripping the leather from his body, he lay it beside the washing basket to carefully clean the following day. He switched on the shower and gratefully moved into the hot stream. He placed his hands on the tiles in front of him and lowered his head, allowing the water to pound onto his neck and sluice down his back. Closing his eyes, he recalled everything from that night in vivid detail.

When he began to fall asleep, he soaped and washed his body, then switched off the shower and dried off. Climbing into bed, he laid on his back, covers tucked beneath his chin, and wished he had another chance to play with Dusty. He knew it was futile, but he wished all the same.

The wish stayed with him over the next few hours because he couldn't sleep despite being tired. When his alarm woke him at seven that morning, he'd probably had around three hours of sleep. Not ideal when he had to contend with two upbeat friends who wanted to know everything about his "date," as they called it.

"It wasn't a date!" Robert stated again when Naomi asked him if he would see the guy again. "I don't even know what his voice sounds like, other than the yips and barks I heard. There were no distinguishable features, which was the whole point. I don't know who he is."

"But you want to."

Naomi stated it with such confidence that Robert made her sort through the box of roses they'd received delivery of. No one liked the job because they always ended up with thorns in their fingers. It served her right for being a pest.

The rest of the day was busy, as was always the case on a Monday morning. Maybe people had plenty of apologising to do for how they'd behaved over the weekend. Robert snorted. It wouldn't surprise him.

The tinkle of the door brought him out from his stupor, and he faced the customer. His heart sank.

"Good morning, Robert. I trust you had a good evening."

Vincent linked his fingers in front of him, no doubt trying to appear innocent. Robert's heart raced, and he hoped Naomi and Finn stayed in the back.

"Good morning, Vincent. How can I help you today?"

He kept his voice even, and though he wanted to retreat behind the counter to give himself some space, he stood his ground.

"I wanted to check on you and make sure everything is all right. You know how things can turn in the blink of an eye. We wouldn't want that to happen to you, would we?"

Robert heard the warning in his tone but refused to be cowed. "Definitely not, but everything is fine, thanks. Would you like to buy some flowers today?"

Vincent roamed closer, touching a flower here and there. "Not today." He stopped in front of Robert. "Be careful, Robert. Be very careful." Vincent smiled. "Have a good day."

Robert clenched his jaw as Vincent left the shop, the threat lingering in the quiet. He rubbed his thumb across the bangles adorning his wrist. How everything could change in the blink of an eye. He'd stayed off Vincent's radar for years by keeping himself to himself, but as soon as he'd taken on the handler job last night, he'd done something he swore never to do—he'd put himself in harm's way. Granted, it was to stop someone else from being hurt, but he'd always prided himself on never getting caught up in the politics or business of others. Keeping his business and nose clean had worked well for him in the past, and he'd promised to continue. One night with Dusty, and his work had gone down the drain.

The worst thing was he didn't regret a minute of it.

His time with Dusty had been precious to him. A reminder of what he'd always aimed for in a relationship, but there was no way he'd be able to find that when those people around him couldn't take him seriously as a Dominant. The pups who had him for one night weren't bothered because it was only *one* night, but there was never any sign any of them wanted more. He'd stopped asking after a while because the refusals were heart-breaking. It was another reason he wouldn't contact the lawyer to extend an unlimited invitation for Dusty to play with him any time. If he did that, he could end up just as broken as before, and he'd worked too hard on reinforcing his heart against the hurt.

"Everything okay, boss?"

Finn's voice broke him from the painful thoughts, and he glanced over his shoulder. "Yeah, all good. I'm away with the fairies today. Must be the lack of sleep that's done it."

"Staying up gallivanting all night doesn't agree with you." Finn chuckled. "I heard the bell. Did we have a customer?"

Robert nodded. "Just someone asking for something we don't have."

He hoped he hadn't lied because if Vincent returned, he was sure it would be for something Robert didn't want to give.

## 10

## HENRY

Henry still buzzed with energy three days later. The experience had been fantastic, and he wanted to do it again. Unfortunately, duty called with it being close to Christmas.

"Cheer up," Freddie said, coming to a stop next to him. "Don't be a sour face in the middle of Christmas cheer."

Henry snorted. "I'm not. At least, I didn't mean to be. I was thinking about when I could next go…do my thing."

"Ah, and the reason for the sad face is revealed. I'm sure you can arrange something between Christmas and New Year. Or if not, straight after New Year. They can't keep you under lock and key for too long."

"Says the man who has so many things to do that he barely has time to visit the bathroom."

Freddie waved his hand. "Not the same. I have expectations of me, as you are aware. Those override anything else."

"Exactly my point, dear cousin."

Henry gazed around the ballroom, watching guests mingle and chat with other patrons. They attended their Uncle William's favourite charity event—a charity that supported those families who spent the holiday in hospital or away from their family. They held this event every year and raised money for those families to help ease the financial burden of this time of year. Henry didn't oppose being there, but sometimes, it felt like he spent all his time with strangers and official people that he never saw his family properly.

Fortunately, he had one more event the following day before he could travel to Sandringham to be with his parents, Mary and her family, and Patrick. A black-tie dinner on Christmas Eve would be his last official engagement until after New Year. The dinner on Christmas Eve was for his entire family, too, so at least he would get to see them. As for Christmas Day, well, the morning would be spent at a church service on the Sandringham estate, but after that, he was free to use his time as he wished. And he wished to spend it with his family.

Family, though, meant Aunt Charlotte and Charles, and it was the only part of the whole celebration he didn't enjoy. There was no telling what her mood would be and if she would censor her words or not. Highly unlikely.

"I'm glad you enjoyed yourself. You appear calmer and more centred, which I never expected," Freddie said, bringing Henry out of his dark thoughts.

Henry sighed. "I can't even explain what it felt like. To have nothing weighing on me. To have the anonymity to be who I am. To forget about the pressures of life. It was… even more than I could have imagined it would be."

Freddie sipped from his glass. "I know exactly what you mean. There's only one person who can get me out of my head, and that's Damon. He knows me better than anyone, even family, I'm sorry to say. I couldn't ask for better in a best friend."

"Without a doubt. But you can talk to me, you know. I know you have Damon, and that's great, but you can talk to me, too. I might not understand everything put on you because you have more responsibility than I do, but I'm here as an ear if you need it." Henry patted him on the back.

"I know, and thank you. Sometimes, it's easier to speak to someone who's not…involved, I suppose."

"I can understand that."

"Ladies and gentlemen, can I have your attention, please?"

Henry and Freddie faced the raised platform where their uncle stood and listened as he spoke about the charity and the spirit of Christmas. Family was important, and Uncle William's speech made Henry think hard about those who didn't have someone to share the special day with, which was Uncle William's point. He wondered if Robert had a family and whether he was spending Christmas with them.

He had forced himself to stay away from the flower shop because he couldn't think of a decent reason to be there, other than to buy flowers for his family, but he could only do that so many times before his family started asking questions. He couldn't get the man out of his head. His mind had even played tricks and made him consider Robert had been his handler because when his pup had leaned against the man, he'd received a whiff of something floral, but he hadn't smelled it again afterwards.

He could visit Robert once more before Christmas to wish them all well. On the morning of Christmas Eve, he would be on his way to Sandringham, and he wouldn't get another chance. Considering his options, he would be better going as he was leaving for Norfolk. He was sure the shop was open, and he could grab some flowers for his mother and sister along the way.

Plan made, he smiled.

"Henry! I'm riding with you this morning!"

Patrick came jogging up, carrying a black bag as Henry was loading his own bag into the car, the crisp winter air surrounding them. Luckily, no snow had fallen.

"I thought you were driving yourself?"

Patrick threw his bag into the boot and slammed it shut. "I was going to, but I thought we could go together instead. We've had little time to talk lately."

His brother was right, but Henry's heart jumped. Could he still go to the flower shop with Patrick trailing along? What would he think of Henry's sudden need to buy flowers? Although he had explained a lot to his brother and cousins, he hadn't said a word about Robert.

"Sure."

They climbed into the car, and Henry drove out of Bagshot Park. The first part of the journey would be fine because it was the same road he would take to Norfolk, but when he turned into Slough, Patrick would ask questions. And he was right.

"Why are we going this way?"

"I have an errand to run first. Who do you think will join us at dinner tonight?"

Patrick snorted. "All the usual people, I would've thought. They love this day as much as Uncle Andrew does."

"It has been a celebration of Christmas for as far back as I remember reading about."

"I wonder how Mother and Father put up with us as children, getting excited about presents yet having to wait until the afternoon to open them."

Henry chuckled. "I don't know, but I can imagine we weren't as much to handle as Freddie, Douglas and George."

"Probably not."

Henry parked near the shop. "I won't be long."

"It's okay. I'll come with you."

Henry's pulse increased. "You don't have to. It won't take me long."

"I don't mind. Gives me some fresh air before being in the car for another two and a half hours."

Henry exhaled and climbed out of the car. There was nothing he could say to dissuade his brother from tagging along, and he briefly considered going somewhere else, but he wouldn't get to see Robert. Steeling himself against the questions he knew he'd have to answer when they returned to the car, Henry stepped inside Floresco.

"Good morning and Merry Chris—" Robert stopped talking when he looked up from what he'd been doing. "Your Highnesses." He bowed his head. "How can I help you this morning?"

Henry took in Robert's appearance. He wore tight black trousers with a purple shirt that was off one shoulder. In his hair, there was a green, sparkly headband with reindeers that bounced on springs whenever Robert moved. Large Christmas trees dangled from his ears, and his eyelids sparkled as much as his green eyes. For a long second, he was transfixed.

"I…um…I need some flowers for my mother and sister for Christmas." He sounded ridiculous, but he couldn't stop looking at Robert's shiny lips.

"Of course. Would you like similar choices to before, or do you have something specific in mind?"

"Similar is good." Henry wouldn't have been able to make a choice if his life depended on it.

"Okay."

Robert busied himself around the shop, picking flowers here and there and fluttering back and forth as he worked. Henry watched him, his attention fixed solely on the man, until his brother whispered in his ear, "Now I know why you wanted to visit. Nice choice, brother."

Patrick chuckled softly and wandered around the shop. "How long have you worked here, Mr…?"

"Robert is fine. I have owned this business for fourteen

years but have worked here all my life. It was owned by my grandfather before I took over from him."

"Fourteen years! You don't look old enough." Patrick winced. "Sorry, that came out wrong."

Robert laughed. The motion of his neck extending as the man lifted his head back to laugh, and the sound of it had Henry shivering in delight. He wanted more.

"It's okay. I'll take it as a compliment. I'm thirty-five, though I have been told I don't look a day over fifteen."

Patrick chuckled. "I'm assuming by jealous friends or family."

"A family joke they never forget." Robert winked at Henry, and Henry's heart danced. "Are these okay for you?"

He held out two bouquets, one filled with purples and pinks, the other with blues and whites. "They're perfect, thank you," Henry said.

"Well, if you're going with flowers, I can't exactly turn up without something," Patrick said. He sighed. "Any suggestions, Robert?"

"Do you want flowers or something else?"

"What else do you have? Not that I don't like the flowers," Patrick quickly added at Henry's frown.

Robert grinned. "We have some Christmas centrepieces or placement decorations?"

"Let's have a look."

Robert wandered over to the shelf closest to the window display and pointed several out to Patrick. While they chatted, Henry watched Robert. The ease with which he moved, the confidence he had, mixed with the soft, elegant movements he made proved to be a scintillating combination. Henry had felt an attraction to other people before, but nothing like this. He needed to find his voice because he was acting like a teenager with a crush. Although he couldn't ask Robert out on a date, he could start a conversation with him like Patrick had.

He continued to watch as Patrick chose two centre-pieces, which Robert took over to the counter and wrapped.

"What are your plans for Christmas?" Henry asked, his heart in his throat.

Robert glanced at him and smiled. "I will close the shop at noon and visit my parents and sisters not long after. I need to get all the presents in the car before I do that, though. It might take me a while. I tend to go overboard with buying gifts for my family."

"Is there no one to help you?"

"No, I gave my staff the morning off to begin their celebrations early. It's the least I could do as they work hard for me." Robert tucked the wrapped vases in a bag and set it on the counter.

"Do you want us to help you?" Henry wasn't sure where the offer came from, but he refused to take it back.

Robert paused and stared at him. "No, it's okay. I can manage but thank you for the offer. I appreciate it."

Henry couldn't look away. Robert's green eyes bored into him, though it came with a slight crinkle of his fore-head. He couldn't get a hold on what Robert's face expressed, but Henry took comfort that he wasn't looking away.

A shrill tone broke through the bubble they'd created, and Robert glanced down and fiddled with the bracelets surrounding his wrists. After a minute, Robert cleared his throat and turned to the till, ignoring the ringing phone. Henry exhaled, his skin feeling tingly and his breathing uneven.

"That will be eighty pounds, please," Robert said, his voice softer than before.

Henry fumbled and held out his card, going through the motions of paying without really concentrating. Once it had gone through, he refocused on Robert.

"Thank you. I hope you have a wonderful Christmas."

Robert smiled. "You, too, Your Highness."

"Henry," he reminded him.

Robert sighed. "Merry Christmas, Henry."

Hearing his name on Robert's lips sent a spark of heat through him. Did Robert feel it too?

"Merry Christmas, Robert," Patrick said from behind him, jolting Henry from his thoughts.

"Merry Christmas, Prince Patrick."

Henry gave Robert a small smile as he collected the flowers from the counter and exited the shop, heaving a sigh. The flowers and Patrick's centrepieces went onto the backseat, and they climbed back in the car.

"Don't." Henry held up his hand before Patrick could say a word. He started the car and aimed it towards their destination.

Patrick lasted all of twenty minutes before he started in with the third degree. "Care to tell me what that was about?"

"Not really."

"He's a nice guy. Have you asked him out yet?"

"No."

"Why not? Is he straight? No, he can't be with the way he was acting. Why haven't you asked him?"

"None of your business."

"I'm your brother. Your happiness is my business."

Henry sighed. "No, it's not."

"I'm older than you. That means I get to check out those guys who might be interested in my younger brother."

"No, it really doesn't. Leave it alone."

Patrick turned towards him and stared. "Why are you against this?" he asked, his voice quieter than before.

Henry concentrated on the road. He wished he could tell him what he'd seen, but it wouldn't make things any easier. Why burden someone else?

"I've hidden for a long time, Patrick. Give me a chance to find my footing first, okay?" It wasn't a lie. Henry had no idea how to go about asking anyone out because he'd never done it. The kiss with Kean was the only time he'd ever kissed anyone, before or since. It wasn't like he hadn't thought about it, but the idea of asking someone out was too much to consider, especially when that someone was a guy.

"Fine. Don't hide from me, though, all right? If you need to vent or talk something through, find me."

"I will. Thank you."

They filled the rest of the journey with conversations about presents, events, plans, and anything and everything else they could think of. Patrick had been right. It had been far too long since they'd been able to talk properly.

It was lunchtime when they finally reached Sandringham. The time away had not diminished the splendour of the place. Apart from Bagshot Park, this was Henry's favourite royal house. He pulled up at the door and switched off the engine. The valet stepped forward, but Patrick held up his hand for him to wait and turned to him.

"Have you brought your suit?"

Henry frowned. "Of course, I've brought a suit. Several, in fact. We're going to need them. Why, haven't you?"

Patrick rolled his eyes. "Not *a* suit. *Your* suit? You know, the playful suit?"

"No! I didn't bring that here. Do you think I'm stupid?"

Henry climbed out of the car and slammed the door shut, wincing when it closed harder than he'd expected. He opened the back door, lifting the flowers and placing them in the crook of his elbow. When he rounded the car, Patrick waited.

"I thought it would be the perfect time to rest and relax for you. I could keep an eye on you while you…be you."

"I can't do that here, Patrick. There are too many people."

Just the thought of it had anxiety ratcheting up his blood pressure. More so when he remembered Aunt Charlotte and Charles would be in attendance.

"Fine. I think you're wrong about them, but it's your

choice," Patrick whispered, a smile in place as their mother descended the steps.

"Boys! I'm glad you made it!"

Victoria opened her arms wide and waved for them to come closer.

"Mother, you saw us yesterday," Patrick said.

"And you've driven over one hundred miles since. You know I don't rest when you're on the road."

Henry stepped forward, kissing her cheek, and held out the bouquet. "I know. I came bearing a gift."

"Oh, these are gorgeous! Where did you find such a stunning bouquet?" His mother beamed and lifted the flowers to her nose.

"A florist I know."

"Ooh, you'll have to tell me about them. Did you know Louisa is considering changing florists to a new shop no one has heard of before? I'm still not convinced it's the best choice, but you know her when she has a bee in her bonnet. If this florist of yours is any good, maybe I could put in a kind word for them?"

Henry's heart dropped. "I think he already does the flowers for Windsor. I helped him set up at the children's Christmas party the other week. Is he not doing a good job?"

"Oh! Is that who made these? Well, in that case, I wholly approve of her choice. That young man was having a trial at that event. His work impressed Louisa, and if you helped, too, I'm not surprised. I'll put in my two cents for... What's his name?"

"Robert. Robert Martin and the shop is called Floresco."

"Wonderful." She linked arms with him, and they wandered inside. "Come on, Patrick."

"But, Mother, I have a gift for you, too!"

Victoria laughed and lowered her voice. "I always love teasing him like this." She winked at him. "Oh, do come on, Patrick." She passed the flowers back to Henry. "Be a dear and hold those for me."

His mother turned and opened her arms to Patrick with a smile. "I'm only playing, dear boy. Thank you for being here, sweetheart. Ooh, it's wrapped." She stepped over to a small side table and rested it on it while she opened the paper. "It's beautiful, and it will look amazing on my dresser."

"It's supposed to be a centrepiece for the table," Patrick said.

Victoria waved her hand. "And it will be, but for my dresser instead. I'm being selfish and refusing to share it with anyone else."

Patrick beamed, and Henry smiled. Christmas was going to be wonderful.

## 11

## ROBERT

Robert needed to stop obsessing over Henry. Photos of the man adorned his phone gallery, and he had many websites bookmarked because of interviews with the prince or general information about him. Henry appeared to be an open book, although Robert wasn't sure that was the truth because there was no mention of a relationship of any kind, and he couldn't believe that. Henry was good at keeping things secret, it seemed.

The problem with his fascination was that Robert's attraction to the man was increasing. The more he found out about him, the more he saw and spoke to him, the more Robert liked who he was. And that meant his heart was getting involved, which was not a good thing at all because who could ever imagine him being with a prince?

"What'cha looking at?"

His sister Ophelia dropped next to him and snatched the phone from his hands.

"Hey! Give it back!"

Robert swiped at her, trying to dislodge the phone from her hands to no avail.

"Ooh, why are you looking at princes?" Ophelia squinted at the screen and zoomed in on the picture of Henry dressed in a pristine black suit, walking next to his brother.

"No reason. It just came up on the search I did. I was curious," he lied.

He knew the minute he'd said it, he'd made a mistake. Ophelia pressed the back button to see what Robert had searched for, and he closed his eyes when she squealed.

"I would be surprised if you didn't see a picture of princes when you searched for Prince Henry. Now, dear brother, why are you searching the internet for a picture of a prince?"

Scrambling to think of a believable answer, he said, "Well, you know I've been wanting the contract for Windsor Castle?" He waited until she nodded. "He helped me with the flowers when we did a children's Christmas party the other week, and he was great. I was curious." He shrugged. "Hen—Prince Henry told me he's worked with his mother in their gardens at home..." he trailed off, knowing he wasn't making any sense.

Ophelia tilted her head to the side and stared at him through narrowed eyes. "You like him," she said.

Robert blew out a breath. "Yeah, but it's weird. I rarely like people without getting to know them first, and I think

I've met him four times. How can I be attracted to him when I don't really know him?"

Ophelia waved the phone at him. "But you do. If anything, you probably have more of a head start than he does—if he's interested, that is."

"What do you mean?"

"Well, think about it. You've been researching him, seeing different pictures of his life, no doubt reading about him. You have a lot of information at your fingertips about this man. Really, you are getting to know him. It just happens to be through the media instead of face-to-face. I know you've explained to me about being demisexual and how you need to have an emotional connection to someone, but I think this *is* your connection. Your brain is getting to know him through the internet, and it likes what it sees, apparently."

Robert thought that through. It seemed plausible, but he'd never experienced it before. Could it work like that? He closed his eyes and sighed because he already knew his answer. The faceless dream man he masturbated to wasn't faceless sometimes, and it didn't dim his arousal.

"What are you going to do about it?"

Robert shrugged. "I don't know."

"Does he feel the same?"

He thought about their interactions and the way Henry behaved around him. "I think so. I thought he visited the shop because it was a test of my professionalism before the family decided about the contract, but... maybe it didn't have anything to do with that."

"The youngest sister can also be the wisest occasionally." Ophelia grinned as she stood. "Come on. Time for lunch."

She sashayed off in the direction of the kitchen and left Robert with his musings. He couldn't believe he hadn't seen it before. He should've known something was happening the minute his faceless dream man became Henry. Now, he needed to decide what he was going to do. There was no way of contacting Henry because Robert didn't have his number, and he was sure if he rang his contact, they would laugh him off the phone if he asked to speak to the prince. The only thing he could do was wait and see if Henry came into the shop again.

If they were going to start something—which was a crazy thought, him with a prince—he needed to explain about his lifestyle choices. He wondered if the rumours of Club Royal were true. If they were, Henry might not be as shocked as other people would be.

"Robert!"

His mother's voice broke into his thoughts, and he rushed to the kitchen, dodging around the Christmas tree. "Sorry, Mama. I was distracted."

"Hmm, by your prince, no?" She winked.

Winnie was fifty-five years young, and after having three children in seven years, she was enjoying the freedom now that they were all grown up and out of the house. While they had been young, she started her custom sewing business, and since they'd left, she had built it up even more. She was in demand. His dad, Zachary, still worked as a postal worker, meaning he was up and out early in the morning, but home just after lunch, depending on how busy his day was. He had started the job when he was eighteen, having declined his dad's offer to work in the flower shop, and had never wanted to do anything else because he said it kept him fit, and he got to meet some pleasant people along the way.

"I can't believe you said something already, you little witch," Robert groused.

"I hope that was witch and not the other word," his mother said.

"It was. Trust me, I know dogs, and she isn't one."

Ophelia frowned at him. "I don't know if I should be offended or complimented about that."

"Offended, definitely." He smirked.

"What's this I hear about a prince?" Zachary asked as they sat down to all the trimmings for their Christmas day lunch.

Robert had arrived at his parents' house the previous afternoon, and although they lived in the same town, he enjoyed spending his Christmas morning with someone, and he stayed overnight. His sisters, however, had arrived that morning. Hadley had brought along her husband, Jason, and everyone had mooned over her seven months' pregnant belly. Hadley and Jason lived in Brighton now and made the trip often, but especially at Christmas. Jason had lost his parents when he was a teenager, yet as soon as Hadley met him, they were both smitten, and Winnie had adopted him.

Robert sighed. "I met Prince Henry when I did the flowers for the children's event a few weeks ago. He helped me out by finishing some sprays for me. He's talented, and we got talking about how he helped his mother in her garden. I didn't see anything of him after that, but a few days later, he turned up at the shop, wanting to buy a bouquet. I thought nothing of it, but he keeps coming back."

"And Robert likes him," Ophelia said with a smile.

"And does Prince Henry like you?" his mother asked.

Robert shrugged. "I don't know. I think so, but it's hard to tell." He laughed self-consciously. "I'm out of practise, it seems."

He closed his eyes and breathed in the scent of the roast dinner, his stomach bemoaning the fact he'd not started eating.

"I think you should be direct and ask him when you next see him," Hadley said. "It worked for me." She smiled at Jason, who blushed and looked at his plate. They were cute together.

The conversation changed to Jason's job, and Robert concentrated on his thoughts again. As he ate roast potatoes, roast chicken, vegetables and more, he ran through every interaction he'd experienced with Henry. He could see points where Henry appeared interested but hadn't done or said anything to show he wanted more. Robert was at a loss, and it confused his dominant self.

The more he thought about it, the more he thought Hadley was right. Robert was a Dominant, and therefore, he needed to be confident in his approach. Similar to when he was dealing with a new pup, he exuded confidence because the pup needed to know who was in charge and who to listen to. But what would happen to the pups

Robert usually helped? Especially the celebrity one? He'd not heard anything from them, but if they called, should he say no because he wanted to speak to Henry, or should he carry on as normal and only stop if he managed to discuss things with the prince? Henry might not even want to try a relationship with Robert. He might be fighting the attraction.

Robert sighed, his mind going in circles. He wished he had a way of sending a Christmas message to Henry, but he didn't. The best idea would be to forget about it until he was back in the shop and hope that Henry would visit again.

It was easier said than done because four days later, after the Bank Holidays, he opened the shop while butterflies fluttered in his stomach and waves of nausea flowed over him. He wished he could blame it on alcohol, but he couldn't.

Finn and Naomi would arrive in a couple of hours, and it gave Robert some time to settle himself down. If they got wind of what was going on, his life would be hell because they wouldn't let up. He set up the till as the door tinkled and glanced up, his usual greeting dying on his lips.

"Good morning, Robert," Henry said, closing the door.

Robert licked his lips, suddenly nervous, which was ridiculous. He inhaled, gathering his confident demeanour and stood taller. "Good morning, Henry."

Neither said anything for a few long minutes, then Robert broke the silence. "What can I get you this morning?" Henry's forehead creased, and his eyes darted around the shop. To save him from buying something he didn't need, Robert continued, "Would you like to join me for a cup of tea? I've not had one yet." It was a lie, but Henry wouldn't know that.

Henry raised his eyebrows. "Don't you have to work?"

"Yes, but there's unlikely to be many customers this close to New Year."

He waited for Henry to answer his original question.

"Yes, please. Tea would be lovely."

"Come on."

Robert turned towards the back of the shop and the tiny break room he'd created. It held a kettle, a microwave, a small counter with a cupboard underneath and a small two-person table and chairs. They didn't need much when there were only three of them working there.

"How do you take your tea?"

"Um…white, no sugar, please."

Robert pointed to the chairs. "Have a seat. It won't take long."

He filled the kettle and set it boiling, all the while feeling a hum of something in the air. Henry's presence lent an almost electrical buzz to the room, and Robert could feel his body wanting to get closer. For him, this level of attraction was unheard of, especially as he'd not interacted with the man as much as it usually took for Robert to attempt anything with other people.

Placing a mug in front of Henry, Robert took a seat opposite, wrapping his hands around his mug.

"Did you have a nice Christmas?" Robert asked.

Henry had taken his coat off and hung it over the back

of his chair, leaving him in a dark red jumper. His hair was mussed as though he'd just climbed out of the shower, and his beard and moustache were neatly groomed.

"It was…eventful." He gave a small smile that didn't reach his eyes. "I'll be glad for a new start to the year."

"That bad, huh? Yeah, my sisters gave me hell for three days, but I had some relief yesterday when they went home."

Henry sipped his brew. "Do you get on well with them?"

Robert nodded. "Very. We're a close family. It's nice."

"I'm close to my brother and mother, but not as much with my father and sister. They're not horrible or anything, but we don't have the same interests, I suppose."

There was one thing Robert hadn't known from what he'd read. "My family doesn't have the same interests as me, but luckily, my friends do. It's always easier going places when you have someone with you."

Henry glanced down at his cup, smoothing his thumb up and down the handle. "I get that. It's not as easy to do things alone."

There was a wealth of information in that tone, but Robert didn't think Henry would appreciate him discussing it right now. "No, it's not easy." He inhaled, readying himself. "Would you like to go out with me sometime?"

Henry's eyes widened when he lifted his head. "I… I… would like to, but I don't… I'm not…" He closed his eyes and refocused on Robert. "I'm not out," he whispered. "I don't know if I can."

Suddenly, Robert understood; Henry couldn't come out. He frowned. "Isn't Prince Douglas gay?"

Henry closed his eyes as if pained and nodded. "He shouldn't... He's... They... Fuck." Henry rubbed his hands over his head, his agitation clear.

Robert rounded the table and stood next to him, sliding his arm around Henry's shoulder and holding him. "Hey, it's all right. Don't worry. I won't tell a soul if that's what you're worried about." Henry stared up at him, and Robert could see the turmoil behind his eyes. He cupped Henry's cheek. "Everything will be okay."

Henry studied him for a moment, then leaned forward and pressed his forehead against Robert's stomach, wrapping his arms around his waist. "I'm sorry," Henry mumbled.

"You don't need to be sorry." Robert ran his hands across Henry's shoulder blades, trying to soothe him. A waft of vanilla reached his nose, and he tamped down on the need to bury his nose in Henry's hair.

Henry lifted his face, resting his chin on Robert's stomach. Robert stared down into the face photographed hundreds of times, and none had done him justice. He threaded his fingers through Henry's hair, and the man's eyelids fluttered. When his eyes refocused on Robert, he saw them drop to his mouth and unconsciously licked his lips. Robert wasn't sure what Henry wanted from this, but he could understand non-verbal language, and this man was aching for a kiss.

Robert lowered his head, advertising his intent with slow movements. He heard Henry's breath hitch, and

Robert's heart pounded. When their lips touched, it felt like a shock went through him. He left soft pecks on Henry's thin lips before pressing harder and encouraging Henry to open his mouth with a flick of his tongue. Henry obliged with a shaky inhale, and Robert slid his tongue inside. He ran his tongue along Henry's and skimmed the tip across the roof of Henry's mouth, catching his rough exhale. Robert tilted his head, giving him deeper access.

Henry's hands gripped at the back of Robert's jumper, pulling him closer. Robert stepped between Henry's spread legs and deepened the kiss further, their inhales and exhales noisy in the silence of the room. Henry tentatively pressed his tongue forward into Robert's mouth, and Robert sucked on it. The result was Henry's head dropping back and his mouth opening further. Henry's reactions were dynamite to Robert's libido, and he felt himself reacting. Robert moved his head to the opposite side, taking Henry's mouth harder.

A tinkling broke through the haze of his mind, and he struggled to understand what it was.

"Hello? Is the shop open?"

The female voice snapped Robert out of his daze, and he broke away from Henry, breathing hard. They stared at each other for a few seconds, then Robert cleared his throat and called, "I'll be with you in a moment!"

"No rush. I'll just browse, thank you."

Robert inhaled unevenly, staring at the prince, looking decidedly dishevelled. "You might want to…" He waved his hand at Henry's hair, though Robert loved the mussed look.

Henry swallowed hard and touched his swollen lips. "Wow."

Robert tilted his head. "Was that your first kiss?"

"Not as such."

Robert received the underlying meaning. "A conversation for another day?"

Henry nodded.

"I have to go." He waved at the door. "Are you staying?"

"I should leave."

Robert was disappointed, but he understood. "You can use the back entrance if you wish."

Henry nodded. "Could I have your number?" Smiling, Robert watched as Henry entered it into his phone. "I've sent you a text, so you have mine. Thank you, Robert."

"What for?"

Henry inhaled and stood. "Making the first move. I wouldn't have known what to do."

Robert bit his lip. "You're welcome."

Henry held up his phone. "I'll call." He hesitated, then pressed a brief kiss to Robert's lips.

He led the way to the back door, allowing Henry to leave with a smile before he wandered through to the shop front.

"Sorry about that. How can I help you?"

Robert didn't know how he was going to pretend like nothing had happened when Naomi and Finn arrived. Henry felt like a newborn foal to him, trembling and stumbling his way through it, but Robert was fine with showing him the ropes, so to speak. He touched his lips, feeling the puffiness of them, and smiled.

When the customer left, Robert checked his phone, grinning when he found the message from Henry. He saved the number and replied with a smiling emoji. He had a voicemail, which he listened to, but his smile disappeared when he heard Elton's voice.

*"I've had a call from the lawyer, Ian Kiln. They would like to arrange another playdate. Let me know what you can do."*

Robert's heart sank. What did he do now?

12

-----

# HENRY

*"Henry! Have you found yourself a master yet?" Charles threw his head back and laughed, then swallowed his shot and poured another one. He carried the drink, plus another for Aunt Charlotte, across to where the woman sat.*

*The second Henry had stepped into the room, he knew he'd made a mistake. Charles on his own was a force to be reckoned with, but Charles with his mother was even more so.*

*"I've heard about these submissive tendencies of yours, Henry. I don't know what you're thinking, but you need to stop right now. No heir to the throne will ever be submissive or gay. You may as well forget about it. You're doing a good enough job as a monitor. Stop trying for more when you'll bring this family down if you do. I'll make sure that never happens."*

*Henry heard the threat in her tone and clenched his jaw against the need to lower his head. Although that was what she wanted him to do while he stood in her presence, it would also allow her further proof of his submission, and he refused to give her that. The evil, vindictive woman would one day get her due. He had to believe that.*

*"I hope you are not also going down the road of your cousin Douglas. It would be a shame to have two disappointments in the family." She crossed her legs and glared at him with a meaning he couldn't help but understand.*

*"I have no need for relationships, Aunt Charlotte. I'm happy as I am."*

*"I'm glad to hear it. There is no need to bring such disgusting behaviour into our precious family time. I can't believe Andrew allowed that boy to be here."*

*The vitriol was dripping from her voice, and Henry was under no illusion who she was talking about: Douglas's boyfriend, Maverick.*

*"He has to pretend to support them, Mother. A king who cannot control his children would be the laughingstock of the country. This way, he can pretend he is inclusive and receive more votes. It's not a bad idea, but it turns my stomach." Charles's face scrunched up, and he rubbed his stomach.*

*Henry swallowed and opened his mouth, but Aunt Charlotte interrupted. "Henry, be a good boy and find your mother for me. I'd like a word." She waved her hand in a dismissive gesture, and though the motion annoyed him, he was glad for the reprieve.*

*"Of course."*

*He exited the room and leaned his head against the wall, gasping for air. Then someone slammed him back against the same wall with a hand resting too close to his neck for Henry to be comfortable.*

*"Remember the warning, Henry. Stay in your lane, or even*

*better, stay unattached. We're not messing around here."*
*Charles's alcohol-scented breath made Henry's eyes water, but*
*he said nothing in return. Charles lowered his voice. "I know*
*you've seen the repercussions of being a fag, Henry. I've seen*
*you lurking in the hallways and the lingering looks you give*
*certain people. Be careful. You never know who the next...*
*problem might be."*

Henry woke, sweat dripping into his eyes and blinding him. He wiped his hand over his face, trying to regulate his breathing. Sleep was the last thing on his mind after he'd received that warning. He didn't think they would kill him in his sleep or anything, but he wouldn't put it past Charles to do something sinister. Henry swung his legs over the edge of the bed and dropped his head into his hands.

Despite the threat, Henry couldn't have stopped himself from seeing Robert again, even if he'd locked himself in the Tower. A smile curved his mouth, glad he'd taken the chance to visit. That kiss... Henry's eyes drifted closed, and he returned to the memory that helped him fall asleep the previous evening. The softness of Robert's hands, the scent of flowers, the taste of his lips, the rasp of his breath. The nightmare receded with every detail he remembered of the kiss he'd shared with Robert.

They'd sent messages back and forth throughout the day—small talk that led to a question-and-answer session. He'd been careful of how he'd worded some things. He was not immune to having someone hack his accounts, however unlikely it might be. Being honest was something he needed to do, but not over the phone. His lawyer had arranged for another pup night for him that night, and he'd made no mention of it to Robert. Henry shook his head. It was too early to think he and Robert were in a relationship and needed to shine a light into the darkest corners of each of their lives. If what they had lasted, he would explain about his puppy side. As far as he was concerned, it wasn't as if he was cheating because there was no sexual aspect to their play at all.

His phone beeped, and he disconnected it from the charger. It wasn't even eight in the morning, but Douglas's message made him smile.

*DOUGLAS: We're going to visit Savill Garden today. Would you like to join us?*

Savill Garden was a botanical garden they strolled around when they had a few hours to spare. Wandering around the trees and gardens was therapeutic. It was a gorgeous spot for a picnic, and one Henry had often taken advantage of.

*HENRY: Definitely. What time?*
  *DOUGLAS: Now?*
  *HENRY: Are you even dressed yet?*
  *DOUGLAS: Um, no.*

*HENRY: How about an hour?*
*DOUGLAS: Perfect.*

Henry chuckled and replaced his phone on the bedside table. He checked the door was locked and jumped into the shower, excited about his life for the first time in a long time. Tomorrow was New Year's Eve. Maybe he was right about it being a new start for him.

His eagerness for the future—one that might involve Robert—had his body reacting, and he soaped his hand before enclosing his cock in it. He leaned his side against the cold tiles, keeping his face out of the spray, and stroked. His eyelids fluttered shut, and a muted groan left his lips. The image of Henry on his knees, staring up at Robert's face as he sucked him, rocked him to his core. He wanted that.

He rolled his forehead against the tiles, turning his back to the spray, and soaped his hand more before returning to fondle his dick. Imagining the taste and the feel of Robert's cock in his mouth and Robert's fingers threading through his hair, holding him in place, had him erupting over his hand with an audible groan.

He panted against the tiles for a long moment, letting his breathing return to normal, and rolled to his back to let the water wash away the evidence. His legs were trembling, but he smiled.

The weather was decidedly cold that day, and he dressed in black jeans, a dark blue jumper and before he left the house, a thick winter coat and waterproof boots. It didn't even faze his mood when he opened the door to the fresh, biting cold air. It wasn't a day for a picnic, but for a walk in the sunshine, it was perfect.

Henry drove half an hour to Savill Gardens and parked to wait for Douglas and Maverick. When they pulled up, understandably, they brought several security men with them. Henry hadn't even thought about that, as distracted as he'd been. He should've brought one with him. It was too late now, but he'd be fine. Douglas was further up the throne line than Henry was, and at least he'd brought some to protect him.

"Good morning!" he said when he climbed out of his car. "This is a perfect day for some fresh air."

Douglas raised his eyebrows at Henry's exuberant greeting, but he didn't let it dim his mood. Let him think what he wanted.

"Morning, cousin. How are things with you?"

"Good, thanks. What made you decide to take a freezing cold walk today?" Henry asked.

Maverick stepped closer. "Someone thought it would blow away the cobwebs of the year and prepare us for the new one. I, on the other hand, would've preferred something warmer."

Douglas draped his arm around Maverick's shoulders and held him. "I'll keep you warm."

The love that shone in Douglas's eyes when he looked down at Maverick was something Henry had always longed for. Someone to accept him for who he was. All the bells and whistles his life and personality consisted of.

Was that Robert? He didn't know, but he would take the chance, anyway.

They began wandering down a path that would weave them through the trees. Douglas talked about the event he and Maverick were currently putting together for those interested in archaeology. It wasn't something that had ever interested Henry, but the animation on Douglas's face as he spoke was enough to get Henry excited about it for him.

"How are things in your neck of the woods?" Douglas asked, raising his eyebrows.

Henry glanced at Maverick and back to Douglas, who shook his head minutely. Douglas had mentioned nothing to Maverick, but maybe Henry shouldn't be worried as Maverick was Douglas's partner after all.

"I've made another playdate for tonight." He purposefully didn't look at Maverick when he said it.

"That's great! I'm happy for you. Is it everything you hoped it would be?"

Henry side-eyed Maverick, seeing a frown on his forehead, though he said nothing. "And more. Being a pup is freeing, relaxing, but exciting at the same time. It's like my body and mind didn't know what to do with itself."

Even then, he could feel the excitement zinging through his nerve endings. He hoped, with everything inside of him, his pup nature wouldn't put Robert off. He wasn't ready to tell him about it, but he would soon because he hated keeping secrets, even those that were necessary.

"Giving someone the reins is hard to do but is the best

feeling in the world," Maverick said. At Henry's frown, he glanced at Douglas, who nodded. "I enjoy sensation play, and giving Douglas complete control to do what he wants to me allows me to feel and nothing else. I don't have to think, I don't have to plan, I'm just me."

"You're really the one in control, though, aren't you?" Henry asked.

Maverick nodded. "Yes. Being submissive doesn't mean you roll over and show your belly to everyone. You know that as well as anyone else from working at the club. It takes strength and courage to let go. I'm glad you've found somewhere to do it."

"What's your handler like?" Douglas asked.

Henry shoved his hands into his coat pocket, the cold a little too much for his extremities. "He's great. Calm, knowledgeable about the club and reminds me to drink." He chuckled.

"I'm glad. You deserve this, Henry." Douglas smiled over Maverick's head at him.

"I didn't think I would ever have the chance at this. I have you five to thank for it. I wouldn't have done it without you prodding me."

Maverick laughed. "I fear for your sanity if you involved those five in your plans. You're a brave man, Henry."

"I think you're braver for becoming part of this family," Henry countered, his high dimmed a little as thoughts of Charles tried to crowd in.

"Nah, I can take on anyone to have Douglas by my side." Maverick and Douglas shared another look, and

Henry focused on the path ahead.

"I kissed someone." His eyes widened. He hadn't meant to say it, but the words had been circling in his head for hours, his own little refrain dancing around.

Douglas stopped, pulling Maverick to a halt, too. "What? When? Who with?"

Henry continued walking for a few more steps, studying the ground as if it held all the answers to his questions, then pivoted on his heel. The security team had stopped far enough away to give them the notion of being alone.

"Remember the florist, Robert?" They both nodded. "Well, we talked a little, and I went to his shop a few times. I never planned on doing anything. I just... couldn't stay away. I went to see him yesterday, and he asked me out." He held out his hand before either could say anything. "I said I couldn't, and he understood, but he kissed me. And it was great," he whispered.

Douglas strode over and enfolded him in his arms. There was a three-inch height difference between them, which meant Henry could hide his face in Douglas's shoulder. He felt a weight lifting from his shoulders and squeezed his eyes shut. He gripped Douglas and said what was concerning him the most.

"I'm scared, Doug."

Douglas pulled back and stared at him. "Scared of what?"

"Aunt Charlotte, Charles, the family, the public, everyone's reactions. Need I say more?"

"They can't do anything about it, Henry. You need to be true to yourself—"

Henry wrenched himself back, throwing his arms wide. "They can do something about it! I've seen it, Douglas! I've seen how they treat people like us! If you'd seen it, you'd be scared, too."

Douglas marched closer. "What do you mean, you've seen it? What have you seen?"

Henry shook his head, rubbing at the headache growing behind his eyes. "I've seen enough to know that being gay won't be acceptable in the family unless you are no longer part of it," he said with a sigh. He dropped his arms to his sides, worn out.

"I don't understand, Henry. I'm gay, and nothing has happened to me."

"Yet."

Maverick rested a hand on Douglas's arm. "Tell me what you've seen, Henry. Actually, don't. Let's take this home. Call the others. I think they're going to need to hear this."

"What do you mean?" Douglas said.

Maverick glanced at him. "This goes much deeper than we ever thought it did, Douglas. We need to figure out what's going on. But not here."

They turned to walk back towards the car, the security team allowing them to pass before stepping in behind them. When they reached the car, Henry said he was okay to drive, but he wasn't, and Maverick knew it.

"Des, could you drive Henry to Windsor, please?"

"Of course, sir."

The security guard opened the door, and Henry slid into the passenger seat. By the time they arrived at Windsor, his head was a full-blown mining excavation. Stress would do that to him. He followed Douglas and Maverick into the building and to Douglas's rooms. When the door closed behind them, Maverick strode over to a small decorative table near the kettle and retrieved something. He wandered back to Henry with a bottle of water.

"Here, take this. If you don't take something now, it will be much worse later."

Maverick handed him some paracetamol and the bottle, and Henry accepted with a small smile. He swallowed the tablets and removed his coat, hanging it on the coat hooks by the door. The door almost bowled him over when it opened quickly after one hard knock.

"Where's the fire?" George asked.

"Patience, dear brother. We need to wait for the others," Douglas said.

The rest of them didn't prolong the wait, arriving quickly, and with Maverick handing out tea and coffee, it wasn't long until they were all seated with equally quizzical expressions.

"Henry has some news we all need to know about," Maverick said from beside him.

Henry inhaled, putting his tea on the table and linking his fingers together. "When I was about thirteen, I witnessed some things that no thirteen-year-old should. We'd been visiting Sandringham because it was close to Christmas. Around eleven o'clock one night, I wandered to the kitchen to get something to eat, but before I could get there, I heard something in a room. The door was ajar, and as any curious teenager would, I peered through the crack." He stared at the floor, seeing nothing but the scene from all those years ago.

"A man hung from the ceiling by his wrists, another locked into the stocks, and yet another spread across the bed. At first, I thought it was the BDSM they'd started telling us about. But their cries were not of pleasure, even I could tell at that age. And what the people were doing to them was nothing but punishment."

An arm wound around his shoulders, but he couldn't see them. All he could see were the faces of the three men. "There were eight other people in that room. People I thought of as family, but they were punishing these men for being gay, for fucking men."

"Who did you see?"

He didn't know who asked, but his mind showed him the images as he spoke. "Aunt Charlotte, Uncle Ernest, Uncle John, Aunt Miranda, three people I didn't know, and Charles. He was only nineteen!" He stared at Christian, hoping his silent apology was received.

Christian blanched and looked away, his face returning to the neutral expression he often wore.

"Fuck. What happened?" Freddie asked from beside him.

Henry stared at him. "Stuff of nightmares until I couldn't take any more, and I ran to bed."

"That morning, you begged to go home, saying there was a ghost in the building," Patrick said, eyes wet.

Henry nodded. "I didn't want anyone to know what I'd seen. But apparently, Charles had always known."

"What makes you say that?" Christian asked in a quiet voice.

"Charles told me the other day when we were at Sandringham. Aunt Charlotte and Charles have been keeping an eye on me and have noticed things. They don't like that, to them, my behaviour implies I'm submissive. They warned me to be more dominant in the future."

"Otherwise…?"

"I don't want to think about that."

Freddie tightened his grip around Henry's shoulders, and Henry sank into it. "I wish you had told me, or anyone. You've spent many years hiding so much. I would've believed you, you know?"

Henry peered up at him. "I couldn't be sure, and by the time I could, I'd pushed it far inside."

"What the hell are we going to do about it?" Christian asked, sitting forward in his seat.

Freddie sighed. "I have no idea, but for now, keep this between us. We need to regroup. Plus," he winced, "I have a meeting I'm late for." He touched Henry's chin in their goodbye. "Stay with one of us if you're worried."

"I will. Thanks."

When Freddie and Christian left, Henry told them about his playdate that night, then left them to their conversation. He needed to get home and get ready, but first, he needed a nap. The stress of the morning had worn him out.

13

# CHRISTIAN

As Christian walked out with Freddie, he felt as if someone had pulled the rug from underneath him.

"Are you all right?" Freddie asked.

"Would you be if you'd just found out your parents were part of this sick practice?"

Freddie said nothing, and Christian apologised. "Sorry, I know they're not *good* people, but I thought they were at least decent human beings if that makes sense."

"Yes, it does. Some people are too good at hiding their true feelings," Freddie said.

If it was a dig at him, Freddie could get lost. Christian had learnt at an early age to show no response to what he witnessed and experienced. It had been drilled into him even more when he'd enlisted. Hiding his emotions was like second nature, although he occasionally slipped around his closest friends.

"I can't believe they could get away with that taking place in Sandringham. There are so many people around at that time of year; surely someone saw something," Christian said.

"Someone did. Henry. That's the problem. If they could scare a thirteen-year-old boy as much as they did, they could do the same to anyone." Freddie sighed. "I wonder how long this has been going on and the extent to which Father knows. I *don't* believe he would have anything to do with it, and I have to believe that if he knew, he would've done something about it. There is no way he would stand for that."

"Let's hope so because if he is, he's gone down in my estimations, and I might just have to do something about it."

Freddie stopped them with a hand on Christian's shoulder. "Don't do anything until we have confirmation, Chris. It might cause more harm than good."

Christian looked away. "I will investigate, but I promise I won't do anything without speaking to you first."

"Good. I don't want to lose you to this. Just because they are...whatever they are, doesn't mean you are like them. You may have come from their genes, but you also have my genes, and you know I would never do something like this. Remember that when you next think you must be like them because YOU ARE NOT."

The fierce words settled inside Christian, and he dropped his head forward. Freddie dragged him into a hug and held him tightly for a long minute. He pulled back and inhaled.

"Where do we go from here?" Christian asked.

"I need to keep collating the information on the different things people have heard about Aunt Charlotte's and Charles's actions and words. I started when things got bad with Douglas and Talon. You know when we thought Charles might've orchestrated it."

"Did he?"

Freddie shrugged. "There's been no evidence of it yet, but I still have plenty of people to talk to. Someone somewhere knows something they don't realise is important. I just need to find it."

"I'll speak to my contacts as well. See if they can come up with something."

"Thanks." Freddie slid his finger underneath Christian's chin and lifted it. "You need this more than anyone at the moment."

Christian tried for a smile. "Anyway, you'll be late for your meeting."

Freddie glanced at his watch and cursed, then jogged down the corridor. "Remember what I said, Chris."

Yeah, he'd remember. He'd remember everything that he'd ever seen and heard and write it all down for Freddie. Knowing himself, he'd heard something he hadn't realised was important like Freddie said. They needed a lead of some sort, and maybe Christian was the one who had it.

## 14

## ROBERT

"We're going to The Den tonight. Are you coming?" Finn asked.

Robert withheld a smile. Despite worrying about being the handler for Dusty without having told Henry, he had decided to go ahead because it wasn't a sexual relationship with Dusty. If it had been, he wouldn't do it. He was sure Henry wouldn't mind once he explained it to him, so he'd agreed to the second playdate.

"Yes, I'll be there at about eight o'clock."

"Woohoo! We'll have some fun tonight!" Finn swayed his hips and danced his way back to the front of the shop.

Robert grinned and turned the music up a little louder. He wasn't a big dancer, but he loved to feel the beat and move however it told him to. There was only an hour left before he closed the shop, and excitement coursed through him when he thought of Dusty. The pup was adorable and had taken to the role quicker than Robert had expected. He was happy to help him achieve that again.

Time flew, and Robert shut the shop, showered and dressed for The Den. He'd told Finn he might not see him beforehand because he needed to "collect" his pup. They were following the same plans as they had the first night.

He entered Elton's office and sank into the seat. "How are you, Elton?"

"I'm good. I'm not sure my heart can stand doing this celebrity thing too often. The stress kills me." He chuckled.

Robert frowned. "I can find somewhere else if you'd prefer? I don't want you getting sick on us."

Elton waved his hand. "Nah. The crux of the matter is that it stresses me out that he's here, but it would stress me just as much thinking he was somewhere else and not as safe."

Robert nodded slowly, an idea forming as dangerous as it might be. A knock sounded before he could bring it up with Elton, and he dragged on his mask and stood. Dusty entered the room, followed by the same two guys as before.

"Good evening, Dusty," Robert said, unable to keep the smile from his voice. "Are you ready?" Dusty nodded, and Robert tied the ribbon to the back of his suit. "See you later, Elton."

"Have a good night."

They strode for the stairs at the back of the club, losing the security men as agreed, and climbed without a word, and when they reached the top, Robert asked Dusty to present.

"Same rules as before," he said to the pup, who looked eager to play.

Robert smiled and wandered over to the mosh, sitting in the same seat as before. He leaned on his knees, reaching forward to scratch at Dusty's head. The pup started because he'd been watching the other pups. Dusty nudged his head forward, further into Robert's hand.

"Are you ready?" Dusty yipped. "Go play."

Dusty scampered off as soon as he'd said the words, and Robert chuckled. When a server came his way, he ordered two bottles of water, a straw and a bowl then returned to gazing at the pups' playful banter. Dusty played with a pup that was brown with white patches. Robert didn't recognise the pup, but he seemed content. Dusty spent his time going back and forth between the pups and Robert, drinking and eating the fudge snacks Robert had brought.

"Have you thought about my offer?"

The silky-smooth but slimy voice came from behind him, and he glanced over his shoulder at Vincent.

"What offer?"

"Oh, that's right. I've not made it yet." Vincent grinned, and a sense of foreboding came over Robert. The man rested his hands on the back of the sofa Robert sat on, bringing his mouth close to Robert's ear. It took everything in him to stop himself from recoiling. "I know who he is," he whispered. "And what a pretty prize he could be."

Robert locked his gaze on Dusty, not wanting the pup

out of his sight, and clenched his jaw. "Leave him alone. It's of no concern to you who frequents the clubs."

"Ah, but that's where you're wrong. I check out all the new happenings around here to ensure my livelihood is unaffected. Can't have that now, can we?"

"What does it matter who he is?"

Vincent stayed silent, and Robert glanced at him. The man chuckled, and a slow smile spread across his face. "You don't *know* who he is, do you? Priceless."

"It doesn't matter who he is," he stated, firming his voice, and returned his gaze to Dusty. "Anyone is entitled to their anonymity."

"Not when it involves me, they don't." Vincent crouched, resting his elbows. "If you don't want me to expose him, you will do as I say."

Robert had known there was a reason for such secrecy, and although he'd been curious, it was none of his business. Now, though, Vincent had made it his concern. His stomach churned as he thought about what Vincent could want.

"And what exactly do you want me to do? I'm not saying I'll do it, but you can ask." He sounded a lot more confident than he felt at that point.

"I want to meet him in person, take him for a trial run, if you get my meaning."

Robert shook his head before Vincent had even finished talking. "Not a chance."

"I didn't think you'd go for that. How about sixty per cent of your business?"

Robert snorted. "Why not ask for the moon?" He

pushed the limit of Vincent's tolerance, he knew, but there was no way he'd give in to the man for something that extreme.

"How about allowing me to leave a few packages at your shop for someone to collect?"

As soon as he heard the words, he knew that had been Vincent's request all along. He'd been using the other ones to soften Robert up. It was the last thing he wanted to do, but what choice did he have? He didn't want Dusty's identity to get out.

"Think about it?" the man whispered before leaving.

Seconds later, Dusty came tumbling up, panting.

"Good boy. Are you having fun?" Robert pushed away the conversation with Vincent, resolved to think about it later. He grabbed the bottle of water and straw and gave Dusty a drink. After, Dusty moved to his side and rested his head on his knee, facing the mats. Robert ran a hand over Dusty's head and back, soothing him until he was ready to go again. He laughed when Dusty and the brown pup collided as they raced back to the mats. The brown pup swiped at Dusty, who got a paw in his face and stopped. When the brown pup moved closer, Dusty retreated, taking a wide berth of the pup, and returned to Robert.

"What's the matter, Dusty?" Robert leaned closer. "Are you hurt?" Dusty whined, pawing at his cheek. "Do you need to have a look at it?"

Dusty yipped. Robert stood, calling for Dusty to follow him, and they entered the bathroom, Dusty rising to his feet. He was a little leery of being there when he knew

Vincent was in the club, but he couldn't avoid it completely.

"It might be a bruise forming if he caught you hard. Go into a stall and remove your mask. I'll pass a wet compress over the door for you to hold against it for a few minutes."

Dusty did what Robert said.

"I know you're voice off tonight, but if you need anything other than what I've given you, you'll need to talk to me."

Dusty yipped.

Robert rested back against the sinks and crossed his arms over his shoulder. He'd not seen the brown pup before, but he hoped it was a coincidence that Vincent was there at the same time. He wouldn't put it past the man to have enticed a pup to rough Dusty up a bit. Despite his words otherwise, Robert would have loved to know who Dusty was. Their dynamic was good, and they meshed well. If it wasn't for Henry, Robert would've considered asking Dusty to be *his* pup, but it was a conversation he needed to have with Henry before he approached Dusty.

The stall door opened, and Dusty came out.

"Are you okay?" Dusty nodded. "Ready for more or had enough?" Robert realised Dusty couldn't answer that without his voice, and he rephrased, "Had enough?" Dusty nodded, and Robert frowned. "Are you badly hurt?"

Dusty shook his head and huffed. "Bruise hurts," he whispered.

Robert raised his eyebrows at the words. He couldn't discern whether he knew the person because a whisper was too difficult to identify, but he hadn't expected Dusty to talk at all.

"Okay. When you get back home, take some paracetamol and maybe ice it again. It should help." He paused. "I'm sorry you got hurt. I know it happens sometimes, but I'm still sorry."

Dusty stepped closer and rested his head against Robert's shoulder, tucking his face down, which must've been awkward because there was a good five or six inches between them. Robert automatically wrapped his arms around him and stroked his back. After a few minutes, Dusty stepped back.

"Come on. Let's get you back downstairs."

As they descended the stairs, Robert caught sight of the clock. Surprised, he stumbled, catching himself on the banister. They'd been there for three hours, and Robert hadn't realised. Dusty's paw came up to rest against Robert's arm, and he glanced at him.

"I'm all right. Missed my step."

They met up with the security men, and Robert said goodbye as they led Dusty away. He pivoted towards Elton's office, removing his mask.

"Don't think about spilling our secret, you hear?"

Robert glanced over his shoulder at Vincent. "Wouldn't dream of it." He smirked and climbed the stairs, ignoring the man. Potentially a dangerous move, but Robert was tired.

He knocked on Elton's door and entered when called.

"I wasn't expecting to see you again. Everything okay?"

Robert licked his lips. "Yes and no."

Elton leaned onto his desk, bringing them closer. "What happened?"

"Dusty got swiped by a brown pup. I think he's bruised his face. I've not seen the pup before. Do you know who his handler is? I didn't stay to find out."

Elton's forehead furrowed. "I don't know off the top of my head. You could check if they're still here."

Robert rubbed at his head. "I can't right now. I'll keep an eye out when I next come."

"Do you think Dusty is all right?"

"He seemed okay, although he said it hurt."

"He spoke?" Elton raised his eyebrows.

"Well, whispered. I couldn't get a fix on who it was if that's what you're asking." Robert grinned.

"Well, you'd be no good as a spy, would you?"

That made Robert's mind go to Vincent. "We may have a problem, though."

"What?"

"Someone knows who Dusty is. At least, I think they do."

Elton sat upright. "What? How?"

"I'm not sure how they found out, but they're threatening to expose him. I received a warning not to say anything to you about it, so keep it quiet for the moment. They're trying to blackmail me into doing something for them to keep the information quiet."

"They can go to hell! Why would you even think about this?" Elton asked.

Robert sighed. "I'm thinking about Dusty. If he's high profile enough, this could be dangerous for him."

Elton studied him. "You care about him."

"Of course, I care about him. I care about all the pups I play with." He fidgeted in the chair.

"What makes him different?"

Robert stared at his hands, wishing he had some jewellery he could play with while he thought. "I don't know. We seem to get along well. There's been no adjustment needed to our dynamic. We fit straight away." He shrugged. "It doesn't matter. If this gets out, he won't come back."

Elton rested back in his chair and rubbed a hand over his chin. "You're not going to tell me who's blackmailing you?"

Robert shook his head. "I shouldn't even be telling you this, but you need to monitor things. Just don't let on you know anything about it." He stood.

"I won't say a word, but you promise me something. If things get bad or you need anything, come to me. It's my fault you're in this mess in the first place."

"If I need you, I'll call."

They said their goodnights, and Robert exited the club, sending a message to Finn and Naomi to tell them he'd left. He hadn't seen them all night but hadn't received a message from either to say they had left. Many things swirled around in his head as he drove home. Dusty. Vincent. Floresco. Henry. He had no idea what to do about any of them.

*ROBERT: Are you free tonight? We can watch a movie until the clock chimes twelve?*

He didn't expect Henry to be free, but he asked anyway. His sisters had invited him to a party with them, but he'd declined. He wasn't in the mood to socialise with lots of people, even if it was to celebrate the beginning of a new year. He'd heard nothing from Vincent, but he wasn't as clueless as to think that was the end of it. Robert had considered calling off the deal with Dusty, hoping it would keep him safe, but it wouldn't stop Vincent from continuing. Even if they didn't play anymore, Vincent still had the information he could use to expose Dusty, and Robert wasn't happy about that. On the other hand, Vincent could be full of shit, but he doubted it. Vincent hadn't got where he was by lying about stuff.

*HENRY: Sorry, I have an event I need to attend, but I can ring you close to the time if you're free?*

Robert grinned. He'd enjoyed recounting the kiss they'd shared and wanted to do it again, but Henry hadn't been around the shop since. His phone rang, and he answered without checking.

"It's not time yet," he said, a smile on his face.

"Mr Martin?" A voice that was not Henry answered him, and he checked the display and winced.

"Yes, I'm sorry. I thought you were someone else."

A musical laugh met his ears. "Not a problem. My name is Louisa, and I'm ringing about the potential contract with the royal family."

"Oh, yes. Hi." Robert facepalmed and inhaled. "How can I help?"

"I'd like you to become our royal florist."

Robert's heart raced, and he held his breath to stop himself from squealing like a girl. "That would be amazing. Thank you so much."

"You're welcome. I would like to invite you to visit with me to discuss the role and what I'd like to see from you, and the help you'd need. I consider it a big job, and I don't expect you to do it all yourself."

"Wonderful. When should I come?"

Louisa laughed again. "Let's get the new year started first. How about 3 January at eleven o'clock?"

"That's fine with me. Thank you for the opportunity."

"Thank you for being good at what you do. I think this could be a brilliant arrangement."

All at once, he realised who he was speaking to, and he became flustered. "I'm glad, Your Majesty." Holy shit, he was talking to the Queen!

"I don't need such formal titles, Mr Martin. Louisa will work just fine."

"Oh, I couldn't. You're…you. It's not…"

"Mr Martin, I would very much like it if you would call me Louisa. In fact, I insist."

Robert inhaled. "May I make an amendment to that?"

"You may."

"Could I still call you Your Majesty in public? I wouldn't feel right not doing so."

Louisa chuckled once more. "That would be fine."

"Thank you…Louisa." Oh my god!

"I look forward to seeing you on 3 January. Have a wonderful day, Mr Martin."

The call ended, and Robert stared in front of him, stunned. He had the contract, and he'd spoken to the Queen of England. Nothing like starting the year off right.

"Are you okay, Robert?" Naomi's concerned voice broke through his haze.

He blinked and glanced at her. "I got the contract."

Naomi squealed. "That's fantastic! I'm happy for you! A double celebration tonight! Finn! Finn! He got…" Her voice drifted away as she ran towards the front of the shop to share the news with Finn.

His phone beeped, making him jump.

*HENRY: If you're not free, it's okay. I can speak to you tomorrow.*

*ROBERT: Sorry, someone rang. You can call me whenever you have a minute, although I will be asleep if it's after 1 a.m. because I can't stay awake past then ;-)*

*HENRY: I'll call at five to twelve. We can watch the fireworks together even though we're miles apart.*

*ROBERT: I would love that.*

·  ·  ·

Robert smiled. Henry was a softie at heart, but he'd known that from the minute he'd seen him with Prince Douglas and his boyfriend at the beginning of the month. He couldn't believe how much had changed in only one month. It was a shame they couldn't spend the new year together, but maybe it was good. It would give them a chance to get to know each other through messages and phone calls.

"Wow, Robert. That's great news! When do you start?" Finn said, wandering into the room.

Robert shrugged. "I don't know yet. I'm meeting with them in a few days to discuss the details."

"What a way to start a new year!" Finn grinned. "I think I need to rub against you with all the luck you're having." Finn moved close and rubbed their shoulders together, holding tighter when Robert pushed him away with a laugh.

"Let me go, you imbecile."

Finn let go but rested a hand on Robert's shoulder. "Truly, though. Congrats, man. You deserve it."

"Thanks." Robert smiled. "Now, get back to work, slacker."

"Yes, boss."

Robert watched as the man skipped down the hallway and disappeared from sight. He inhaled and exhaled, then stood. He had work to do before he closed the shop at three o'clock. There were never many people who wanted flowers on New Year's Eve, but there were some, and he'd give them all a chance to grab a last-minute apology or celebratory flowers before he sent Finn and Naomi on their way and closed the shop for the final time that year. He had New Year's Day off and could relax until 2 January, then whittle for the day before his meeting with the Queen. What would Henry say when he told him? He didn't have long to wait to find out.

15

# HENRY

"I spoke to Father about the Dominant and submissive roles." Freddie's voice was a faint whisper near his ear. "At first, he didn't want to hear it. He said he couldn't understand why we needed to change it. I explained that in regular clubs, the roles of Dungeon Monitors didn't have to be a specific designation; they only needed to do the job. Then, without naming names, I got him to realise not everyone in the family is a Dominant."

Henry glanced at him, heart racing. "And the result?"

Freddie's smile stretched lazily across his face, Damon's showing a similar expression. "He's changing the rules."

Henry closed his eyes and inhaled through his nose, withholding any outward emotion. After so long, things were changing for the better within the royal family. Unfortunately, it didn't stop him from needing to hide; he just didn't need to be as strict. Charles would be gunning for him no matter what; therefore, he needed to be careful. At least others would benefit from the change.

"That's great news."

"How are things with you?" Freddie sipped his champagne.

Henry thought about his message conversation with Robert and smiled. "Good. I, um, I've met someone."

Freddie raised his eyebrows and faced him. "Yeah? Can I ask who he is?"

Henry wrinkled his nose, debating if he could explain. He glanced around to ensure no one was close enough to hear them. "He's a florist. I met him when he did the flowers for the children's event at the beginning of the month." His cheeks heated, and despite having tanned skin, he knew it would be visible. "He kissed me," he whispered.

"That's fantastic. Are you going to see him tonight?"

Henry shook his head and waved his hand, indicating the room they were in. "I'm here, aren't I? I'm going to call him near the time, though."

"Forget about that. Go to him. You have—" Freddie checked his watch, "just over three hours to get there. You can do it. I'll cover for you." He elbowed him. "Go get your man."

It wasn't impossible to drive from Sandringham to Windsor in three hours, but it would cut it fine. Henry rubbed a hand over his mouth and chin.

Freddie nudged him again. "Go."

"Henry, why waste the chance?" Damon added.

He placed his glass on a nearby table and exhaled. "All right. Let's hope this isn't a mistake." His heart pounded so hard, it hurt as he said goodbye to his cousin and slipped out of the party. He'd make it up to Uncle Andrew and Aunt Louisa. Jogging down the corridors of the main house, he finally exited into the cold winter air, realising he'd forgotten his coat but refused to turn back and fetch it. He raced across the driveway to where he'd parked his car in the garages earlier that day and climbed in, glad he kept his keys with him the entire time.

The engine growled into the silence, and he grinned at his dishevelled reflection in the rearview mirror. He couldn't believe he could be so reckless as to race to Robert's side without even warning him he'd be there. Hopefully, it would be a pleasant surprise for him.

Time stretched on and on as he drove the one hundred and twenty miles home. It felt like he'd never arrive, and with every minute that ticked closer to midnight, the flutters in his stomach increased. It was only when he entered Windsor that he calmed a bit, although a new emotion swept over him: fear. Fear of being rejected. Fear of Robert not being home. But not even the fear of someone seeing him could stop him from pulling into a parking space and switching off the car.

He checked his watch. He made it with ten minutes to spare. Did he go straight up there now, or should he wait until closer to the time? He squinted up at the shop, seeing it in darkness, but a warm yellow light escaped from the windows of the room above it. Knowing Robert—or at least someone—was there settled one of his fears. His phone buzzed at five to midnight. He'd set it to notify him of the time, so he didn't forget to ring Robert, not that he was far enough away from Henry's thoughts for that to happen.

The alarm gave him an idea. He climbed out of the car and dialled.

"Hey, are you having a good time?" Robert's voice made him smile, and he wandered down the alley to the back entrance to Floresco, the chilly wind biting through his suit jacket.

"Hi. Yeah, it's been good." Well, it was until he'd left. "Are you ready to start a new year?"

"As ready as I'll ever be. It would've been nice to celebrate it with you here."

Robert spoke hesitantly as if he didn't want Henry to feel bad about not being with him. Henry smiled.

"Do me a favour, Robert. Open your back door." *Hurry, I'm freezing.*

Robert paused. "Why?"

"Humour me." He gritted his teeth to stop them from chattering.

He heard rustling on the other end of the line and additional sounds from inside the house in front of him.

"You realise it's nearly midnight. If I get chopped into little pieces because there's a murderer hanging around, it'll be on your conscience forev—"

The door swung open, and Robert's shocked face and unfinished sentence stood before him. He wore leggings and a large fluffy jumper that ended just above his knees and looked extremely warm and comfortable. Henry pulled the phone away from his ear and ended the call, slipping it into his pocket. Robert's arm dropped to his side as he continued to stare.

"Surprise?"

Henry wasn't sure if it was a good one or a bad one with the wide-eyed expression on Robert's face.

"What…? I thought you were in Norfolk?"

"I was."

"What are you doing back here?"

Henry shrugged. "I wanted to see you."

A smile spread across Robert's face, and he stepped out of the door until he was toe to toe with Henry. He peered up at him. "This is the best surprise ever."

Henry stared into the bright green eyes of the man who had sneaked into his heart when he hadn't been ready for it. He lifted his hands and cupped Robert's jaw, smoothing his thumbs across his cheeks.

"Happy New Year," he mumbled, lowering his head.

A firework lit up the sky and boomed into the quiet, making them both jump and knock their heads together. With a laugh, Henry stared at the rainbow colours covering Robert's face and closed the distance, taking Robert's mouth as he'd always imagined he would. He sipped from his lips, then invaded and explored his mouth until he needed to break away for air. The steam from their breaths melted into the sky, and he felt a shiver go through Robert's body.

"Can we go inside?" Henry asked.

Robert nodded. "Please."

Robert gripped hold of the lapels of Henry's jacket and

walked backwards, obviously trusting Henry to guide him in the right direction because he didn't look over his shoulder.

"Step," Henry warned.

Robert lifted his foot and stepped over the threshold, tugging Henry with him, and closed the door with a thump. As soon as they were in the warmth, Robert pressed Henry against the door and kissed him again, lifting onto his tiptoes and wrapping his arms around his neck. Henry slid one hand between Robert's shoulder blades and the other down to the curve of his ass. They pressed together, their mouths and tongues exploring, tantalising, tasting. Henry groaned when Robert pulled back but kissed down his neck to the collar of his shirt.

"Too many clothes," Robert said, and cold air filled the gap between them when he stepped away.

Henry went to move closer, but Robert grabbed his hand and dragged him up the stairs; Henry laughing when he tripped on several steps along the way. He had no time to see his surroundings because Robert was in front of him again, holding his cheeks.

"Do you want me? Do you want this?"

Henry would get on his knees and beg if he had to, but there was something he needed to say first. "Yes, I do, but I need to tell you something. I've...never been with anyone before." He stared at Robert's shoulder instead of in his eyes, embarrassed by the revelation he was still a virgin at thirty-one.

"I guessed as much." When Henry raised his eyebrows in question, he said, "You said you'd been hiding. I assumed that meant you hadn't been with a man before."

Henry cleared his throat. "I haven't, but I've also not been with a woman."

Surprise flickered through Robert's eyes before it disappeared, and a smile curved his mouth. "Just means I can take my time and spoil you, doesn't it?" Robert's forehead creased. "Do you know if you prefer to top or bottom?"

"I'm…" Henry inhaled. Apart from his family, he'd told no one about this. "I'm a submissive, and I'd like to try bottoming."

Robert tilted his head and gave Henry a chaste kiss. "Thank you for trusting me. I promise I will never divulge any information you tell me here. This is a place of safety. Somewhere you can be yourself. I will never throw that back at you."

Henry's heart resumed its normal rhythm with his words, and he kissed him. He pushed everything else aside —his role as a prince, his family's expectations, the public's constant presence—and reacted as his body and mind wanted to. That night, he would be just Henry.

The kiss went from slow and soft to heavy and rough within seconds. Robert turned Henry around and started walking, leading them somewhere deeper into the apartment. He hoped the bedroom. Henry chuckled when his shoulder crashed into a door frame, and Robert apologised before continuing. Robert slid his hands up and over Henry's shoulders, pushing the jacket off and letting it fall to the floor. He tugged at the tie around his neck, pulling it free and throwing it somewhere, all the while kissing Henry, making him lose his mind. When Robert jerked his shirt from his waistband, he inhaled in short, sharp bursts, his body shaking from the arousal flooding his nerve endings. This was what he'd been missing all these years. He'd managed fine with closing his eyes and using his hand before, but now…he didn't know if he could be without it, and they hadn't even reached the best part yet.

Robert undid all the buttons on Henry's shirt and pushed it off, sliding his hands across his skin, from his neck to his waist. Henry needed to feel Robert against him and gripped the hem of Robert's jumper in his hands and yanked it over his head. Robert laughed at the move and skimmed his hands over Henry's chest, pausing with his palms over Henry's nipples and moving his hands in small circles. The dual sensation made Henry bite off a whimper and drop his head back.

"On the bed on your back," Robert said, pushing against his chest.

Henry crawled onto the bed, resting on his back with a pillow beneath his head. The corners of Robert's mouth curved, and he reached for Henry's shoes, which he'd forgotten he still wore. Robert pulled them off and his socks, and climbed onto the bed, crawling like a pup would on the floor until he rested over Henry, braced on his hands and knees.

"Hey," Robert whispered.

"Hi." Henry smiled, loving the attention Robert showed him.

"Do you know the traffic light system?" Robert asked, dipping down and kissing his sternum.

"Yes." It was as ingrained as how to tie his shoes. Not that Robert would know that.

"Tell me."

"Red to stop, yellow to pause and check in, and green to continue."

"Good. Use them when I ask or if you need to at any point. Understand?"

"Yes, sir."

Robert smirked. "Glad to hear you have manners."

Henry stared up at him, wanting him. He shivered when he thought about what they were going to do. His body ached, reaching for Robert in a visceral way. He needed more. Opening his mouth to ask, he stopped when Robert lowered his head and licked, nipped and sucked his way down Henry's chest and stomach. Each touch created goosebumps, and Henry gripped the cover beneath him.

Robert crawled backwards, his fingers dancing across the skin of Henry's waist along the path of his trousers. With a glance at Henry, Robert threaded the belt through the clasp, undoing the buckle and sliding it free from the loops. Henry watched as Robert fingered the supple leather with narrowed eyes before setting it aside. Not on the floor, as Henry had thought he would, but on the bed. Henry raised his eyebrows, but Robert winked, returning to Henry's trousers. He unfastened the clip and drew the zipper down, far slower than Henry wanted him to. Remembering what Robert said about taking his time,

Henry tried to relax into it but couldn't help wanting more and faster.

Robert must've realised because he tapped Henry's hip and tugged the trousers off when Henry lifted to give him access. It left him in only his boxers, and Henry could see his cock straining at the thin confines.

"Beautiful," Robert murmured while sliding his hands up Henry's thighs, eyes on his groin. When Robert reached his shaft, his hand conformed to the shape, sending darts of pleasure up Henry's spine.

Henry bit his lip, his chest heaving, but his eyes never left Robert, whose fingers slipped beneath the waistband and lifted it over his aching cock. Robert met his gaze and leaned down, swiping his tongue over the head once. The sight of Robert closing his eyes and savouring his taste with a hum of delight sent tingles all over Henry. He tightened all his muscles to stop from thrusting up or finishing too soon.

Robert licked his lips, his focus centring on Henry again, while he dragged his boxers off and away. For a second, Robert stepped away, and Henry worried, but Robert stripped off his clothes and came back to slide his naked body over Henry's.

Robert's body was smooth and silky to the touch, and Henry couldn't resist unclenching his fists and skimming his fingertips over the dark, blemish-free skin. Robert rose, caging Henry with his arms and stared at him, his mouth curving.

"Is this okay?"

"More than okay," Henry said.

"Colour?" Robert reminded him.

Henry's cheeks flushed. "Green, sir."

"Glad to hear it. Let me know if I'm going too fast." Robert smirked. "Or too slow."

With their mouths sealed, Henry could do nothing but feel. His eyelids closed of their own volition, but this time he wanted more. He dived into Robert's mouth, holding his head in place to taste every inch. When he felt light-headed, he pulled back, gasping. Robert rested their foreheads together while they regained their breathing.

"You are…" Robert said and sighed. "There are too many words to describe how amazing you are that I can't pick the best one. Amazing will have to do."

"But I've not done anything."

"You don't need to. You are gorgeous, nice, oh, far too many words." Robert kissed him again. "Let me show you."

Robert leaned across the bed and opened a drawer, and Henry's cheek flared with heat, knowing what he retrieved. When a foil packet and a tube landed next to him, he stared at the ceiling, trying to cool his embarrassment until Robert slid his hands over his thighs.

"Colour?"

"Green, sir."

The tube squeaked as the lid came off; Henry would know the sound anywhere. He wasn't sure if the ceiling was the best choice to study because he didn't know what Robert would do next, so he lowered his eyes to meet Robert's.

"There he is," Robert said.

At his words, Robert leaned down and sucked the head of Henry's cock into his mouth while a finger rubbed against his pucker. Henry's nose flared. He'd fingered himself before but never had anyone else close enough to do it for him. It was a completely novel sensation yet similar all at the same time. He stared at Robert's bobbing head as he took more and more of Henry's cock each time he lowered. Robert wrapped his free hand around the base of Henry's shaft, stroking in time with the suction, sending Henry higher and higher.

Henry re-gripped the covers and curved his body when the tip of Robert's finger pressed harder against his hole. He knew enough to bear down, allowing Robert entry. The burn was minimal, but he knew it would get worse with more fingers—or a cock. Knowing that was a possibility tonight sent lightning along his nerves. Robert doubled his speed when he pressed two fingers into him, and Henry rocked his head against the pillow. Maybe he should have spent more time stretching himself, using bigger dildos or something. It never crossed his mind.

Robert lifted off, laving his tongue around the head and flicking against the nerves underneath. Henry jerked and wrenched on the bed but gritted his teeth and with-held his orgasm.

Robert's eyes had darkened, and sweat beaded on his forehead, and Henry was sure he looked the same, maybe worse.

"Do you want to come like this? With my fingers in your ass and my mouth on your cock?" Robert asked. "Or do you want my cock in your ass?"

Henry groaned and squirmed against the intrusion, wanting more but also wanting to fly. Wanting Robert was what Henry ultimately wanted.

"You. I want you."

Robert smiled. "Good. Bear with me a little longer while I get you ready."

"Please, hurry."

"As quickly as I can, but I need you ready. I refuse to hurt you more than necessary."

Several long minutes later, with Henry's skin soaked with sweat and his breathing uneven, Robert raised his head. He reached for the condom, opened it and rolled it on before Henry could blink, then slicked it up.

Henry stared into Robert's eyes as Robert pressed forward. He winced at the burn but didn't complain. His nails gripped Robert's arms, undoubtedly leaving nail marks, but he wanted this more than anything.

Robert's face was a mask of determination until his balls rested against Henry's ass. Breath heaving, Robert lowered himself to his elbows, pressing a kiss to Henry's mouth.

"Colour?"

"Green. So fucking green."

## 16

## ROBERT

It took everything in him not to burst out laughing at Henry's words. He'd never heard him swear before, and he would bet every penny he had that it didn't happen often. Robert inhaled a few times before rising once more to his hands. The sensation of Henry squeezing around his cock sent shivers up his spine to the base of his neck, which sent goosebumps all the way back again. It was like a vicious loop.

"Please," Henry said, trying to move.

"All right. Hands on the headboard."

Henry gripped the wooden slats, and Robert could see his knuckles whiten. He lifted Henry's legs, resting them over his arms to open him further, giving Robert better access. He licked his lips, the sight of where they joined intoxicating. He withdrew and thrust, withdrew and thrust, gaining momentum. Henry whimpered and took everything Robert gave him, but Robert wasn't happy. He pulled out, much to Henry's displeasure if the growl was anything to go by.

"Onto your knees, chest to the bed."

Henry quickly obeyed, stumbling to get into position. When he was where Robert needed him, Robert rested a hand on Henry's spine and aimed his cock for his pucker. Resistance met him for a few seconds before he pushed through the ring. He groaned as he slid deep and paused when he was as far inside as he could go.

"Colour?"

"Green. Please, Robert. Please. You feel so good. I want to feel you."

Henry babbled some more, becoming more incoherent as he went, and Robert smiled. He withdrew and drove forward without respite, repeatedly impaling Henry and, if Henry's noises were anything to go by, in the right place, too.

"Stroke yourself, Henry. I want you to come with me."

Henry repositioned his arms, and Robert could see one moving at a faster rate than what Robert was, and he picked up his speed. Prickles of pleasure darted around his groin and spine, increasing with every thrust.

"That's it, Henry. I want you to spill all over the bed for me." Henry's ass clenched, and Robert grinned. His lover liked dirty talk. "Your ass looks divine taking my cock. You should see it stretched perfectly for me to drill."

"Oh, god. Please!"

Robert held Henry's hips and increased his speed, his

orgasm barrelling towards him. "Come with me, Henry. Come *for* me! Fuck!"

Robert continued his punishing pace until he felt Henry spasm around him, wringing more of Robert's climax from him. When his body stopped jerking with aftershocks, he withdrew, panting, and rested his forehead on Henry's spine. At least, until Henry listed to the side and collapsed. Robert chuckled and leaned over the man, nuzzling him with his nose to Henry's chin. But other than a half-hearted attempt to say something that ended in just a hum of noise, Henry rested his hand on Robert's head.

Robert smiled and climbed off the bed, stumbling a few steps before getting his legs to work properly. He hadn't come that hard in years. Solo acts only go so far, and never did it make him come as hard as that.

He wrung out a warm, wet cloth and padded back to the room. Henry was still in the same position, and Robert cleaned him up after a brief flinch. He put the flannel on the bedside table and manoeuvred Henry from on top of the covers. As quick as he could, he stripped the cover and recovered it with a clean one, then laid it over Henry's body. He threw the cover in the washing basket, returned the flannel to the bathroom and checked he'd switched everything off around the apartment before climbing into bed next to the prince.

Henry was dead to the world when Robert pulled him into his arms, but Robert was fine with that. In the morning, he would run him a bath because he'd be sore, and they'd decide what their plans were. They didn't have to talk about years or even months down the line, but Robert wanted to have some sort of idea about where they were going with this. Henry wasn't out. Currently, their relationship would be a secret. The notion was fine with Robert, but he refused to hide for years. A few months, he could understand, but not years. He knew Henry had a difficult life, but surely there was something they could do to make it better.

Robert inhaled Henry's scent and snuggled down. Those decisions and worries weren't for tonight. Instead, he needed to enjoy having a prince in his arms because he wasn't sure how often it would happen.

Robert woke, overheated and crushed in someone's arms. It took him several seconds to realise who was behind him. He hadn't been the little spoon for ages, and the thought made him smile. He wriggled, attempting to move the band of arms around his waist, but they wouldn't budge. Rolling his head into the pillow, he smothered his laughter. After regaining control, he turned his head to the side and called Henry's name. To begin with, all he received was an exhale and a nuzzle of Henry's face into the back of his neck. After several more tries, Robert slid his hand between them and wrapped it around Henry's cock, which was hard and waiting for Robert, it seemed.

He didn't stroke. Instead, he rubbed his fingers against the sensitive nerves beneath the head of his cock continuously. One of two things was likely to happen. One, Henry would wake when the pleasure was too much, or two, he would wake once he climaxed. Either way, he'd wake up.

Henry's hips twitched, and his limbs trembled as Robert teased him, enough that Robert encircled his own cock and stroked. He felt precome slide down his fingers from Henry's cock, but he wasn't in the best position to stroke Henry. What Henry needed to do was wake up, and he would give him a morning treat.

Robert stroked his own dick, twisting his hand to catch the nerves as he rose and again before he lowered. He rubbed his crack against the base of Henry's cock, giving him more stimulation, which in turn sent himself higher. His movements increased as his arousal flared. Henry's cock trembled in Robert's hand, and more precome slicked his way.

Henry woke as he climaxed, his arms tightening for a second before releasing, and Robert stroked twice more before he found his release.

"Good morning," Robert said, breath heaving.

"Good morning to you, too." Henry pressed a kiss to Robert's jaw. "I wasn't expecting to wake up to that."

Robert rolled over to face Henry, grimacing at the sticky mess they'd made. "Well, it was that, or I'd have to chop your arm off. You're surprisingly strong."

Henry frowned, and Robert chuckled. "Your arms were closed so tight, I couldn't move. I found a way to move you."

Henry's eyes widened. "God, I'm sorry. Did I hurt you?" He moved away a few inches.

Robert rested a hand on his chest. "I'm fine." He paused and stared at the prince. "How are you is the question?"

Henry didn't answer him straight away, and Robert appreciated that he took the time to think about his answer.

"I feel great. Relaxed, content, happy. But when I think about what will happen outside these walls, and I feel panic closing in."

Robert understood the feeling. "You don't need to worry about anything at the moment. We're going to have a long soak in the bath, get dressed, and we're going to sit around all day and relax." He stopped. "Do you have anywhere to be today?"

Henry's forehead creased. "No, although I should call my cousin to let him know I'm okay. He's the one who persuaded me to come to you last night."

Robert smiled. "I'm glad he did. I wasn't expecting us to go that far, but I don't regret a minute of it. Are you okay with everything that happened?"

Henry grinned. "Without a doubt. Can we have a repeat soon?" He nuzzled his face into Robert's neck.

Robert tilted his head to the side, giving Henry more access. "After you've had a rest. Your ass will smart for a little while because it's not used to it, but we can do other fun stuff."

Henry's face lit up like an excited child—or an excitable puppy. Robert wondered whether pet play was something Henry might be into. He added that to a long list of questions he would eventually get around to asking. Robert leaned in for a kiss and pulled away, several long minutes later, panting.

"You're dangerous." He chuckled and slid from the bed, pulling a face when he felt the dried come on his skin. "Let me run a bath, and I'll shout when it's ready."

He glanced back at the bed as he passed through the bathroom door, smiling at Henry laid out naked with his hands behind his head. "See something you like?"

"I think we both do," Henry said.

Robert laughed and entered the bathroom, setting the water running in the bath before using the toilet and washing his hands. He frowned at his reflection when he thought about the conversation he needed to have with Henry about Robert's pups. If they were serious about each other—which on Robert's part, he was, and on Henry's part, it was unlikely he wasn't—he needed to explain sooner rather than later, especially as he'd booked another playdate with Dusty for the middle of the week. He didn't want to keep it from Henry but wasn't sure how to broach the subject.

Of course, there were rumours about the royal family being part of a BDSM club, but how much of it was true, and how much was a fabrication of the media? Did he want to risk his relationship at such an early stage? But if he didn't explain it straight away, would it be worse when he eventually did? He shook his head and put the thoughts aside. He'd think about that another day when Henry wasn't waiting on him.

"Bath's ready!"

He'd put in plenty of bubbles and laughed when Henry bounded into the room. His mannerisms reminded Robert of an eager pup. Holding out his hand, he waited for Henry to grip him to climb into the bath without falling. Once Henry was situated, he told him to scoot forward and joined him, spreading his legs on either side of Henry's body and encouraging the man to lean back against Robert's chest.

Once they had settled, Henry let out a sigh.

"Everything okay?"

Henry nodded, his hair brushing against Robert's chest. "Everything's great. I love having baths. It's usually when I read…"

Robert waited for Henry to continue and, when he didn't, asked, "Read what?"

Henry didn't answer straight away. Instead, he twined their fingers together and played with them. When he finally spoke, his voice was as soft as a whisper. "I love reading romance novels. The ones on my shelves are male/female books, but I have a hidden box with gay romances. I lock all my doors when I'm taking a bath, so no one finds me with them. No one is allowed in my bedroom. Ever. I'm scared of the repercussions of being gay, but I can't stop. I don't want to stop."

Robert wrapped his legs over Henry's, sliding his free arm over his chest, holding him as completely as he could in their present position. "You shouldn't have to stop. Can you tell me why you're scared?" His heart broke for the man who had much to give.

Hesitantly, Henry explained the situation with his evil

aunt and cousin and other members of the family. He told him about all the little things that had been said and done over the years, making Henry a big bundle of nerves about the whole thing. To say it annoyed Robert was an understatement. He was furious, and even that didn't cut it.

"Why has no one done anything about them?" he asked. "Surely, if she's vocal about it, they can pin something on her or her son."

Henry shook his head. "Nothing has ever been confirmed."

"What about you?"

"Who would believe a thirteen-year-old boy?"

"Many people."

Henry shook his head again, turning to the side. "They'd spin it enough that it would seem like the men wanted it. They're not stupid enough to leave witnesses."

"That's not true. They've left you."

"Yeah, and look where it's got me. I'm terrified to live my life. I'm scared to say anything out of turn. I don't know how Douglas does it." Henry rested his head beneath Robert's chin and exhaled.

"You said he's in a relationship?" Henry nodded. "That could be why. He has support from his partner and you."

"He was like it before he had Maverick. He's never been quiet about being gay. He must be strong to ignore it all."

"Or he could be just as scared as you are," Robert said.

Henry lifted his eyelids, staring at Robert. "Maybe."

"What does life look like to you?" Robert asked, trying to steer the conversation in a different, happier direction.

"What do you mean?" Henry traced Robert's nose and upper lip.

"Take me through a day in the life of Prince Henry."

The corner of Henry's mouth curled. "Depends on what I have planned, I suppose. But, generally, I'm free to do as I please. I often help my family or cousins out when they need something, or I attend events like the one last night. Other than that…" Henry paused, laying his hand against Robert's chest. "I keep to myself a lot."

"Ahh, a lone wolf." Robert chuckled. "You seem more content around your brother and cousins." Robert's eyes widened as he realised what he'd said. He swore in his head and felt himself flush. He hoped Henry wouldn't pick up on his observation.

Henry glanced at him, a small frown creasing between his eyes. "How would you know? You've never seen me with them."

Robert inhaled and winced. "I may or may not have been searching the internet for pictures of you."

Henry let out a loud laugh. "You did? That's nice to know. I couldn't find anything about you when I searched for you."

Robert poked him with a finger. "You didn't search for me. Stop telling tales."

"I did! Do you know how many other Robert Martin's there are in England? I'll tell you. A lot. And I searched through each one to find one that matched your face."

Robert's heart soared. He leaned forward and covered Henry's lips with his own. It was an uncomfortable position, but he needed Henry to know how much he meant to him. When his neck spasmed, he winced and pulled away, rubbing at it to ease the tension.

"The water is getting cold. Let's get out, and we can get some breakfast."

Henry leaned forward, and Robert climbed out first, grabbing a towel for Henry and drying him off. He rubbed it over his hair. Though it wasn't really wet, it meant some of the water made it easier for Henry to style it. While Henry did that, Robert dried himself and cleaned the bath.

As he walked into the bedroom, Henry stood, staring at his clothes. "I didn't think things through. I don't have any clothes other than these."

Robert chuckled. "Don't worry. They're probably not your style, but I have some oversized clothes that will probably fit while we're inside. You can always change back into the suit when you need to leave."

He wandered to his chest of drawers and rummaged through until he found some joggers Finn had left behind, which looked like they might fit, and a huge T-shirt that Robert liked to sometimes wear to bed. He handed them to Henry and shrugged.

"Try. If you don't like them, I won't be offended."

Henry rested them on the bed and dropped his towel. Robert stared for a minute, enjoying the physique of the man before finding his own clothes. He tightened his lips when he saw Henry.

"Yeah, not quite your style, but they'll work for now. It's not like we're going out anywhere," Robert said.

Henry brushed a hand down the front of the T-shirt

and smiled ruefully. "I don't mind. I don't think I've ever been this dressed down, though. It kind of comes with the territory."

Robert strode over to him and linked his hands behind his neck, his heart thumping harder when Henry automatically slid his hands behind Robert's back. "I like you like this. You're relaxed and calm. You're less…" Robert couldn't think of the right word.

"Uptight?" Henry grinned.

"No." Robert tilted his head. "I don't know. Less starched, maybe." He laughed. "Sorry, that was a terrible example, but I can't think of a better one."

"I don't mind. It's true. I feel like I can be more like myself when I'm with you." Henry's shoulders tightened, but he said nothing more.

"Come on. Let's eat. I can make a mean beans on toast."

Robert threaded his fingers through Henry's and aimed for the kitchen. He pressed a kiss to Henry's lips as he pushed him into a seat and flicked the kettle on. By the time breakfast was ready, Henry and he had already finished one cup of tea. Making a second, Robert set them in front of their seats and sat.

"Eat up."

"Yes, sir."

Robert raised an eyebrow. "It's like that, is it?"

Henry smirked. "Not really. I'm not as submissive out of the bedroom, although I do like allowing others to take point when we're in a bigger crowd. I try to slink into the background for most events and speeches." He took a bite of toast, chewed and swallowed. "When it comes to normal, daily life, I—"

He cut his words short when a phone rang. It wasn't Robert's ringtone, so he assumed it was Henry's. The man jogged into the bedroom and returned with the phone to his ear.

"Good morning, Mother. Yes, I'm sorry I couldn't be there." He paused and listened. "Right." Paused again, and his shoulders dropped. "Yes, I understand. I'll be there as soon as I can." He closed his eyes and rubbed at his forehead. "Yes, Mother. I love you, too. Bye."

Henry closed the phone, and Robert tried to remember that Henry had a whole life Robert wasn't part of at that moment.

"I'm sorry. Mother wants me back at Sandringham. Apparently, there's an event happening tonight that she wants me to be part of. They've set up a party for the family."

"It's okay. You need to be with your family. Do you need to go now, or can you spare another hour?"

Robert already knew the answer, but it didn't stop the disappointment from winding its way through his body when Henry shook his head.

"I'm sorry."

"It's fine. We'll get some more time together." He stood and wrapped his arms around Henry's waist, staring up at him. "When you're back home, let me know. We'll sort something out."

Henry lowered his head, and they kissed, soft, sweet

and delicious. "I'm definitely coming back for more of that."

Robert smiled. "Yes, you are."

He kept the smile on his face until Henry waved at the end of the alley towards the front of the shop, then he sagged against the doorframe. Being with a prince was not the easiest of timetables to manage.

17

## HENRY

Trying to get time to spend with Robert was more difficult than Henry had expected. For all his words about being free to come and go as he pleases, it wasn't strictly true. He had his role at Club Royal to think of, which was why he hadn't seen Robert in three days, since he'd left him on New Year's Day. They had messaged back and forth, and Robert had told him Aunt Louisa had given him the contract for Windsor Castle. He was happy for him.

The bass of the music vibrated through his leather-soled shoes, and he crossed his arms and studied the occupants of the main area of the club, checking to make sure everything was running smoothly. He'd been on shift for an hour already, but he was ready to leave. He wanted to visit Robert, but that wouldn't happen for another two days. His mother had asked for his help in the garden the following day, and he'd arranged for a playdate for Dusty that night. He had cleared his Thursday schedule, though, so he could go to the shop to see him.

He waved across the room to get Douglas's attention and moved his finger in a large circle to show he would do a walk around. Douglas gave him the thumbs up, and Henry stepped down from what he called the "lookout" position. There were always at least two monitors in the main area, walking the floor, and another four monitors would make the rounds on the other areas within the club. Naturally, Henry preferred the pet play area, but they all swapped around to keep them from getting bored.

Uncle Andrew had made an announcement at the club meeting the previous day, explaining the new rule that the royal family members did not have to be Dominants any longer. A murmur of disquiet had trickled around the room, but Henry couldn't tell if it had been good or bad. The king had also made a point of stating the harassment rules, telling the family in no uncertain terms that they would not tolerate anyone harassing someone because of their preferred role.

Henry had caught Charles's eyes at that moment, and the visible hatred had him trembling. He'd forced his gaze away and refocused on his uncle. Despite the proclamation, which Henry wholeheartedly agreed with, he wasn't sure if he could do it. He knew George had already spoken with his father about him being submissive before the meeting, but the memories of what he'd seen still played in his mind every time he thought about coming clean.

The club appeared to be in fine form, and he weaved his way towards his post, greeting and stopping to talk to those who asked him a question. Before he stepped up, someone gripped his upper arm in a tight hold and crowded against his back.

"You may have persuaded the king to change his opinions on submissives, but you won't change mine," Charles said in his ear. "And I see you've also found someone who's willing to give it to you up the ass. Congrats."

A photo appeared before him. It was dark and difficult to see some aspects, but what wasn't was him and Robert kissing outside Robert's house when he'd arrived on New Year's Eve.

"Where did you get this?"

"Doesn't matter." Charles tightened his grip. "Do you really want to bring him into this because you're getting higher and higher on my list of people that need to be taught a lesson?"

The ominous words sent a chill through Henry, and he closed his eyes.

"That's what I thought." The photo disappeared. "Stay away from him and keep your nose clean. It's how you've lived this long. Why ruin a good thing?"

Charles let go and melted into the crowd seconds before George stepped to Henry's side.

"What did he want?"

"To make my life hell as usual." Henry swallowed hard and climbed onto the step, facing the crowd. George joined him.

"What do you mean?"

Henry explained about going to see Robert and them agreeing to make a go of things. Then he repeated what

Charles had said. He didn't bother keeping it a secret because they knew everything else.

"What the hell? We've got to figure out a way to stop this. To stop them. We're fucking royalty. We should be able to do something!"

"Calm down, George. I know what you're saying, but we have to be careful. We don't know how many people are involved in this."

"We need to speak to Dad. He knows they're on shaky ground, but he prefers his enemies as close as his friends. A direct threat like this needs to be discussed."

Henry knew George was right, but he didn't know if he could expose himself as much as he would need to. "Let me think about it, George. I'll make a decision in a couple of days."

George sighed. "All right, but can I at least tell the others?" Henry nodded. "Hey, look at me." Henry did. "We're going to fix this. We have to." He slid his finger from under Henry's chin and smiled. "We're the Scandalous Six. We can do anything." He winked.

Henry huffed a laugh and shook his head. "You're a menace."

"Takes one to know one," George replied and jumped off the step, merging with the crowd.

Henry smiled, though it dimmed a little when Charles's threat returned. He didn't want to put Robert in danger. He didn't know the best course of action. Every which way he turned, someone would get hurt. There were too many people he needed to protect and only one of him. It was too much pressure. Maybe he should let

Charles do what he would with him, and no one would need to worry.

Despite the dire thoughts of the previous evening, Henry had a wonderful day with his mother. Patrick had joined them for an hour, then left them to their gardening. They were weeding and cutting back, which was a big job for a garden as large as his mother's was. Henry was glad they'd chosen a cooler day because he worked up a sweat, regardless.

"Have you seen any more of your young man?" Victoria asked.

Henry dropped the tool he'd been holding and stared at her, heart pounding in an uneven rhythm. "What?"

"Robert, isn't it? He sounds like a nice enough fellow from what Louisa told me."

His mother continued to pull the unwanted green stems from the soil as if she hadn't dropped a bombshell on him. When he said nothing, she glanced up at him and smiled.

"You're my son, Henry. I've always known. I thought you would come to me if you needed anything, so I left it alone. All your life, you've been missing that spark, but when you spoke to me about Robert, it flared to life. And I began to hope." She rested her hand on his. "What's stopping you from being who you are?"

Henry dropped his gaze and clenched his jaw. He

couldn't tell her. If he did, she'd try to go up against Aunt Charlotte, and it scared Henry that she might lose.

Victoria sighed. "Do you at least talk with the others?" Henry nodded. "That's something, I suppose."

Henry could hear the disappointment in her tone, and he hated it. "I'm a submissive, Mother." The words tumbled out, and he wrinkled his nose and squeezed his eyes shut.

"Oh, I know that, too." She chuckled at Henry's startled look. "There's not much that gets past me. Being in this family makes me see things that others probably wouldn't. I'm glad Andrew has changed the rules. They were hard on many people, but now they get to be who they want to be. Including you."

Henry felt tears gathering at the back of his eyes, but he sniffed and held them back. He hadn't realised his mother was so observant, and he wondered what else she had found out.

"I know being gay and submissive is seen by some as weak and below our station, but they're wrong. There is nothing weak about following your heart. It takes great strength, in fact. Take Douglas, for instance. He fights every day because, every day, people are posting about him and Maverick, telling them they're abominations and all manner of ugly things. But he stands up with Maverick by his side and lives *his* life. Nobody has the right to tell you who you should or shouldn't be."

Henry sat back on his heels, staring into the distance. His mother's words were a balm to his soul, but the voice and images of his past were too loud. He couldn't brush them aside as others could.

"All I'm saying is that I'm here if you need me. And you know the others are there for you, too."

Victoria continued pulling the weeds while Henry thought about her words. He couldn't bring himself to spill his secrets yet, but she gave him the confidence to say he might be able to one day.

"Thank you," he said instead.

Her words stayed with him throughout the afternoon and evening when he dressed for his playdate. Excitement coursed through him, although a little voice told him he should've explained this side of him to Robert before continuing the sessions. He would tell him, but he needed this freedom one more time, so he was calm enough to talk through everything.

As usual, he met his handler in the owner's office and followed him to the mosh. There weren't as many pups this time, but he saw the same brown and white pup from his previous visit. He would stay away from him. Although he hadn't received a bruise from the swipe he'd received, his cheekbone had been tender for a day or two.

There were another two pups, both completely black save for their white and black ears and tails. They could almost be twins. To begin with, Dusty stayed by his handler's side, resting his head against his thigh. He felt uneasy for the first time since he started these visits, but he couldn't pinpoint his reasons for the feeling. He closed his eyes and focused on the feel of his handler's hand stroking over his head and neck.

Something soft bumped against his paws, and he blinked and stared down at the ball. He glanced across the mats and saw the two playful pups wagging their tails at him. Batting the ball back, Dusty watched as they fought over it for a moment, then sent it shooting back Dusty's way. It went past him, and Dusty chased after it and nudged it back again. This time when the ball came towards him, the two pups came with it, and they tumbled over each other to reach it.

"—decided what you're going to do? I've given you more than enough time to think about it."

Dusty tilted his head and stopped playing, hearing the tone of the voice and not liking it.

"It's not just me I have to think about, Vincent. I have my staff to consider if things go wrong."

"Robert, Robert, Robert. What am I going to do with you? Someone has been keeping secrets."

Dusty froze and watched the unknown man, Vincent, pull out his phone and show his handler something. His handler rubbed his head and sighed. When he spoke, it held weariness and was a voice he'd recognise anywhere.

"Why do you need me, Vincent? I'm sure you have plenty of other people more willing to do your bidding."

"Yes, but what fun would that be? You have twenty-four hours to decide, Robert."

When the man left, Dusty scampered over to his handler.

"Hey, Dusty. Would you like a drink?"

The tone had changed, and Dusty didn't hear Robert's voice any longer. He heard a higher-pitched, more singsong sound. Unwilling to wonder anymore, he nudged away the hand and batted at his handler's mask.

"What are you doing, Dusty?" His handler pushed him away and lowered his voice. "You wanted me to stay anonymous."

Dusty pawed at him again.

"Are you sure?"

Dusty yipped.

His handler removed his mask, and there sat Robert. It thrust Henry back into the present, and he stumbled back. He sat on his ass, staring at the man he'd come to know so well. Or so he'd thought. How could he keep something like this from Henry? Then he smacked himself mentally. Wasn't he doing exactly the same thing? Wasn't he keeping a secret from Robert? He couldn't deal with it and stood, walking towards the stairs.

"Dusty, wait!"

He didn't. He jogged down the stairs and motioned to his security guards that they were leaving. He'd give himself that night to go through everything in his head, and he'd visit Robert and explain everything the following day, but he needed peace firstly.

They exited into the night sky and headed for the car.

"Dusty!"

He climbed in the car and shut the door before Robert reached him. How could he not have known? Robert's green eyes were distinctive, but he'd not been interested in who it was, had he? He'd wanted what he could get and forget about anyone else. As they reached a dark road, Henry removed his mask and rubbed at his face.

"Is everything okay, Your Highness?"

Henry bobbed his head. "Yes, thank you. It's just been a long day."

They deposited him at Bagshot Park and drove away. He wandered through the hallways on muscle memory alone, and once he'd shut and locked his door, he sank to the floor, resting his arms on his knees.

Robert was his handler. Robert was in the lifestyle. Robert was *a* handler.

He huffed a laugh. They were even more perfect for each other than he'd originally thought. Why had he run away tonight? Looking deep inside, he couldn't find an answer, but he needed to if he was to have answers to Robert's questions the following day.

He reached for his phone.

"Patrick? I need some help."

Patrick offered to call the others, and Henry agreed. He might as well tell them all at the same time, and they could all call him stupid for walking away. He knew he was, but it hadn't stopped him from leaving without a goodbye.

Soon, the Scandalous Six sat around his living room and stared at him, open-mouthed.

"You can say it. I'm an idiot."

Freddie was the first to speak. "No, you're not. You'd received a shock and needed to regroup. That's not being an idiot. That's being clever. You need to get your thoughts in order before you can explain what they are."

George sat forward. "I know you have to speak to

Robert, but what is this guy on about? What did Robert have to decide about?"

"It must be something to do with his shop because he mentioned his staff," Henry said.

"Is this Vincent guy trying to get him to sell it?" Douglas asked.

"I doubt he'd do that. He's happy there." Henry stood, pacing in front of them as he spoke. "It was his great-grandfather's business. He's unlikely to let it go without a fight."

Patrick spoke from where he was leaning against Henry's desk. "Who knows about you two?"

Henry stopped. "Our relationship? No one but you. Our friendship? More people." He froze. "Shit!" He slammed his hand against the nearest wall.

"What?" Christian asked, coming to stand with him and checking over his hand.

"Charles knows."

Curse words flew through the room.

"How the hell did he find out?" Douglas said.

Henry shook his head. "I've no idea *how* he found out, but he cornered me last night at the club, showing me a photo of when I went to Robert's." He cleared his throat. "We kissed outside his apartment. Apparently, someone caught it on camera."

"But who?" Christian asked.

"What about Vincent? Do you think he could've done it? Could he be working with Charles?" Freddie said.

Henry went over the conversation he'd heard again in his head. It didn't sound like Vincent was working for someone else, but that didn't mean he wasn't. But he did show Robert something.

"He showed Robert something on his phone. Do you think it was the same photo?" Henry said.

"It's possible. If they're working together. If they're not, it has to be something incriminating for Robert to react like you said he did," Patrick said.

"I need to see Robert. If Charles has somehow started in on Robert, I need to stop it. I won't let him get caught up in Charles's vicious games."

"What are you going to say about Dusty?"

Henry paused. "I'm going to turn up as Dusty and hope he'll let me in before I reveal myself. I'd prefer to do it off the street if possible." He strode to the door.

"Do you want us to come with you?"

"No. I'll be fine. Although..." He glanced at George. "Would you mind coming?"

George raised his eyebrows but nodded. "Sure. If you think I can help."

"It's just in case I can't explain the submissive issues within the family. I struggle with that a lot."

"I can do that," George said, a small smile in place.

Henry looked past him to Patrick, who was staring at the floor. "Patrick..."

His brother glanced at him and curved his mouth, though the smile didn't reach his eyes. "I'll be here when you get back. I'm always here if you need me."

Henry couldn't stand his brother looking forlorn and strode over to him, throwing his arms around him. "I'm sorry for not including you in all of this. It's not because you don't have my back. I promise. I know you're here for me, but I'm…scared of my own fucking tail. I need you to be strong for me so that when I fall, I know you will catch me."

He whispered the words for Patrick's ears only and held on as he felt Patrick's tears. They stayed that way for a few minutes, then Patrick pulled back. His eyes were wet, but he stood tall. With their goodbye action, he left the room. Freddie said goodbye and motioned he would speak with Patrick and trailed after Henry's brother. After a brief goodbye with the rest, he and George climbed into Henry's car and aimed for Floresco.

He hoped he wouldn't be too late.

## 18

PATRICK

Patrick strode down the hallways of his home, trying to hold his emotions in until he reached his own wing of the house. He was of no use to his brother. Instead, he would hide away and lose himself in his music.

"Pat, wait up!"

Freddie's voice stopped him, and he waited until the footsteps caught up. "What's up?"

Freddie raised his eyebrows. "You know what's up. How are you doing?"

Patrick dropped his gaze to the floor and scuffed his foot along the tile. "I'm fine."

"No, you're not. Talk to me."

Patrick exhaled. "There's nothing to talk about."

Freddie stepped closer, his shoes entering Patrick's vision. "Talk to me." He lowered his voice until Patrick could do nothing but obey.

"Not here." He spun and wandered through the corridors until he reached the north wing of the building. He entered his sanctuary, holding the door for his cousin. "Do you want a drink?"

"No, I'm good."

He said no more, but that more than anything got Patrick talking.

"I feel like Henry doesn't want me to be part of his life—at least this part of his life. I understand being unsure about it in the beginning, but I thought it would change when he was used to it. But still, he wants George and not me." He dropped into a seat. "I know I'm whining and acting like a kid, but he's my brother. I want to help him."

"He knows that, Pat. He knows you're there for him, but you have to let him find his way to you."

Patrick remembered the words Henry had whispered, *"I need you to be strong for me so that when I fall, I know you will catch me."*

"How can I help him when I don't understand what he's going through?" He stood and strode over to the piano, sitting on the stool in front of it. He lifted the fallboard and began moving his fingers along the keys, sending music through the air.

"Do you *need* to understand what he's going through?" Freddie asked, coming to stand next to the piano. "Can you not just be there for him no matter what you know or don't know?"

Patrick considered his cousin's words. Henry was under no obligation to tell him anything, brother or not. He wanted to know because he wanted to help Henry, but he didn't need to know. Freddie was right. He should just support him and pick up the slack if Henry needed him.

He wished he could help more than he was. This thing with Robert was surprising, but he wished them well. He knew Henry liked Robert. If he could be the missing link between both sides of his personality, then Patrick hoped they would find the way through any issues.

As for Aunt Charlotte and Charles, well, Patrick was at a loss. Charles had buried himself deep inside Henry's psyche, and they needed to figure out a way to set him free.

"Do you think Henry will need therapy?" he asked Freddie, his fingers still tinkling with the keys.

"It's possible. I would be surprised if he didn't, but I have noticed since he's found his pup and is free to express it, he has been calmer and more centred. It's almost as if he's able to focus on the here and now instead of on the past."

Patrick considered that. "What do you think about Robert?"

Freddie grinned. "I think the man is good for Henry. From what Douglas told me of their first meeting, he saw sparks fly straight away, and that was before Douglas knew Henry was gay."

Patrick smiled. "I noticed a similar thing when we visited before Christmas. There was a charge in the air when they were in the same room. I'm hoping they can work it out."

"I'm sure they will. If Robert is as good a handler as

George said he was, then his day-to-day personality can't be much different."

"He's nice, and I don't think he'll take any shit from Henry." Patrick chuckled.

"I doubt it will be Henry that gives him shit. It'll be the rest of us."

They shared a laugh.

"Thank you, Freddie. You are always the voice of reason."

Freddie rolled his eyes. "I try."

## 19

## ROBERT

When he tried to follow Dusty from the building, a look from one of the security guards made him stop. Robert knew he couldn't make a fuss in front of all the people in attendance and backed off. Instead, he jogged to Elton's office and knocked.

"What happened?" Elton said as soon as Robert entered.

"What do you mean?" How did Elton know something was wrong?

Elton waved a hand towards him. "You look like shit, and you should be with Dusty, shouldn't you?"

Robert sighed and dropped into a seat, running a hand over his hair. "Yeah. Something came up, and Dusty changed his mind about seeing who I was. As soon as I took my mask off—after double-checking he wanted me to, I might add—he freaked out and left."

"Do you think it's someone you know?"

Robert shrugged. "It's possible."

"Why did he ask you to remove your mask?"

"Vincent paid me a visit while we were in there, threatening to expose Dusty and me with my…new friend," he finished with a shake of his head.

"New friend?" Elton held up a hand. "Never mind. We need to get this Vincent thing under control. I think we need to speak with the lawyer. They need to be aware of the potential fallout of the situation; otherwise, they'll have our ass."

"Agreed."

"I'll call him in the morning. You get yourself home."

Robert had no idea what to do about Dusty, but as he didn't know who it was, it had to be left in Elton's hands for now. He wished he knew why Dusty had run from him.

Making his way home, he climbed the steps to his apartment with heavy feet. He needed someone to talk to about it, but there was no one he could involve because of the NDA he'd signed. It would be a long night for him.

He flicked on some music and allowed the notes to work their way through his body as he removed his leather. Cleaning off in the shower made him feel a little better, but not much. He dressed in leggings and another oversized jumper before nuking some popcorn and settling into the sofa to watch TV. He didn't see a minute of it, too engrossed in his thoughts and replaying the images from the night to make sense of the pictures on the screen.

Failure. He felt like a failure for some reason. As if he'd

ruined Dusty's experience, and he didn't like it. He always did his best for the pups, but he'd fallen short with Dusty, and he didn't know why. That was the worst thing about it all. He didn't know what he'd done to make Dusty run. If he didn't know, he couldn't fix it. Even if he knew who Dusty was in real life, he wouldn't tell a soul, but he didn't see how that could be because he didn't know any celebrities.

He could probably discuss it with Naomi and Finn as long as he kept any specific details out of it, but it was late. He'd think about it and, if he decided to go ahead, would ask them tomorrow.

A knock had him double-checking he'd read the clock correctly, then jogging down the stairs to the door. He checked the peephole first and stood back, hesitating before opening it.

"Dusty. What are you doing here?"

Robert glanced at the pup and at the man beside him who had his coat pulled up over his lower face. His stomach churned. How did Dusty know where he lived? And why had he brought a friend? Hopefully, Robert wasn't about to be burgled or murdered.

"Can we come in, please? We want to stay anonymous to anyone who could be watching." It was the man who spoke, not Dusty, and Robert took a second to get a feeling of the two. "We won't hurt you. I promise."

Robert sighed. "Can't do much about it if you are going to, in all honesty. Come on in." He stepped back, opening the door wider to allow them both inside. Climbing the stairs to his apartment, he shook his head, resigning himself to whatever was going to happen. They probably worked with Vincent and were here to rough him up. That was an idea he'd never thought of before.

"Have a seat. Do you want anything to drink?"

The man shook his head and unzipped his coat.

"Holy shit," Robert said. "I apologise, Prince George. I didn't know it was you..." His words faded away as he flicked his focus to Dusty, trying to follow the connection between the prince and Dusty when Dusty removed his mask.

Robert sank into the armchair, grateful it had been behind him because he'd not checked. "I do know a celebrity," he murmured, staring at Prince Henry.

Henry dropped to his knees in front of Robert. "I'm sorry I left earlier. I was shaken. I was angry because I thought you couldn't trust me with the knowledge of what you did until I realised I had done the same thing. I...I was stupid. I should've stayed and spoken to you." He sighed. "I didn't want anyone finding out this part of me until I'd figured out if it was something I wanted to continue, but when my handler was so good, I couldn't resist coming back time and again." He smiled. "I dreamt of it being you, but never did I imagine it would be. Can you forgive me?"

Robert's lips curled, though his mouth barely moved. "I forgive you. I have to say, though, I don't know where we go from here."

Prince George sat on the sofa across from them. "If I may be so bold, we have a lot of different aspects to discuss tonight."

Robert frowned. "What do you mean, Your Highness?"

"George, please. Firstly, may I say that it's lovely to finally meet you. Your reputation preceded you."

Robert widened his eyes. "You're the one who requested me?"

George nodded. "I did. I'd heard good things. Anyway, we think there are some things going on with you that are related to some things happening to Henry. For instance, Vincent Dwyer and our cousin Charles seem to be aiming for a similar result."

"What result?"

"To get what they can out of an unpleasant situation."

Robert rubbed his head. "I don't understand."

Henry rose from kneeling and sat next to George. "You know what I told you about Charles and what happened when I was younger?" He saw George glance at Henry with raised eyebrows but nodded at Henry. "Well, he cornered me the other day and showed me a picture of you and me kissing outside here on New Year's Eve. He threatened to expose me if I didn't heed his words."

Robert sat back, his shoulders dropping. "Vincent showed me the same picture tonight. Which one took it? My bet is Vincent or one of his goons because he's been telling me he knew who you were since your first night as Dusty. He didn't tell me who you were but taunted me with the knowledge."

George narrowed his eyes. "I bet he followed you home, Henry."

Henry nodded, staring at the floor. "Probably." He rubbed a hand over his chin. "It shows that they're working together at least. What do they want? Well, I know Charles wants me to pretend I'm not gay and keep my mouth shut about what I saw. What about Vincent? Has he said anything?"

"Yes. He wants to leave packages at the shop and have other people pick them up. I don't know what will be inside, but I bet it's drugs or money or something along those lines."

"Fuck, Robert. Don't even consider that."

"I won't now. I was on the edge of saying yes."

Henry rested back and stared at the ceiling, his head on the back of the sofa. "I'm sorry I brought this to your door."

"You don't need to be sorry. We need to figure out what to do. But before that, why did you need to bring the cavalry with you?" Robert nodded towards George. "Not that I don't appreciate you being here, but what did you think I was going to do?" He had a teasing tone to his voice, and Henry knew he wasn't mad.

Henry leaned forward and covered his rosy cheeks with his hands. "I don't know. Maybe for moral support more than anything."

"I'm in a similar situation to Henry," George said. "Not only am I bisexual, but I'm also a submissive. I know how much of a toll this is taking on Henry, and I wanted to support him through it. No one should go through this alone."

Robert thought about the different pieces of the puzzle that needed to be slotted into the right places before they could do anything about either of their adversaries. "I think we need a drink." He rose. "Tea, coffee, juice, beer or vodka?"

George grinned and rubbed his hands together. "I knew I liked you. Vodka would do me great, thanks."

Robert glanced at Henry, who had a small smile on his face as he watched his cousin. "Tea for me if it's no trouble."

He wandered into the kitchen and set the kettle boiling. As he went through the motions of making drinks, he considered what Henry wanted from him. Did he still want a pup and handler role only, or would he want to find someone else while they kept their romantic relationship? Those answers weren't as important as the ones about their steps to thwart Vincent and Charles. What was the best option?

It was the question he asked when he carried the drinks to his guests.

George sighed. "I think we need to bring the rest of us together." He glanced at Henry, who nodded. "Collectively, we should figure something out."

"The rest of you?"

"The Scandalous Six! Have you not heard of us?" George said, throwing his arms wide. "We're famous!"

Henry threw a cushion at him. "Shut up. George coined the collective name, though none of us have agreed to it. It's me, George, Patrick, Freddie, Douglas and Christian. We've always been close and go to each other for advice on a lot of things."

"Ah, okay." The description reminded him of the photo

he'd saved onto his phone when he'd searched the internet for Henry.

"I'm sure we can get them together over the next day or so," George said.

Robert shook his head. "I have less than a day to give Vincent an answer."

Henry stood and strode to the window. "Fuck this shit. What the hell is wrong with people?"

It was a rhetorical question, but the way Henry's voice broke as he spoke had Robert standing and wrapping his arms around him.

"The world fears new things. They can't handle change. They need order, not chaos, but they don't realise that by accepting everyone, order will resume."

"Nicely put," George said from behind them.

Henry spun in his arms and leaned back against the low windowsill. "When did you get so wise?"

"Right about the time my mother gave birth to me." Robert winked.

"Cocky shit." Henry pecked him on the lips, though his eyes advertised exactly what he wanted. "I'll call Patrick and Christian. George, call your brothers. Let's see if we can get together tonight."

"I'll grab some more drinks. Is anyone hungry?"

"I'd murder someone for a Chinese," George said.

"A man after my own heart. Hmm." Robert tapped his chin. "Have I chosen the wrong prince?"

Henry came towards him, and Robert retreated to the kitchen with a laugh that tailed off when Henry caged him with the counter to his back. There was something exciting about Henry being forceful and overbearing. He bit his lip and tilted his head back to meet Henry's gaze.

"Care to rethink your decision?" Henry asked.

Robert's tongue swiped over his lips. "No. I'm happy with the prince I have."

Henry fastened their mouths, cupping his hands to the back of Robert's head while he plundered his mouth. Robert allowed the tension-filled kiss for a few seconds then pushed against Henry, pinning him against the counter and took charge of it. He slowed them down, tasting, tantalising, teasing until soft noises escaped from Henry's throat.

Robert lifted his mouth, wiping Henry's bottom lip with his thumb. "We will sort this out, one way or another." Henry nodded. "Now, what would you like to drink?"

Henry started to answer when George stepped into the room. "No need to worry. Christian said he'd grab Patrick and get security to swing by the Chinese on the way here."

Robert straightened. "They're coming here?"

"Is that a problem?" Henry asked, standing upright.

"I need to tidy up. The place is a mess!"

Robert began picking up things from the floor and tidying the coffee table. He hadn't expected them to come here. He thought they would meet somewhere else. Was his house secure enough?

Henry grabbed him around the waist and paused his movements. "Robert, you don't need to tidy up, and this place is secure enough. Freddie and Douglas will bring their own security team, anyway. We'll all be fine."

"But having so many royals under one roof…I've seen

the movies, Henry. That's when people strike to hurt you! When you least expect it!"

"Robert!" Henry held his face in his hands, waiting until Robert focused on him before saying, "We're good. Relax."

"Says the member of the royal family," Robert murmured.

He sat on his armchair, and Henry dropped to the floor by his feet. Robert didn't hesitate to put his hand on Henry's head, smiling when Henry dropped his cheek to his knee. Dusty was never too far away, Robert surmised.

They put on a comedy film while they waited, and laughter filled his small apartment. When George's phone rang, he jogged down the stairs and let in their family. Robert inhaled and stood, his legs and hands trembling at having royals under his roof. He tried to push aside his worry and greet the men, who were much larger than life. He'd met Douglas before, but none of the others. He could see the family resemblance when they all stood together.

The scent of Chinese food had his stomach growling, and he clutched at it with wide eyes. "Sorry."

Douglas chuckled. "Sounds like a plan to me."

Robert frowned. "What does, Your Highness?"

"Eating first. Dealing with assholes after."

They all agreed, but Henry said, "It's going to get mighty confusing if you call them all Your Highness, Robert. I'm sure they're all happy to be on first name terms."

"Definitely. We get enough royal shit everywhere else. We don't need it from family," Patrick said.

Robert raised his eyebrows at Henry, but he shrugged with a quirk to his lips. He liked the idea of being their family, but the idea also scared the hell out of him. He concentrated on handing out plates and making drinks for those who wanted them. While they ate, they put another comedy on, and Robert watched from the corner of his eye as each cousin interacted with the others. Despite the hierarchy, they appeared to be on the same level, even Freddie, though he seemed quieter than the others, more watchful.

When they'd finished, they'd all tidied up, much to Robert's consternation. He made a fresh round of drinks, and they settled around the room. Robert sat in an armchair with Henry at his feet, Patrick, Douglas and Christian squashed on the sofa, Freddie took the other armchair, and George sat by Freddie's feet.

"Right, let's get this sorted. What's going on?" Freddie asked.

Henry and Robert explained the situation as well as they could understand it. While they did, the men cursed and lamented the day their aunt was born.

"I think we need to figure out some potential routes we could go and follow them to their possible conclusion. If we take it methodically, we might be able to choose the best one without having to go through with them in real life," Freddie said.

"What about telling Mother and Father?" George asked.

Douglas shook his head. "They know what Charles tried to do to me, though there was no proof. I don't think they're going to help as much as we'd want them to. Their hands are tied more than ours are."

"What about someone else? Like Uncle William?" Patrick said. "He's not as close in line to the throne and may have more connections than we do."

"That's an idea. Okay, if we did that, what are the potential outcomes?" Freddie asked.

"Him saying no," George said.

"Someone finding out we talked and exposing Henry," Patrick said.

Robert watched as they batted ideas around the room with limited input from himself. He didn't mind because they were a force to be reckoned with. He wouldn't ever want to be pitted against them. None of them believed they had much to give to the conversation, but the further they went, the more they realised the pitfalls and positives of their ideas.

"I think the best idea would be to speak with Uncle William. Even if he doesn't help, he might give us an idea of which way to go," Douglas said.

Freddie nodded. "I agree, but it's up to you two." He stared at Robert and Henry in turn. "You're the ones going through this, and although we know there are likely to be repercussions that fall on all of us if something happens, you will be the primary focus."

Robert glanced at Henry. "I'm happy to do whatever it takes to get Vincent off the streets and away from us, and Charles out of all of our lives."

Henry nodded. "I doubt the latter is possible, but if we could get rid of one issue, it would help."

"All right. I will call him first thing in the morning because I know he wakes at something stupid like four o'clock, and I'll give you all a status report at a more reasonable hour. Robert, let us know if Vincent is in contact before your time is up."

"I will."

The men stood, each giving Henry a goodbye before leaving.

"I should've asked if it was okay for me to stay," Henry said.

"I would've been sad if you had gone." Robert smiled. "Let's get some sleep."

"Is that all?" Henry smirked.

"Maybe you should follow me and find out."

## 20

HENRY

Henry followed him into the bedroom, the sway of Robert's hips hidden behind his jumper, much to his disappointment. Robert whirled around, and Henry came to a halt when he was toe to toe with him. Robert slid his hands up the leather suit Henry had forgotten he wore. He'd said he hadn't wanted any of them to see him like this, but when he'd spoken to them earlier that night at home, he hadn't thought about it. Same when they arrived here.

"What's got you thinking hard?" Robert asked.

"I'm more comfortable in my pup suit in front of others than I expected to be."

Robert smiled. "You're getting used to it. It's a part of you now. It means you're content." He spun Henry in place, unbuckling the straps Henry patiently buckled himself those many hours ago.

As his fingers tugged, skimmed and slid over his suit,

Henry closed his eyes and lost himself in the bliss of being touched and held as if he meant something. When Robert removed his suit, it left Henry in his skin-tight onesie, which was pulled off soon after. Henry, left in his boxers, yanked at the hem of Robert's jumper, dragging it over his head, and did the same for his leggings.

They stood there in their underwear with their arms around each other, and Henry had never been so content. Robert understood every part of him now and didn't shy away from him. He took everything that was thrown at him, thought about it and made a decision about what he wanted to happen. Henry was blessed to share Robert's life. He hoped they could stay this way, and nothing that happened outside of this room would tear them apart.

"Let's have a shower. I bet you were sweltering in that suit."

Robert placed their phones on the bedside table, then grabbed his hand and tugged him towards the bathroom, where he proceeded to wash every inch of Henry's body. Their cocks stood to attention, but neither did anything about it. Henry wasn't in a rush. Robert switched off the shower, dried Henry with a soft towel and led him to bed. He expected Robert to throw him on the bed and devour him, but instead, Robert lay down and crooked a finger at him. Once Henry settled against Robert's side, with Robert's arms securely around him, he sighed.

"I know I teased you about doing more than sleeping, but I think we both need to sleep more." Robert pressed a kiss to Henry's head.

Henry's heart swelled with the care and devotion

Robert had shown in the past few hours. He'd cared for his family when they had invaded his home, he'd looked after Henry, knowing he needed more than just sex, and he'd given Henry the time to collect his thoughts without pushing.

"Thank you."

Robert replied by tightening his arms and kissing his head again. "Sleep. We'll wake up refreshed and, hopefully, full of ideas."

Henry didn't think he'd be able to sleep, but his phone woke him, the ringing tone peeling through the silence and making him jump. He fumbled for the device and put it to his ear when he saw his brother's name.

"Hey, sorry to wake you. Freddie spoke to Uncle William. He wants to meet with us to go through a few things. Would you be able to get to Windsor in an hour?"

Henry cracked open his eyes again and blinked several times to stop his eyes from rolling back in his head. He cleared his throat. "Yeah, we'll be there."

"All right, see you in a little while."

Because of his current location, the drive to Windsor would take around five minutes, so he had plenty of time to spend with Robert before his life became a free for all. He rolled over, smiling when he found Robert eyeing him. The corners of the man's lips curved, and Henry enjoyed the unlined, relaxed face staring back at him.

"Good morning." Henry threw an arm over Robert's waist.

"Morning. Are you having to leave?"

Henry sighed and snuggled closer, his eyelids fluttering shut. "In a little while. Uncle William wants a meeting in an hour."

"I'll lend you some clothes unless you want to arrive in a pup suit?"

Henry's eyes sprung open. "No! What would Uncle William think?"

"That you're happy, and he doesn't care how or why?"

Henry paused. "Yeah, I suppose. But no, I couldn't do that. It's a different matter being in front of my brother and cousins, but not my uncle."

"Are your brother and your cousins in the lifestyle as well?" Robert asked.

Henry hesitated. Technically, he couldn't tell Robert about the club because he hadn't signed a club-specific NDA, but he *had* signed *an* NDA. Maybe he could get away with it.

"There is something else I need to tell you, but I shouldn't because you haven't signed an NDA about it. I know you signed an NDA about what happened at The Den, but this one would be more specific. That being said, I trust you to keep this to yourself."

He glanced at Robert, hoping the severity of the situation was evident in his eyes. Robert studied him for a moment before nodding.

"I won't tell a soul."

He returned his head to Robert's chest. "What do you know about Club Royal?" He felt Robert jerk, then settle.

"Only what I've heard and read about in the media."

"A lot of that is true." He paused, allowing that to sink in. "The Club is owned and run by the royal family, and they give every person in the family a mandatory membership. Whether they use it is up to them, but for the most part, they do. I'm one of twelve monitors who keep the guests safe, and up to recently, the rules for the club had been that the heirs to the throne needed to be trained as a Dominant and in BDSM to the highest level. I'm trained as a Dominant, though I don't want to be."

Robert blew out a breath. "Wow. The rumours about the club are widespread, but no one could confirm anything."

"It's because of the legally binding NDAs everyone has to sign regularly. People can allude to a lot of things, but no one will ever confirm anything."

"You said something had changed recently. What?"

Henry smiled. "Freddie has convinced Uncle Andrew to change the rules regarding royal family members. They no longer have to train as Dominants and become Monitors if they don't want to. They can be submissives if they want to be."

Robert tightened his arms. "That's great news."

"It is." Henry hesitated. "I don't know if it will change other people's views of us, though."

"You mean your cousin."

Henry nodded and continued to slide his cheek against Robert's chest, the heat transferring onto his skin, and the scent of him enfolding him.

"I doubt they will ever change their minds. They seem set in their ways and principles, and I don't think even a royal proclamation would stop them from following that."

Robert inhaled. "In some ways, you have to commend them."

Henry lifted off him and stared. "What!"

"Calm down. I don't mean to commend them for their misguided thoughts. I mean, they're sure that their ideas are right that they're willing to stick with them and fight for those beliefs. It takes some strength to stay true to your core belief when those around you oppose it. Think about it. I'm not saying it's right."

Henry leaned on his elbow and stared at nothing. "It's true in some ways. We proclaim people should accept everyone for being who they are, to be inclusive and true to themselves, then argue that someone else shouldn't have certain views. You're right. I can see how they're staying true to their beliefs, but it doesn't mean I have to agree."

"I'm not saying it's right. Not at all. In fact, it's not. But maybe if we figure out *how* they think, we might be closer to recognising the best route for us to take."

"Good idea." Henry sighed. "I suppose we should get ready to leave."

Robert smoothed his hands over Henry's back. "I won't be able to come with you."

Henry lifted his head. "Why not?"

"I need to open the shop. I don't have anyone who can do it for me."

Henry sat up. "It's okay. We'll be fine." He said the words, but his shoulders lowered, and his stomach dropped. He'd hoped to have Robert there with him to help him through the discussions they were about to have.

They dressed in silence, with Henry borrowing some clothes, and Robert stopped with his hands on his hips.

"Hold on." He grabbed his phone and put it to his ear. "Hey, Granddad. Sorry if I woke you." He listened for a moment and smiled. "I'm glad. I wondered if you could open the shop for me today?" He nodded. "Great. Yes, I'll explain it later." He glanced at Henry. "Thank you." Ending the call, he locked gazes with him. "I'm coming with you."

"You don't have to."

"I know, but I want to. It's not fair making you sort it all out when I'm involved as well. Besides, I want to support you. You're going to be outing yourself to your uncle. It's the least I can do."

Henry's eyes widened, and his heart raced. "Oh, my god. I am. I hadn't thought about it like that. What the hell am I going to do?"

Robert caught him around the waist and brought his pacing to a halt. "You're going in there strong and honest, and you're telling him the truth of who you are. There is no shame in that. As far as I'm aware, your uncle seems fine with gay men. I wouldn't worry at all."

"But I've not even told my father! My mother figured it out, but my father doesn't know. Shouldn't he know before my uncle?"

Robert gave a small smile. "I think these are extenuating circumstances. Your father will understand once the story is out in the open."

Henry still worried, even with Robert's reassurances. He couldn't help it. Spending so much time hiding himself from everyone—except his mother, apparently—made him jumpy. Robert drove them to Windsor, meeting George on the driveway.

"Bright early morning for us all," he said with a grin.

"Have you even been to bed?" Henry asked.

George winked. "Maybe."

They wandered down the corridors, and Henry hadn't even realised he held Robert's hand until the man squeezed it. His heart missed a beat and continued pounding at a rapid pace. He needed to forget about what other people thought. Many people supported him and would support him if they knew. He needed to calm down. Robert squeezed his hand again, and Henry returned the gesture with a smile he was sure was barely visible.

Freddie had sent them a message to tell them to meet in his rooms, and they headed that way. George knocked, then barged right in without waiting for an answer, and Henry rolled his eyes at him.

They greeted everyone, including Maverick and Damon, who Henry hadn't expected to be there but was happy they were. The only person they waited on was Uncle William, who turned up several minutes later.

"Good morning, all of you. I hear you may have a problem or two. Frederick, would you mind if I made myself a cup of tea?"

"I'll get it for you, Uncle William. Have a seat," Douglas stood.

"Thank you."

William Sutcliffe was an imposing man when he stood. He was as tall as Henry, and they were of similar appearances as were most of the family. The genetic markers ran deep through their family. His uncle was fifty-five years old, and he and his wife had four children of their own, including Alice, who was non-binary, and Helena, who was a lesbian.

Now that Henry had the reminder at the front of his mind, he knew Uncle William wouldn't care he was gay. It was a stupid thought brought forth from the fear Charles had him cowering under.

"Thank you, Douglas." William took a sip and sighed. "Perfect." He rested the cup on his knee and glanced around the gathered people. "Who's going first?"

Freddie shared a look with Henry and began to speak. He went through everything they knew about what had happened with Douglas, Maverick and the guy who had been hell-bent on creating a nightmare for them, Talon. Henry spoke about what had happened when he was younger and the things he'd seen and heard. George took over and spoke about his own experiences, which no one had known about.

"Obviously, all of that is awful, but something else must've happened for you to bring it to my attention now," William said, draining his cup.

Henry inhaled, and Robert took his hand. He smiled at him and focused on his uncle, who raised his eyebrows. He ignored the question in his eyes and explained the issue he and Robert currently dealt with. When he finished, he was exhausted.

William blew out his cheeks in a large exhale. "Well, that's a right pickle you've got yourself into, isn't it?" He scratched his chin. "We know Vincent and Charles are in cahoots because the picture appears to be the same one— we don't know for sure, but it seems like it is. As for Charles, I think he wants to be lord of the manor. His mother wants nothing more than to have her children on the throne, but she knows it won't happen. They're trying to discredit you all, making you seem like monsters to the public. The problem they don't see is that it's showing *them* in a poor light, not you."

"What do we do about Vincent?" Henry asked. "Robert has to give him an answer today."

William stayed silent for a moment, lost in thought. "Stall him. Tell him yes but say you'll only do it if he signs an NDA about the picture and the knowledge he has."

"What if he says no? He could threaten to release the picture." Robert gripped his hand.

William leaned forward. "Do you have a problem with your relationship going public?"

Henry peered at Robert. If anyone had asked him several weeks ago, he would've told them to go to hell. Now, though, he decided he no longer wanted to hide. He wanted to be free of the burden. He smiled and glanced at his uncle.

"No problem at all."

Robert tapped his shoulder. "No! You don't want to do this. What about Charles?"

Henry faced Robert. "I have family who will support me. Charles and Aunt Charlotte are scaremongers. I don't want to live like that anymore. Not now that I've found you."

Tears brimmed in Robert's eyes but didn't overflow. "If you're sure, then I'm with you all the way."

Henry kissed him and turned to his uncle. "It's fine."

"If Vincent says he's going to release the picture, let him. He can't link you to being the pup, Henry. He couldn't have any proof of that from what you've described. You did a great job of hiding it in public. Although I would suggest from now on to do it within the security of the club." William raised his eyebrows.

"Yes, Uncle William. I'll speak to Robert about it later."

"As for Vincent, he'll either be gagged because of the NDA or behind the times by releasing the picture. He won't benefit from either. Even if you say you'll do the job for him but refuse afterwards, he doesn't have a leg to stand on. He won't be able to talk about it because he's signed the NDA."

"And if he doesn't sign, I won't agree to work with him, and he'll release the picture that won't matter to us," Robert finished.

"Exactly." William grinned. "To make it even better, you could release a statement now and beat him to it, then he'll have a picture worth nothing."

"What about Charles?" Freddie asked.

The rest of them had been silent for the time he and William had been discussing things.

"Charles is a little more difficult to deal with. We have no solid proof that he's doing any of these things, even if we *know* he is. If we can get something to stick on him, we'd be golden, but as it stands, there's nothing much we can do."

"I'm concerned about Henry's safety when our relationship is public knowledge. Charles threatened him more than once." Robert rested his elbows on his knees.

"I would suggest increasing your security for a little while, Henry, but you could also threaten him back. Write your statement, lock it away and say we will deliver it to the police should something happen to you. You've shared the knowledge with us now, and although we only have your word on it, they are less likely to do something the more people know about it." William growled. "I wish I'd known about it then. I would've done something straight away."

Henry sat back on the sofa, staring at the ceiling. A weight had lifted from his shoulders, and he could finally breathe again. On top of that, he'd found Robert, who he couldn't imagine being without, even though it hadn't been too long since they'd begun. He wanted to shout his newfound relationship to the rooftops.

And he could!

He jerked upright. "Yes, to the announcement. I want to do it now. As soon as possible. I need to speak to Father first, but I want the world to know." He refused to hide any longer.

Although when it was over, he'd hide away, but only because he couldn't take too much of people focusing on him, and he'd already had that enough today.

21

## ROBERT

As soon as they confirmed the announcement, things got a little crazy. Henry and Robert drove to Bagshot Park and sat down with Henry's parents for a late breakfast. Princess Victoria was all smiles and happiness, joy seeping from her pores as she congratulated them both. Prince Patrick Senior was stoic but gave his blessing, especially after they had explained the reason the announcement was happening so quickly. When the information came to light about what Henry had seen, his mother had burst into tears and pulled him into a hug, murmuring in his ear.

Before they left to return to Windsor, Princess Victoria pulled Robert aside.

"I can see you love him very much. Don't be afraid of who you are, of who he is. His life is uncommon, but he's just a man underneath it all. Don't fear the bullies who try to bring us down because they will try, but if we can stick together—if you two can stick together—everything will work out fine."

Robert nodded, unable to say a word from the thickness in his throat. Victoria hugged him.

Henry's parents would meet them at Windsor in an hour, which was when William had arranged for the press conference to start. Henry dragged Robert, laughing, down a corridor until they reached another wing of Henry's house. The moment Robert entered, he knew this was Henry's area. The decoration was different, darker but more comfortable, and he felt at home immediately.

"I need to get something else to wear," Henry said, striding towards another door. "As much as I appreciate the clothes you lent me, I think I need something that actually fits." He chuckled as he unlocked the door and disappeared.

Knowing how much Henry needed his inner sanctuary to be untouched, Robert stayed in the living room and sank onto the sofa. Everything had happened fast. He needed a second to catch his breath.

Princess Victoria was correct. Robert loved Henry. It was why he was going ahead with this whole charade, despite being an insignificant person in the grand scheme of things. He knew this would protect them both, but he couldn't help but wish they were back in their little bubble above his shop. Being outed as the lover of a prince hadn't been on his to-do list that day, but at least he wore clothes that accentuated his features and had put makeup on.

He pulled out his phone and dialled his mother.

"Hey, Mum. Yes, everything's fine but put the news on in an hour."

"Why?"

"Just do it and make sure Hadley and Ophelia know about it, too."

"Sometimes, dear boy, you worry me with your mysterious words." She sighed. "Okay, we'll be watching."

"Thank you. I love you."

"Love you, too, sweetheart."

"You could've invited them," Henry said, making Robert jump.

"I know, but Mum would've kicked up a fuss about not having time to prepare. It's better this way. Forgiveness is easier than permission." Robert smirked.

Henry raised his eyebrows. "I'll remember that."

He glanced at his watch. "I'm going to call the shop to let them know."

Henry drifted closer, resting his hands on the back of the sofa and leaning down to capture Robert's mouth in a sweet kiss. "Thank you for this. I'm sorry it's making you into a puppet of sorts."

Robert slid his arms around Henry's back, tugging him down until he straddled Robert's legs. The weight of him settled something inside Robert. "This would've happened no matter when we announced our relationship, wouldn't it?" When Henry nodded, he continued, "It doesn't matter because no one can prepare for standing in front of a room full of journalists and detailing who they're sleeping with." Robert smiled to show he was joking. "This helps us both because it means we'll be too much in the public eye for anything onerous to happen."

Henry wrapped his arms around Robert's neck, resting their foreheads together. "You deserve more than I can give you."

"I deserve the man I love," Robert whispered.

Henry lifted his head, eyes wide, tears pooling. "You love me?"

"How could I not? You're the kindest, most unselfish person I've met, and we fit. Our personalities fit, our beliefs fit, our sexual preferences fit, our kinks fit. Who could ask for more?"

Tears overflowed as Henry joined their mouths in a blistering kiss that would've taken them to the bedroom had it not been time to leave.

Henry stared at him as Robert wiped away his tears. "I love you, too." He sniffed. "I never, ever thought I'd have this. I expected to live my life alone, but when I saw you at the children's Christmas party," Henry shook his head. "You were a lighthouse in the night, guiding home a lost ship." He snorted. "That sounded corny, but you get my idea."

"I love that description. You helped me to remember what it's like to have someone support you no matter what." Robert kissed him again. "This is going to be a fun story to tell our grandkids."

Henry's eyes lit up. "You want children?"

Robert nodded. "I'd love them, but only if you do."

"Hell, yes! I'd always loved the idea of having loads of

kids running around a house. Having a large family myself, I want that for my—our—children."

"My family is not huge, but I can see the appeal from how you interact with your cousins."

Henry's phone rang. "It's Freddie." He climbed off Robert after a quick peck on his lips. "Yes, we'll be on our way in a few minutes."

As Henry finished getting ready, Robert called the shop and gave them the same cryptic message about watching the news. Then it was time to leave.

A driver waited for them in the driveway, and Robert raised his eyebrows but said nothing as he slipped into the back seat with Henry. As soon as they sat, Henry threaded their fingers together.

"We're going around the back of Windsor so no one can see us before we give the announcement."

Butterflies swarmed in his stomach, but he held tight to Henry's hand. He'd faced worse situations than this. Telling the world he was sleeping with their prince was less scary than facing off with Vincent, and that was something he would have to do that afternoon. Nothing like getting everything done in one day. He snorted, and Henry gave him a questioning look.

The twenty-minute journey appeared to take forever, but finally, they pulled up outside the back of the building. Henry stepped out first and held the door for Robert. They held hands as they entered the building, and a staff member ushered them into a room that held the king, the queen consort, Frederick, Douglas, George, Patrick, Christian, Prince William, Princess Victoria, Prince

Patrick Senior and several other people Robert recognised but hadn't been introduced to.

His heart hammered as he realised how many eyes were on him—them. Henry squeezed his hand, and Robert glanced up at him. The serene smile Henry gave him went a long way to settle his nerves, and he smiled, straightening his back, refusing to cower to those who might do them harm.

"Henry, I'm glad you're here. Robert, nice to see you again." Queen Louisa approached them and brought them each into a hug, one after the other. "I'm happy for you, Henry," she whispered in the prince's ear but loud enough for Robert to hear.

Henry smiled and kissed her cheek. "Thank you, Aunt Louisa. That means a lot."

"And as for you, dear boy, thank you for helping him find his way." She cupped his cheek for a second, then stepped back. "Are you ready?"

"Do you know what you're saying, Henry?" called George, sporting a grin.

"No, I'm going to wing it," Henry retorted.

He heard a few gasps amongst the crowd, but both Queen Louisa and Princess Victoria clapped their hands and smiled. The door opened for them, and blinding lights flashed. Henry squeezed his hand again, and Robert inhaled.

They stepped to the podium, and Henry let go. Robert had a moment of panic before Frederick took his arm and held him in place beside him when Henry strode forward. The rest of the family took their places in a semi-circle behind Henry, showing their support but allowing Henry to do this alone. As Henry had told him earlier, he needed to show his strength; otherwise, he'd be shot down. Figuratively.

Henry's voice rang out through the room. "Thank you for coming on such short notice. I have some news to share, which I will do in a moment. After that, I will take a few questions." He paused. "I am gay." Gasps and murmurs went around the room. "I'm not saying this for any other reason than to stop some unkind people benefitting from giving out this news before I was ready. I wasn't ready, but I'm standing here anyway, opening my life for scrutiny, so those people receive nothing. This is my life, my decision, and no one will take it away from me." Henry glanced to the side, not looking at Robert, but as if he was checking to make sure he was still in his perimeter.

"No one should have to come out on live television. No one should have to come out at all. Coming out shouldn't be necessary. Being gay should be as secondary to a personality as being straight. For that to happen, things need to change." He inhaled. "I would like to introduce my boyfriend." He stared at Robert, a smile curving his mouth, and held out his hand.

Robert's heart pounded, and his hands trembled, but he stepped forward and clasped his hand in Henry's. Henry squeezed him, then let go and wrapped his arm around his waist before turning back to the journalists.

"This is Robert Martin. He owns a flower shop called Floresco. When I first met him, I knew my life would never be the same, even as I fought against it. Hearing that gay people are an abomination is hard on anyone, including me."

Robert rested his head on Henry's shoulder when his voice cracked.

"I will not willingly allow another person to go through that if it is within my power to stop it. This man is by my side and gave me the strength to fight back. Thank you."

The volume rose as journalists shouted questions, and Robert winced. Henry leaned down and whispered, "Just a few more minutes, sweetheart."

"Yes?" Henry pointed at and focused on a journalist in the front row.

"When did you know you were gay?"

"I had an idea when I was ten years old but didn't really understand it at that age. I suppose I should say twelve or thirteen. Somewhere around there." He found another journalist.

"Who told you gays were an abomination?"

Robert exhaled and bit his lip. What was Henry going to say to that? He could hardly point the finger at his aunt.

"Someone who should've known better."

Robert raised his eyebrows at that and tried to withhold a smile. He was in front of the country at this point.

"Robert, what's it like being with a prince?" A laugh circled the room.

He started, not having expected someone to want to ask him something. He fumbled. "Overwhelming. Public." Everyone laughed. "No different from any other person," he finished with a smile.

The questions continued until King Andrew put a stop to it some twenty minutes later.

"Thank you for taking the time to visit us and hear our wonderful news. I hope you will celebrate this event with us and help us recognise and support the LGBTQ+ community among us."

Their supporters filtered back into the room behind the podium, and the doors closed. Henry let out an audible sigh, and Robert wrapped his arms around him.

"You were amazing."

Henry huffed a laugh and tucked his head into Robert's neck, inhaling. "Thank you for being with me. I'm sorry if you'll be inundated now. I should have left the shop name out of the speech."

Robert brushed it aside. "It doesn't matter. It might be good for business."

"You'll have to take on more employees," Douglas said from beside them.

They pulled apart and greeted Henry's cousin.

Douglas clapped Henry on the shoulder. "You should've brought me into the speech. You know I wouldn't have minded."

"I know, and thank you, but this was about Robert and me."

"Speaking of shops, though, I better get back. If people flock to the shop, Granddad will get overrun," Robert said. "Plus, I'm not sure what time Vincent will be there."

"All right. I'll come with you." Henry guided him over to his mother.

"No, you need to stay here and finish up whatever stuff

they say you need to do. This announcement wasn't the only thing you had. I'll be fine."

"I'll go with him, and we'll take some security, too," Damon said.

Robert glanced over his shoulder and saw Frederick's best friend standing a few steps away. "You don't need—"

"That would be great. Thanks, Damon," Henry said, giving Robert a significant glare. "You need someone with you now that I've outed you to the country. At least for a few days until it dies down."

Robert opened his mouth to argue, but the worry in Henry's expression softened him. "All right. We'll talk about this more later, though."

Henry smiled and kissed him for a lot longer than Robert thought he would in front of members of his family. Robert's cheeks were scorching by the time he left Henry's side and was shown through the corridors to a car by Damon. A driver and a security guard climbed into the front seats, and if Robert wasn't mistaken, another two or more guards followed in a second car.

"It will only be for a short while until their attention moves onto something else. At the moment, you're bright and new, but soon, they'll find another shiny toy." Damon's words brought him a little comfort, and Robert acknowledged them with a word of thanks.

The drive was five minutes—he could've walked it— but finding somewhere to stop was next to impossible. The flower shop was several people deep away from them, and Robert told them to stop, and he'd get out from there.

"That won't happen," Damon said, grinning.

Robert rolled his eyes and huffed, crossing his arms over his chest. "Pull around the back if you can get the car down the alleyway." He pointed out the entrance, which was covered by people, too. Soon, two security guards from the car behind them came walking past and spoke to and cajoled people into moving so the car could get past. Flashes of cameras, shouts of Robert's name, and banging on the car made him understand exactly what the royal family had to deal with. He hoped his granddad was okay.

The car barely fit down the alleyway, and once it was in the car park, they climbed out. Robert glanced at the other car and saw it had stopped right in the entrance, blocking anyone else from coming down. Some people tried to squeeze past, but the car doors opened, stopping their progress.

Robert rushed to the back door, letting himself in with the key and let Damon and one security guard inside. The rest stayed outside. When the door closed, he leaned against it and exhaled.

"Robert! You could've warned me. I was expecting a leisurely day back at a job I love, and after your speech, things went frantic. I have Finn standing at the door and only letting in two people at a time. It's crazy."

Robert hugged his granddad. "I'm sorry, Grandad. I should've warned you more than I did, but I honestly didn't expect this." He waved his hand towards the front of the shop and let his hands drop again. "Granddad, this is Damon Winchester. He offered to escort me back here."

"Nice to meet you, sir. If it's no trouble, I'd like to stay for a little while to ensure there are no issues."

His granddad shook Damon's hand. "Of course, it's no bother. You might need to get your hands dirty, though. We're busier than we've ever been."

Robert's eyes widened. "No, he doesn't need to work, Granddad! Sorry, do whatever you need to do. Ignore him."

Damon chuckled. "I don't mind helping at all. We can get two of the security guards to take care of holding people back and letting them in and out of the shop. That will free up your staff to do what you pay them to do."

Robert let out a sigh. "That would be great, thanks."

Damon went off to sort that out, and Robert banged his head against the wall a few times.

"Have you spoken to your parents yet?" Granddad asked.

Robert shook his head by rolling it on the wall. "They can grill me later. I have work to do."

They spent the early afternoon working twice as hard as they'd ever done, then it calmed a bit. He let Finn and Naomi finish for lunch and sent his granddad home for a rest. Damon had been fantastic and had helped customers with their decisions as much as he could. Robert thought the customers were just as happy to get to speak to the heir's best friend as they were to be in the shop of a prince's boyfriend.

"You can head off now if you want to. Thank you for your help."

Damon smiled. "You're welcome, but if it's all the same, I'll wait for your staff to come back before I leave you. Although, I'll disappear in the back and make a cup of tea if that's okay?"

Robert chuckled. "Yes, of course. Help yourself."

Damon patted him on the shoulder as another customer entered. Robert lifted his head and froze. He panicked for a second, wondering why the security guards had let him past, but realised they would've been told to allow him entry.

"I would say I'm happy to see you, Vincent, but I'm not," Robert said. Damon flicked his focus to Robert and stepped to the side, though he didn't turn around.

Vincent's stony gaze studied him. "I assume from the press conference I saw that your answer is no."

"You would be correct."

"That's not the only photo I have, Robert. Do you really wish for Prince Henry's kinks to be visible for the world to see?"

Robert's heart raced, but he kept his cool. "I'll make a deal with you, Vincent. You sign an NDA about these photos and the information you know, and I'll store your packages."

Vincent narrowed his eyes. "Why would I do something like that?"

"Because you need my help. I've heard about the police closing down some places where I'm sure you were storing items. You must be running out of 'lockers.'" He surrounded the word with finger quotes.

He watched Vincent's jaw clench and release, clench and release until he nodded. "Okay. Get me an NDA, and we have a deal."

Robert couldn't believe the guy had caved. Telling the man he was desperate hadn't been smart, but it had worked. He rummaged under the counter where he'd placed an NDA for just this moment. He placed it on the counter, put a pen beside it and stepped back.

"There you go."

Vincent drifted closer, dragging the piece of paper towards him. Robert studied him as the criminal read through the document. It was the same version of what Robert had signed at The Den, with a couple of small caveats in it to ensure Vincent had no loopholes to find.

When the man signed his name, Robert let out a breath. Damon pivoted around and removed the NDA from Vincent's hands before saying anything.

"You will leave this property and never return. You have signed away your pictures and knowledge. You have nothing left to threaten Robert with. He will *not* be working with you."

"You little shit! You made a deal!" Vincent's eyes bulged from his head as his fist smashed into the counter.

He continued to rampage, but the security guards grabbed him before he could do any damage to the shop. Robert exhaled when the door closed behind them.

"I don't know if he'll come back or not, but at least you have the legal aspect on your side. I might suggest getting a restraining order, though. It will help a little."

"Thanks, Damon. I appreciate it."

The shop was quiet when Damon left to make his tea, and Robert sat in his chair and stared at his shop. His life was going to change, that was for certain.

# HENRY

After Robert had left, Henry's parents had ushered him into a room with Uncle Andrew and Aunt Louisa, along with some other members of the family. He hadn't been sure what the plan was from there, but he wished he could be with Robert. After announcing to the country, and possibly the world, about their relationship, it seemed poor form to leave him to deal with the ramifications of that alone.

"Now, Henry, we need to discuss a few things before you can go," said Uncle Andrew. "I know things have been difficult for you for years, but we need to get this sorted."

"I know. Thank you for supporting me with this."

Someone nudged his shoulder, and he glanced at them. Douglas held out a small bowl, and Henry took it with a frown. When he looked inside, there were various squares of different flavoured fudge. He grinned at his cousin and mouthed his thanks. At a chuckle, he peered to his other side, cheeks darkening when his mother shook her head at him with a smile.

"There are likely to be some repercussions from this announcement," his uncle continued. "I'm in no way saying you shouldn't have done this. Quite the contrary, but it won't be taken lightly."

"I understand. I thought it would be easier to kill two birds with one stone, so to speak."

Uncle Andrew leaned forward, resting his elbows on his knees and linking his fingers. "William told me about the conversation you all had." The king pierced Henry with his gaze. "I wish you had felt comfortable enough to come directly to me about it."

Henry's cheeks heated again, and he dropped his gaze to the bowl in his hands. "I'm sorry. I wasn't sure what to do. They scared the life out of me with their threats, but it was only when I had Robert to protect that I realised how much I needed to figure it out to be free."

His mother rubbed her hand up and down his spine, much like she used to do when he'd fallen and skinned his knees. "You did what you needed to at the time. No one can fault that. You were a child."

"Regardless, we now have to predict what they will do," Uncle Andrew said and sat back. "That is never a straightforward thing to do with her."

Henry understood the undertones about not using names amongst family. They couldn't be too careful about who she had coerced to work with her.

William took a seat on the other side of him. "Don't forget to write that statement I mentioned. It will go a long way to protecting you."

"We will assign three guards to you for the time being. We'll see what the ripple effect is and change the number depending on if things get better or worse." Uncle Andrew stood.

"What about Robert?" Henry asked.

Andrew smiled at him. "We will afford him the same security as if he were a member of the family. There will be additional guards at his shop for at least the next few days. Maybe more." Andrew pulled him into a hug and patted his back. "I wish you every happiness."

"Thank you."

Louisa came to stand before him. "I like him, Henry. It was one reason I chose him for the contract. I'm glad you have him, and vice versa. Take care of one another, but also remember, we are here for you both. If you need anything, just ask."

"Thank you," he repeated, voice hoarse.

He sank into his seat again, his mother pushing the bowl of fudge into his hands. While he chewed the sweet treat and listened with half an ear to what his mother and Uncle William were discussing over his bent back, he watched those around him. He noticed the expressions of happiness, nonchalance and sadness, then several with expressions of anger. Many of the latter were cousins he rarely saw. When Freddie dropped into the seat opposite him, Henry leaned further forward and recited the names to him, asking him to keep a note of them. Freddie pulled out his phone, tapped away at it, and nodded again.

His mother gained his attention when she rose from her seat. "I'm going home now, dear." She wrapped her arms around him and whispered, "Charlotte is here. Be careful, my son." Pulling back, she raised an eyebrow at him, and he nodded.

"Safe drive, Mother. I'll be home a little later after I've checked in on Robert."

She patted his cheek. "Take your time. I'm happier now that I know someone else is keeping an eye on you." She winked.

Henry chuckled. "Thanks." He rolled his eyes.

His father, who he'd spoken to earlier that day and who had given his wholehearted blessing, squeezed the nape of his neck as he passed and slid an arm around his wife as they exited the room.

Henry sighed. "I'm going to seek out George. I wanted a word before I left."

"He's in his room, I believe," Freddie said. "I overheard him saying he'd stayed long enough with the family." Freddie grinned.

"We can overwhelm people when we're all together like this," Uncle William said with a laugh. "Speaking of which, I'm leaving, too. Well done, Henry. I'm proud of you."

They said goodbye, and Henry wandered the corridors as he checked his phone. He'd received a couple of updates from Damon in between him helping Robert, which made

Henry chuckle. Neither he nor Robert had mentioned Vincent yet, so Henry assumed he hadn't visited.

"You should be ashamed of yourself."

Henry froze, ice trickling down his spine. He lifted his head. Aunt Charlotte, Uncle Ernest, Albert and Charles were standing before him, and he wasn't sure what to do.

"You are dragging your family through the mud. How dare you show us up! You are nothing but an abomination."

Henry sucked in a silent breath and held it, trying to push aside the hurt those words caused. "You have no right—"

Aunt Charlotte stepped forward, throwing her hand in the air. "I have every right when it affects my family! You are the fifth person within the next generation to stamp your heritage into the ground. Do you think your ancestors would have allowed this to happen?"

It was a rhetorical question, but one Henry would answer. "They may not have acknowledged me, but at least they would have understood," he said, losing his cool. "How many of *your* ascendants were gay with or without public scrutiny? How many took male lovers and hid it? How many didn't hide? We are not the first in the family to be like this, but we *are* the first to be proud of it."

"And that right there is the problem, *Henry*," Charlotte spat.

"No, *you* are the problem."

Henry spun around at Aunt Charlotte's gasp, and Uncle Andrew, Uncle William, Aunt Lou, Freddie and

Douglas all stepped from the shadows. How long had they been there?

"You have spewed nothing but vitriol for years, Charlotte. It ends now. You are no longer welcome at family events. If I require your presence, you will hear directly from me."

"But—"

The king slashed his hand through the air. "No! I've had enough! I have no problem at all with Henry or Douglas or George or Helena or Alice—all of whom you mentioned in your tirade—or anyone else who might want to try something new. You are causing problems in my kingdom, and I won't allow it."

Henry dared not look at Aunt Charlotte, and his gaze found Albert's. Instead of the disgust he assumed he'd find, Albert's expression was pained. After several seconds of a staring contest, Albert moved to cross the distance between them.

"Albert, what do you think you're doing?" Aunt Charlotte screeched.

Henry kept his gaze locked with Albert, unsure of his plan, but when he came to a stop in front of Uncle Andrew, Albert held out his hand and lowered his head.

"Please forgive me for my part in this. I have never wanted any harm to come to anyone, especially the LGBTQ+ community. I thought staying quiet was the best option, but I realise now that was the wrong choice. I am, after all, part of the community my mother is trying so hard to ruin."

Henry glanced at Aunt Charlotte when a gasp

sounded, and her hand covered her mouth. Transferring his gaze back to Albert, he saw Uncle Andrew grasp his hand and pull him into a hug.

"You are more than welcome to distance yourself from those you do not wish to be associated with," Uncle Andrew said.

"Thank you. I apologise for everything."

"The only apologies you need to make are to yourself for putting yourself through this."

"Albert! Get back here right this minute! You are not part of *that* community. You have a wife at home waiting for you."

Albert closed his eyes and whispered. "Do I have your support?"

Uncle Andrew lowered his voice. "Evanna will always have sanctuary if she needs it."

Albert's eyes flew open at the king's words, though Henry frowned.

"Albert!" Aunt Charlotte hissed.

His cousin pivoted to face his mother. "I have a wife who was once a man. Evanna is a transwoman."

"What?"

The screech echoed around the corridors, and Henry winced when he realised how many people had probably heard this interaction.

"We have already moved out of the house. You don't need to worry about that."

Charlotte's face twisted and darkened. "Now, I understand why conceiving a child was so problematic." She sneered. "I think this *disease* is catching too many people around here. I'll be glad for the fresh air."

She whirled around, and if she'd been wearing a skirt, it would've arced around the people surrounding her. Head held high, she marched down the corridor, clicking her fingers as she went. Charles narrowed his eyes on them before following his mother. Uncle Ernest shot a pained glance towards Albert, then startled when Aunt Charlotte shouted his name and hurried after her.

Henry exhaled and slumped against the wall nearest him. His legs were trembling, his heart racing, and he could barely breathe, but he also felt lighter. George came to a standstill next to him and cupped his nape.

"Are you all right?"

"I don't know."

He glanced across at Albert, who Uncle Andrew was talking to in low tones. His cousin looked defeated, and although Henry wanted to help, he couldn't at that moment. He needed space.

"Come on. Let's go to my rooms. We'll get some peace and quiet for a while."

He allowed George to guide him to a room and settle him in a chair. However long later, George pressed a warm cup into his hands and sat beside him. They said nothing, both seemingly lost in their thoughts. Henry's phone broke the silence, and he pulled it from his pocket.

*DAMON: Vincent is sorted. He signed the NDA, and the guards escorted him off the premises. Robert will need a restraining order to cover all bases, but he should be free from him now. I'll be heading home soon, but I've been told the security that is already here will stay until they organise a shift change. Hope everything went okay with you.*

*HENRY: Thank you, Damon. You went above and beyond for us today, and I appreciate it.*

He placed his phone on the arm of the chair instead of calling Robert like he wanted to. He required a few more minutes of peace before real life entered the fray. He needed to remember to get a gift for Damon to thank him properly for everything he'd done for them.

Henry finished his tea and turned to George, resting one knee on the sofa and an arm along the back. "I hadn't realised you'd told anyone else about being bisexual."

George grimaced. "I hadn't. Charles overheard me talking to a friend the other day, and obviously, told on me. Father approached me when he'd been told of the rumours going around. I didn't see the point in denying anything."

"Does your dad know all of it?"

George nodded. "I decided to get everything out in the open at the same time. Saves my heart from having palpitations every time I'm asked a personal question."

Henry snorted. "That it does."

"Freddie said you were coming to see me. Did you need something?"

"No. Actually, I was coming to make sure you were okay."

George chuckled. "And the Wicked Witch of the West interrupted your plans."

"Yes." Henry lowered his head. "I had no idea about Albert. I'd always assumed he would take her side. He and Evanna have been married for ten years. How much of a burden that secret must have been to keep this long." He sighed. "I'm glad he took a stance. He must've feared for her life."

"He's not the only one. You were well into your one-man spiel when I came along. I knew you had it in you, but I was never sure if you'd let it all out."

Henry smiled. "Me neither. I hadn't planned to say anything. I was going to let her words roll off my back and finish my journey to your room, but the knives kept slicing, and I snapped."

"Not a bad thing. The result was a good one."

Henry bobbed his head. Aunt Charlotte being banished from family events was a good thing, but he wondered whether it would make things worse, not better. If she wasn't where they could see her, what would she get up to?

He stood, grabbing his phone. "I'm going to find Robert. If the place was as busy as Damon said it was, he's going to need to relax, especially if the same thing happens tomorrow."

When the driver arrived to take him home, he messaged Robert, letting him know he was on his way to him. He hoped the man wasn't already asleep, which given the time of day, he shouldn't be, but he wouldn't blame him if he was. Robert replied with a smiling face emoji, and Henry grinned. He tilted his head and asked his driver to detour to a shop he knew sold massage oils. The shopkeeper had conniptions when he turned up, but they were pleasant and helpful, and Henry was soon on his way again.

By the time he arrived, he realised he didn't have any clothes to change into in the morning again. He'd have to make do with what he wore today. It would be fine for the journey home. Robert opened the door in a satin dressing gown with leggings underneath—the weather was not conducive to warmer clothes yet—and Henry thought he looked amazing. The man pulled him inside and pressed him back against the closed door.

"I missed you today," Robert said, sliding his hands behind Henry's neck. Henry nuzzled his nose up the column of Robert's neck and sank his teeth into his jawline as Robert's head dropped back on a sigh.

"I miss you always." He kissed the bite better and grabbed Robert beneath his thighs. Robert's breath hitched, but he wrapped his legs around Henry's waist and held on as he climbed the stairs to the apartment. "I have a gift for you."

Robert raised his eyebrows but said nothing, not even when Henry laid him on the bed and unwrapped his dressing gown. A bare chest greeted him once the satin fabric slipped to the bed. Henry couldn't help himself and kissed from the waistband of the leggings up the centre of Robert's body to his mouth. When their lips met, he'd expected to be taken deep and hard in a kiss Robert controlled, and it surprised him when Robert let him lead.

Henry kept the kiss soft, a seduction rather than over-heated arousal.

When they pulled away, Henry lifted off him, dragging Robert's leggings and underwear free, and licked his lips at the sight. Robert shuffled to remove the gown and threw it to the floor.

"On your stomach with your head on the pillow, arms by your head."

Henry expected Robert to balk at the order, but he gave a small curve of his lips and did as he'd asked. The expanse of pale skin taunted him, and he couldn't wait to get his hands on Robert. He grabbed the small bottle of essential oil from his pocket, where he'd left it to warm up, and removed his clothes. He climbed up the bed to straddle Robert's thighs, then clicked the tube open and squirted some lavender-scented liquid into his hand. As he rubbed his hands together, the smell increased, perme-ating the room. He felt Robert inhale and pause before exhaling again, but he didn't move position.

Henry placed his hands on Robert's lower back and massaged the oil into his skin. He made his way over his back, monitoring those areas which appeared tight or provoked a reaction from Robert. It was as calming for him as he hoped it was for Robert.

When Robert began pushing back against Henry, and therefore, his ass was pressing against Henry's cock, his movements stuttered, and Robert seemed to take that as his cue to reverse their positions. Before he knew it, Henry was beneath Robert, and Robert kissed him like his life depended on it. Robert held his head and tilted it where he wanted it as his tongue and lips devoured him. Henry couldn't keep his eyes open. Letting Robert take his breath seemed like a good idea until he grew lightheaded, and he pulled back with a gasp.

Robert chuckled and braced himself above Henry. "Time for your reward."

## 23

## ROBERT

"And what reward might that be?"

Robert grinned at the light sparkling in Henry's eyes. Being away from him for the few hours that afternoon and evening had made Robert wish he didn't have to work, but it was a great distraction, and they had finally sorted things with Vincent. He hadn't arranged the restraining order yet, but he planned to the following morning.

Tonight was for them.

Robert felt loose and relaxed as he teased Henry, kissing, licking and nipping across his skin, tonguing the valleys of his muscles, flicking at his nipples. Henry's cock pooled precome on his stomach, and Robert hadn't even reached his belly button yet.

He tongued the fleshy dimple, licking the precome off as he went. By the time he'd reached Henry's groin, the prince was squirming beneath him, mumbles of incoherence falling from his lips. Robert pushed Henry's legs wider to accommodate his shoulders and licked a stripe up the underside of Henry's cock, watching as it twitched and dripped more fluid. He encircled the base and curled his tongue around the mushroom head, the bitter taste coating his mouth. Resting his thumb against the nerve bundle, he made small, fast circles then added more sensation by flicking his tongue against Henry's slit.

Henry bucked and trembled, and Robert knew he was close to his breaking point. Robert continued his ministrations, staring up at Henry's face to watch for the point of no return. When Henry reached it, Robert sucked him to the back of his throat and swallowed, breathing through his nose as Henry came in several powerful bursts of fluid. Robert didn't particularly enjoy the taste of come, which was why he preferred having his cock in the back of his throat when he came—less to taste—but he wouldn't stop doing it. The wonder on Henry's face was worth the price of a bitter aftertaste.

Henry laid gasping, splayed out with his eyes closed, and Robert smiled from his kneeling position. He climbed off the bed and took a drink of water, then manoeuvred Henry around the bed to get the covers from beneath him. After rolling Henry to his side, he crawled behind him and pulled the covers over the top, tucking them in around them. The apartment got chilly overnight sometimes.

"Thank you," Henry said, his voice low and sleepy.

"You're welcome."

Robert pressed a lingering kiss to the nape of his neck and wrapped his arms around the man he loved.

He jerked awake at a crashing sound, followed by shouting and pounding on the front door. Robert shook Henry awake and jumped out of bed, sliding leggings on as he headed for the door.

"Mr Martin! Wake up!"

A voice shouted through the door, and he ran down the stairs, flinging the door open. The first thing he noticed was the scent of smoke.

"What's wrong?"

One of the security guards who had been sitting outside the building on duty tried to pull him out of the building, but Robert yanked his arm back.

"What's wrong?" he asked again, raising his voice.

"The shop is on fire. You need to get out."

Robert's heart stopped. "What?" he whispered.

"We have to get you out. The fire's spreading too quickly." The security guard tried to get him out of the building again, but Robert avoided him and ran up the stairs to where Henry was fully dressed and grabbing both their shoes.

"I heard. Get some clothes on quickly. I doubt we have much time," Henry said, his face a shade of anger Robert had never seen him wear.

While Robert grabbed a jumper and shoved a couple of things he couldn't do without into a bag, Henry put his phone to his ear.

"There's a fire. We're just leaving. I'm bringing him home. I don't know. Yes, send a car, please. We probably won't be able to leave straight away."

Sirens pierced the silence, and they descended the

stairs and raced out into the night. A night that wasn't dark any longer. They jogged down the alleyway, past the roaring, blistering flames that were consuming Robert's livelihood. The security guard herded them to the opposite side of the road, and Robert sank to the ground. Despite the fire engines arriving faster than he'd expected, the flower shop was a shell of its former self. He closed his eyes and prayed they could save his apartment. Not only because it was his home, but because there were many items inside he would hate to part with.

Henry sat beside him and wrapped a blanket around them both, holding Robert close. "I'm sorry."

Robert frowned. "Why are you sorry?"

"I have a feeling this was Aunt Charlotte's doing in a roundabout way."

Robert sighed, watching the flames reach for the sky and the water beat it back. Anger curled inside him. "She won't win. Yes, this hurts, but it's all immaterial. I can replace everything. If this is the best she can do, bring it the fuck on."

Smoke wafted their way, and the sounds of orders being shouted, water pouring, engines running, and the buzz of conversation surrounded them. The red and blue flashing lights, the white headlights of cars and the yellow and orange flames kept away the dark night. He couldn't believe it was all gone, but there was no denying it.

"I'll ensure everything gets replaced," Henry said, his voice strained.

Robert turned to him, cupping his cheek. "The insurance will replace everything. All I need you to do is stay with me. Don't go getting any silly ideas about being a bad influence on me or trying to save me from your aunt. Get out of your head, Henry. I know you."

Henry gave a small smile but didn't argue. Robert dropped a kiss on his lips and rested his head on Henry's shoulder. They watched the firefighters work their magic until they called the all-clear. One firefighter strode over and crouched in front of them.

"Mr Martin?" He glanced at Henry, raised his eyebrows, then focused on Robert. "The fire is out, but we still need to secure the building and ensure it's safe. It didn't get into the apartment, although there is likely to be extensive smoke damage. You won't be allowed back in until tomorrow at the earliest. Is there anything desperately you need from the apartment?"

"No, I grabbed what I needed most." He pointed at the backpack.

The firefighter nodded. "You will need to give a statement to the police, but that can wait until tomorrow. I'm sorry for your loss."

"Thank you."

Henry pressed his lips against Robert's temple. "Shall we head to my house? I have a car waiting."

Robert nodded twice in slow succession. He stared at the remains of his shop and steeled his resolve. "If it was her, she won't win," he repeated.

He stood, shouldering the backpack, and held out his hand. Henry's forehead creased, but he accepted. They wandered down the street, away from the bustle of the fire, with two security guards following them. A black town car waited further down, and as soon as they approached, the driver climbed out and opened the back door. They slid inside, and Robert jumped when he saw Patrick waiting inside.

"Is it bad?" Patrick asked.

Henry nodded. "The shop is gone. The apartment will be okay, though."

Patrick rested a hand on Robert's knee. "I'm sorry. We'll figure out who did this."

"I think we already know, don't we? Or at least, we have two potential suspects: Charlotte or Vincent." Robert tucked his backpack beside him and tugged at his sleeve as he had no jewellery to play with.

"I agree," Henry said. "The sooner we get someone to look into this, the better. We need to find whoever started the fire."

Patrick sat back as the car pulled away from the kerb. "Father rang me a few minutes ago—remember he has contacts at the police. They said from what they could gather, mainly from what your security guards said, they watched the property and saw a homeless man walking past. The guy threw a firebomb through the window before either of them could react. One guard went after the guy but lost him. The other guard came for you."

"And with all the flowers in there, it would easily set alight," Robert said. His emotions were all over the place, but anger and sorrow were the most prevalent. "I need to call Finn, Naomi and my family. I don't want them hearing about this on the news."

"Do you want to wait until we get settled at home before you do it?" Henry asked.

"Yeah, I will. I doubt I'll sleep much more."

Robert let the conversation of the two brothers wash over him as he watched the streetlights pass by. He wasn't angry at Henry for what happened, but he was a little pissed off that the royal family hadn't been able to stop Charlotte's actions before this. From what he gathered from the several conversations he'd taken part in, Charlotte was the bane of the family, but they couldn't ever pin anything on her or her son. Something needed doing. Fast.

They pulled up outside Bagshot Park, and before they'd even opened the car doors, Henry's mother was there, pulling Robert into her arms.

"I'm glad you're okay. I was worried something had happened to you both when Patrick woke us and ran out with barely a reason."

She tugged Henry into a hug, too, and ushered them all into the house.

"We're fine. Mother, as much as we'd like to talk to you right now, Robert needs to contact his family so they don't worry. I'm going to get him settled in my rooms." He faced Patrick. "Would you mind filling them in, please?"

Patrick nodded. "Sure. I'll come by in a little while and see if you need anything."

"Thank you."

The brothers touched each other's chins and parted, Henry leading Robert down a long hallway and around several corners until Robert lost his bearings. Henry opened a large ornate door and ushered Robert inside, closing it behind them. He dropped into the nearest chair, which happened to be a comfortable sofa, and pulled out his phone, staring at it.

"Do you want me to call them?"

Robert blinked up at Henry, who had come to sit beside him. It took him a second to understand what he'd said. "No, it's better if I do. If you call, they'll worry something happened to me. I'm just tired."

Henry wrapped his arm around Robert's shoulder and slid closer. "I'm here. Whatever you need me for."

Robert stared at him and realised those words applied to more than this scenario. Henry had always been there for him, no matter what the problem was. Also, Henry didn't care less about Robert's dominance and the way he looked. Well, didn't care was probably the wrong words, but he believed in him and trusted him as a Dom, which was more than many people did. The temporary pups didn't count; they were content with using him for their needs for one night, not for a relationship.

"You see me." The words were soft, and Robert slid his hand to Henry's jaw and around the back of his head, pulling him down for a kiss. There was a distinct scent of smoke on their clothes and skin, but Robert didn't mind at that moment.

When they pulled away, Henry frowned. "What do you mean, I see you?"

"I feel like we had this conversation, or I planned to have this conversation. My mind is a little fuzzy. Let me call my parents, and we'll discuss my words. Is that okay?"

Henry smiled. "Of course. Would you like a drink?"

"Tea would be wonderful."

Henry rose, and Robert watched his actions for a moment before refocusing on his phone. He dialled and held it to his ear, wincing when his mother answered in a frantic voice.

"What's happened?"

"I'm fine, Mum. Sorry to wake you, but I needed you to know before someone else did. The flower shop burnt down." His mother gasped, and he could picture her expression with a hand over her mouth. "I'm with Henry at his house at the moment, but we're both fine. We stink of smoke, but we've no injuries or anything."

"Oh, my god. What happened?"

"We don't know much. We'll be talking to the police tomorrow. They should have some more information for us."

"And you're sure you're okay?" When his mother worried, she worried worse than several parents put together.

"We're fine. I promise."

Winnie sighed. "All right. I suppose there's not much more you can do tonight. Get some sleep."

"I'll try." He closed his eyes. "I'm going to ring Finn and Naomi now, so they don't turn up for work tomorrow."

"Okay, sweetheart. Ring me in the morning, all right?"

"I will. Love you, Mum. Say hi to Dad for me."

"Love you, sweetie."

He ended the call and exhaled, then put it to his ear again, going through the same conversation with Finn.

"I'll wake Naomi. You get some rest," Finn said.

"Are you sure?"

"Yeah, it's fine. Besides, she'll keep you on the phone for hours trying to get more information from you."

Robert chuckled. "True. Thanks."

"No problem. I'll speak to you tomorrow."

By the time he'd finished, his tea was lukewarm but still a welcomed drink. He downed it in several long gulps and placed the cup down again.

"Thank you for that." Robert smiled at Henry.

"You're welcome." Henry threaded their fingers together. "Would you like a bath or a shower?"

"A bath would be great."

"Come on."

Henry pulled on Robert's hands, and they wandered through the rooms to the bathroom. It was only when they stood in the large room and Henry locked the door that Robert realised he'd not paid attention to Henry's inner sanctum. The prince hadn't even flinched when they'd drifted through it.

Henry leaned over the bath, but Robert tugged him aside. He needed to look after Henry. When he thought about what could've happened if the security guards hadn't been outside, it made his heart and head hurt. He switched on the bath after depressing the plug and added a few drops of bath liquid. The calming scent of lavender filled the room. Robert faced Henry and undressed him. Not as a tease but as a promise. A soft smile played around Henry's lips. When he was naked, Henry returned the favour and undressed Robert, then Robert switched off the taps and helped Henry into the bath before sliding in behind him and pulling his lover against his chest.

In the bath, their height difference didn't matter. Henry was the perfect height to rest his head back on Robert's shoulder. Silence reigned, but Robert needed to explain his earlier words.

"When I first got involved in the BDSM community, everyone assumed I would be submissive because I loved wearing jewellery and makeup and what they saw as girly clothes. They made many comments as I began my training to be a Dominant. In fact, it had taken me months of searching before I found someone willing to train me. Everyone before him assumed I wasn't serious. But Elton could see something in me, luckily."

"The owner of The Den?"

Robert nodded. "Yeah, we've been friends for years, though not as close as many people assume we are. He's been there through all the relationships I've had and was there to commiserate every time another failed because the sub couldn't take me seriously."

"They're idiots."

Robert chuckled and sighed. "But you see all of me. You saw me at work when I was overwhelmed and stressed, but you made things easier by following my instructions as if you knew it would help. You saw me at The Den before you even knew it was me and let me take care of you. You saw me after you knew it was me, and you still didn't care and gave me a chance. You saw me in my apartment, surrounded by the things I had carefully found to make it my own, and you didn't try to change me. I have exposed all the different facets of my personality to you, and you still want me."

His voice broke at the end because his emotions had risen to the surface. Henry turned his face into Robert's neck and pulled Robert's legs over his own so they were intertwined fully.

"The different facets of your personality are what I love about you. No matter what anyone else says, no one else would've been happy with you because you were made for me. What annoys other people, I love. What scares other people, I love. You are who you are, and you're perfect to me."

Robert's eyes closed, and he whispered, "Thank you. I love you, too."

"I know you do. It's why we work well together. I would love for you to join me at the club one night. You can see what I do when I have to be a Dominant."

Robert slid his hands over Henry's chest. "Do you still have to do that with the king changing the rules?"

Henry was silent for a moment. "That's true. I don't know. I've not spoken with him about it yet."

"Maybe you should. But yes, I'd love to visit the club. I'd be able to find out if the rumours are true." He waggled his eyebrows when Henry glanced at him, then laughed. "Are you going to be my pup there?" Henry froze, and Robert was quick to reassure him. "You don't have to. I wasn't sure if it was something you'd like to explore in your own domain, so to speak."

"Maybe. I might have to speak to George first."

"George?"

Henry flushed. "He's been helping me work through my thoughts on the whole thing. Aunt Charlotte and Charles have twisted my thoughts into knots, and I'm slowly unravelling them. I hope I can be your pup at the club soon."

"However long it takes, I'll be by your side. And if you'd prefer to stay going to The Den, that's fine. Elton will be more than happy to have you there. Although, we might have to tell him who you are if Vincent hasn't already. I told Elton about the blackmail."

"Let's leave that decision for another day when I'm not turning into a prune."

They laughed, then Robert washed Henry's hair and body, cleaning away the smoke, and Henry did the same for Robert. When they were finally wrapped in ankle-length, fluffy dressing gowns, they wandered through to the main room, where Patrick waited for them. Luckily, Henry had checked his phone before they exited; other-wise, his brother would've seen a lot more of them than he wanted to.

"Feeling better?" Patrick asked.

"Much better, thanks." Robert smiled.

"Mother wanted to know if it was all right to invite your parents for lunch tomorrow?" Patrick's mouth twitched. "I said I'd ask."

Robert's eyes widened. His mum would love it, and his sisters would scream in excitement. His dad probably wouldn't mind either way. He nodded.

"Good luck," he said.

## 24

## HENRY

"**W**ouldn't it be better to make it dinnertime? We have to speak to the police in the morning," Henry said. He sat beside Robert, as close as he could get.

"I think that's why Mother suggested it. She didn't want you getting too involved with the police and forgetting to eat." Patrick grinned. "You know how worrisome she can be."

"I know. All right, but could you ask her to arrange it as a late lunch, say one o'clock? It will give us time to sleep and sort out the police statements."

Patrick nodded. "Sure thing. Robert, would you like to ask your parents, or would you like Mother to call them?"

"I'll do it!" Robert jumped from his seat and grabbed his phone. "They'll be expecting me to give them an update, anyway." He glanced at Henry. "Can I use your bedroom to call?"

"Of course."

He watched as Robert disappeared into the bedroom and closed the door behind him. He doubted that was for any other reason than he wanted to give them privacy to talk. It was the kind of thing Robert would do without making a fuss about it.

"He's good for you," Patrick said.

Henry peered at his brother. "He is. I've never felt this way about anyone before, even…" He averted his gaze.

"Kean. Yeah, I know."

Henry studied Patrick. "How did you know about Kean?"

"You studiously avoided looking at him at certain times, mainly when we were around other people, but when it was just a few of us, you'd follow him around the room with your eyes." Patrick cocked his head. "Why did you never reach out again?"

Henry stared at the fabric covering his legs, picking at a stray thread, and wrinkled his nose. "I pushed Kean away, not willing to let him suffer along with me if something happened because of Aunt Charlotte and Charles."

Patrick nodded. "That puts things into perspective."

"I couldn't see him again after that. I ignored him and sent a message through Freddie to stay away. I haven't seen him since, except from afar."

"Doesn't matter now, though I thought it was a shame at first because you would've been good together. But not as good as you are with Robert. I hate to think what would've happened had you been with Kean when you met Robert. I have a feeling you'd have broken Kean's heart."

Henry glanced at the door Robert had gone through, his heart so full, he was reluctant to think it could hold any more love. "You might be right." He cleared his throat and approached a subject he knew he needed to address. "I'm sorry I didn't come to you before I first came out to you all."

Patrick waved his hand through the air. "It's fine."

"No, it's not. You're my brother, and I should've known you'd have my back no matter what. And I *do* know that, but it's difficult. I feel different from the rest of you. You'd speak about certain things, and I wouldn't get the rush the rest of you explained. When George explained he felt the same, it was as if I had been…" He sighed. "I don't know, accepted, maybe. It's not the right word, but you understand my meaning."

"I get it. I do. I won't deny it hurt that you went to George instead of me, but I understand why you did." Patrick stared at his linked hands, his thumbs fiddling as he did when he was unsure.

"I'm sorry. I won't do it again."

Patrick squinted at him. "Yes, you will because if that's what you need, you do it. Don't come to me to make me feel better. You go to the person who can help you best." He grinned. "Then come to me after."

Henry smiled. "Deal." He stood, meeting Patrick in the middle for a hug that should've happened a long time ago. "Anyway, how're things with you? Did things not work out with Matilda?" he asked when they pulled away and sat next to each other.

Patrick had been seeing Matilda for several months, though he denied they had a relationship. According to Patrick, they were just friends with benefits, but Henry had seen how Patrick looked at her. He'd wondered whether they would stay together, but he hadn't seen her in a few weeks.

"No, they didn't. She wanted more than I was willing to give."

"But you liked her. Why wouldn't you want more?"

Patrick exhaled in a rush. "I don't know. It was too comfortable. Too organised. Everyone kept pushing us together, and she loved the idea of a relationship, but I can't commit to her because…" He sighed.

"You want more," Henry guessed.

"I want what you and Douglas have," Patrick whispered. "I probably shouldn't hold out for it, but I couldn't ever see that being Matilda and me."

Henry squeezed his shoulder. "You have to stay true to yourself. If I've learnt nothing else in these last few weeks, it's that."

Patrick stared at him, a smile curving his mouth. "You've bloomed under Robert's careful tending, Henry."

Henry snorted and pushed him away. "Ha, ha, hilarious."

"Come on! I had to get a flower joke in there somewhere. It was the perfect opening."

"Hmm." Henry's focus turned to the bedroom when the door opened. "Everything okay?"

Robert smiled. "Yeah. They're over the moon to be invited, but I told them your mother would be in touch with the details in the morning. I hope that was okay?"

"Not a problem," Patrick said, standing. "I'll let you get some sleep." He pulled Henry into a hug again and gripped him. "I don't want to think what could've happened tonight. I'm glad you're both okay."

Henry returned the pressure, feeling like he was finally the brother he should've been all these years. "No more secrets," he said, pulling back.

Patrick placed his forefinger under Henry's chin and slid it forward, lifting it a little. "No more secrets," he promised.

Henry returned the gesture and peered at his brother as he strode out of the room. There was a sadness to his gait that Henry hadn't noticed before. When had Patrick lost the joy in his life? He had been on par with Douglas in the mischievous category as they were growing up.

"Are you okay?"

Henry smiled at Robert, who stood beside him. He wrapped his arm around him. "I'm great." A yawn overtook him. "But I'm tired." He chuckled. "Let's get some rest."

Their sleep was once again interrupted the following morning when Patrick knocked on their door. Henry grumbled as he rose from the bed, throwing on the dressing gown he'd worn the night before. Unlocking the door, he rested on it as his eyes blinked up at his brother.

"Sorry. Mother asked me to let you know the police are here for your statements."

Henry stifled a yawn. "What time is it?"

"Nearly ten o'clock."

Henry groaned but agreed. They'd only slept for five hours, but it would have to do. They could go back to bed after lunch with their parents if they needed more.

"Thanks. Tell them we'll be down shortly."

"Will do. Sorry, again."

"Payback is a bitch, I'm told." Henry winked and closed the door, blocking out the cursing Patrick aimed his way.

"I'm up. I'm up," Robert said, throwing his legs over the edge of the bed.

"Sorry, but the sooner we get this sorted, the sooner we can get back to bed." Henry climbed onto the bed behind Robert and slid his arms around his neck, nuzzling his face into the side. "I love how you smell in the morning."

Robert laughed. "What sweaty?"

"No, I can smell *you*. Nothing artificial blocking anything but your unique scent. If I could bottle it and carry it around with me, I would."

"I wouldn't recommend it. I'm sure the media would love that titbit of information."

Henry chuckled. "I'm sure they would." He pulled back. "Would you like to join me in the shower?"

"Is that a good idea when we have to be in a meeting soon?"

"No, but I'm asking, anyway."

Robert's mouth curved. "Okay, but if we're late, I'm blaming the prince."

"Deal."

They were later than planned, but Henry was sure the police didn't mind when his mother had entertained them in their absence.

"Good morning, sweetheart." Victoria kissed his cheeks as she did every morning and did the same to Robert. "Would either of you like something to eat while you talk?"

Henry glanced at Robert. "I'm good, although I'd love a cup of tea. Robert?"

"Tea would be lovely."

"Not a problem."

She bustled over to a small table to the side of the large sitting room, asking the police officer if he needed another drink as she went.

"No, I'm good, thank you, Your Highness."

Henry reclined on the loveseat opposite the police officer, and Robert dropped beside him, though turned towards Henry and rested his arm along the back. Henry slid down a little, getting more comfortable. Robert's finger played with the short strands of hair at the base of Henry's neck, and it was all he could do to stop himself from purring at the sensation.

"What do you need from us today, Officer...?" Henry asked.

"Henderson. Ted Henderson, but please, call me Ted." He waited while Victoria gave them their drinks and left the room with a wave. "First, I'd like to hear about what happened last night."

Henry and Robert filled the officer in on the events of the previous evening, from when they'd been woken by the security guard banging on the door to when they arrived home.

"Do you have any ideas who might have done this?"

They glanced at each other, and Robert nodded. "I've made an enemy of Vincent Dwyer recently."

The police officer visibly winced. "Ah, okay. How did that come about?"

Robert explained about the blackmail, leaving out certain aspects of the story to ensure Henry stayed protected, no doubt.

"I also want a restraining order against Vincent, although that might be too little too late now."

Henry reached for Robert's hand, squeezing. "It's never too late. It's better to be safe."

Robert's eyes softened, and he rubbed his thumb behind Henry's ear. "Okay." He turned back to the officer. "I want to get it organised."

"Understandable. I'll arrange for it to be filled out, and you can either come to the station to sign it, or I can bring it back here, whichever is easiest for you."

"Thank you, Ted." Robert sat forward, reaching for his tea, and Henry felt bereft at the loss of his hand on him.

"I think I have everything I need. Do you have anything else to add or any questions?" Ted's eyes flicked between them, and both shook their heads. "Great. I'll leave you to your day. I'll be in touch soon."

"Thank you." Henry showed Ted to the door, and a staff member waited in the hallway to show him to the exit. "Thank you, Grace."

He returned to the seat and dropped into it, leaning his

elbows on his knees and his head into his hands. Robert's hand rubbed up and down his back, and Henry turned into him. Robert enfolded him in his arms, and Henry had only ever felt as safe in his mother's arms before. Robert pulled him against him and rested back against the seat so that Henry was resting on his chest. He slid his arms around Robert's back and closed his eyes.

"What's wrong, Henry?"

Henry squeezed his eyes tighter as if that would keep all the ugliness away from them. "I want to live our lives without all this crap hanging over us," he said into Robert's chest.

"I know. We will. We just have to get over these few hurdles first." Robert stroked his fingers through Henry's hair and kissed his head. "The first hurdle being lunch with our parents."

Henry chuckled. "This is going to be fun. I can't wait to meet your family."

"You say that now. I'll ask you again afterwards."

"My opinion won't change unless they're horrible to you."

Robert kissed his head again. "You don't need to worry about that. They're great. They might be a little shocked at my appearance, though."

Henry lifted his head. "Why?"

"Because I don't have makeup or jewellery on."

Henry bit his lip. "Come with me," he said after a momentary pause.

They strode down the hallways back to Henry's wing of the house and entered his rooms. Henry led the way to his bedroom, locking the door behind them on autopilot. He drifted to the chest of drawers he'd hidden a gift in and pulled it out. His heart raced. He'd never bought something like this for anyone before, except his mother, but he hoped Robert liked it.

"What's this?" Robert asked when Henry sat beside him on the bed and offered the wrapped box.

"A present."

Robert frowned but took the box and unwrapped it. The crease between his eyes deepened when he saw a black box. He lifted the lid and gasped, a hand covering his mouth. Henry hoped that was a good thing, but his heart didn't like to assume.

"Are they okay? I wasn't too sure if they were the right style for you or not."

Robert threw his arms around Henry's neck and kissed him, the kiss short and sweet until it wasn't. He wanted Robert to lay him down and ravish him, but they didn't have time. He pulled back.

"I love them. Thank you."

"I can't do anything about the makeup, I'm afraid. Unless you want to ask Mother?"

"God, no! I can't ask your mother to borrow her makeup! These will be great."

Robert focused on the box again and inspected each bangle before slipping it on his wrist. There were ten in total, each one having a different crystal design on them. Henry had spent over an hour discussing the crystals' meanings with the store assistant before choosing the ones he thought worked best for Robert.

"Each crystal has a different meaning or helpfulness. Amazonite helps with intuition and hope, carnelian restores vitality and motivation, aquamarine enhances clarity, citrine revitalises and cleanses, blue quartz calms the mind, celestite calms and uplifts, fire agate gives courage and protection, red aventurine enhances creativity, red jasper promotes stability and balance, and rose quartz is for love, peace and compassion."

"They're beautiful. I have some crystals of my own at the apartment, but I never thought to buy something that I could have with me all the time. They're gorgeous."

Henry touched them. "They look great on you."

Robert cupped Henry's face, the bracelets jingling. "I love them. Thank you."

"You're welcome."

Robert leaned forward and joined their mouths, licking along Henry's lips until he opened, then dipped inside. Henry wrapped his hands around Robert's waist, closed his eyes and let himself feel. Everything had been on a downer for them recently, but he hoped things would get better. Robert rested their foreheads together and smiled.

"We should get ready for lunch. I'm sure my parents are already here, impatient as they are."

Henry grinned. "Let's go meet the parents."

Robert snorted. "You won't be saying that after you've met them."

They got themselves sorted, making themselves more presentable than they had been, and wandered towards the dining room his mother had said they were eating in.

Surprisingly, it was their private dining room instead of the one they usually used for guests.

The closer they came, the louder the voices were, and Henry glanced at Robert, who shrugged and rolled his eyes.

"I warned you."

Henry's heart pounded, not because of the noise, but because he was about to meet his boyfriend's parents. He hoped they would like him because he wasn't sure he could give Robert up if they didn't. He certainly wouldn't allow Robert to lose contact with them because they were together. Everything hinged on him making a good impression.

They entered the room to a sight he never thought he'd see—his mother arm wrestling with, who he assumed, one of Robert's sisters. Henry took in the rest of the room: his father talking with two men in the chairs by the fireplace; Robert's mother bustling around the table, adding plates to it with another sister's help; and Patrick, Finn and Naomi watching with rapt attention and chatting.

"Ophelia!"

Robert's voice whipped across the room, inviting everyone's gaze to them.

The sister, Ophelia, glanced over her shoulder, though she didn't stop arm wrestling his mother. "What?"

"Let go right this minute!"

"Robert Martin, don't talk to your sister like that," Robert's mother scolded from her position at the table.

"Victoria agreed to take part. She can make her own decisions, you know."

Robert's face darkened as heat filled his cheeks, and he rested his forehead against Henry's shoulder, closing his eyes. "I told you. I warned you this would happen. But nobody ever believes me."

Henry chuckled, receiving a half-hearted backhand from Robert. "This is perfect."

Robert raised his eyebrows, resting his chin on Henry's shoulder as he stared at him. "You're insane," he whispered.

Henry leaned over and kissed him. "Insane about you."

Robert burst out laughing. "That's corny."

"But it made you laugh."

Robert smiled. "That it did. Are you ready for whatever else they're going to get up to?"

"Bring it on." Henry grinned.

Robert narrowed his eyes. "Mother!" he called and chuckled as Henry's smile dropped. "Would you like to meet Henry?"

"You're mean," he whispered.

"May as well get it over and done with straight away."

## 25

# ROBERT

Robert couldn't believe his sister was arm-wrestling with Henry's mother. A bloody princess! What the hell was she thinking? He wanted to facepalm but refrained. He'd warned Henry. Now, they had to deal with his crazy family and hope Henry's family didn't think they were insane.

"Relax. Everything will be fine," Henry murmured at his side.

Robert tried to keep from snorting at that and smiled at his mother as she approached. "Good morning, Mum."

"Oh, darling boy. I'm glad you're okay." She dragged him into a chokehold, and he let go of Henry to keep himself upright.

"I'm fine." He pulled back. "Mum, this is Henry. Henry, my mum, Winnie."

"Nice to meet you, Mrs Martin."

His mother yanked Henry into a similar hug Robert

had received, and Robert covered his mouth with his hand to stifle his snigger.

"Pfft. Call me Winnie." She released Henry and cupped his cheek. "I'm glad you're all right, too."

"We're both fine. I promise. If I was concerned about Robert's health at all, I would've insisted the paramedics check him out. The security guard got us out in time."

Winnie exhaled and closed her eyes. "I don't want to think about what could've happened, so let's get something to eat."

"Mum!" he hissed. "This isn't your house. You can't come in here and boss everyone around like you can at home."

Tinkling laughter sounded, and Princess Victoria stepped forward. "I said she could do whatever she wanted to ensure her family felt welcome here. If she wants to fuss around you, let her. She needs to have her mother's instincts calmed before she will settle. Trust me."

Victoria slid her arms around Henry, her son having to lean down so she could reach. She whispered into his ear, and Henry nodded in reply, then they parted with a smile each. The princess turned to him.

"I'm glad to finally meet you properly, Robert. I've heard such wonderful things about you."

Robert bowed his head. "Thank you."

"Patrick, dear! Come and meet Robert."

Robert swallowed hard as Henry's father strode across the room, followed by Robert's dad and granddad.

Patrick Senior held out his hand, and Robert shook it,

the grasp firm but not punishing, which made Robert feel better.

"Nice to meet you, sir."

"You, too. Henry, have you met Zachary and Joseph?"

Henry stepped forward, gripping his dad's and grand-dad's hands in turn. "I haven't had the pleasure yet. Thank you for coming."

"I never would've believed Robert would catch a prince, but he always managed to surprise us," Zachary said with a wink.

Robert rubbed a hand over his face. "Dad!"

Henry's free hand slipped into his and squeezed, though he was still talking with his dad and granddad. Despite Henry's opinions of himself, he truly was of royal bearing because he made conversation with the best of them, winning his family over. By the time they'd been introduced to everyone and were sitting at the table, everyone appeared to be best friends. It was more than he could've hoped for. But he relaxed too soon.

"Henry, are you into this tying up and ordering people about thing?"

"Mum!" He slapped his hands over his eyes. "Oh, my god!" He pierced a steely glare on her. "You don't go asking about that part of people's lives. How many times do I have to tell you? It's none of your business!" He turned to Henry. "I'm sorry. Ignore her."

"What? I wanted to make sure you had someone who could give you what I know you need." She shrugged. "Mothers don't care if the questions are intrusive. They just want answers. Am I right?" She glanced at Victoria.

"I agree. Although with a small caveat that I don't need to know every minute detail about your sex life." She winked. "It's still of interest to me."

Robert dropped his forehead to the crook of his arm and groaned. "Please don't discuss our sex life at the table."

Laughter rang around the room, and Henry rested a hand on Robert's nape. Robert sat upright again and locked eyes with his boyfriend. Henry wore a serene smile, but it was the look in his eyes that had Robert pausing. He was happy, and that made Robert ecstatic. Robert cupped Henry's jaw, staring into him, and closed the distance between their lips.

"I love you," he whispered a second before they touched.

The kiss was soft and full of electricity that they could easily take further, but present company dissuaded that from happening. Henry dropped another kiss to his lips and smiled.

"I love you."

A sniffle caught his attention, and he glanced at the table, feeling his cheeks heating from embarrassment. All the table's occupants were staring at them with varying degrees of smiles, but his mother and Henry's were dabbing at their eyes.

"To answer your question, Winnie, I am in the lifestyle, the same as Robert." He glanced at him and inhaled, and Robert knew exactly what he was going to do. "I'm a pup, and Robert is my handler."

Robert waited with bated breath for the reaction to the announcement. He knew his family wouldn't care either way, but he also hadn't explained the lifestyle in any detail. They would undoubtedly have questions.

"I'm glad you could finally tell us, son," Patrick Senior said. "I've seen the submissive side of you come out occasionally when *you* didn't realise you did it, I think. I have been waiting for you to talk to one of us, and when you didn't, I was ready to ask you about it, but Victoria changed my mind. She told me you'd tell us when you were ready." He reached across and covered Victoria's hand with his own before continuing, "It doesn't matter to us, Henry. Being part of…what we're part of means you accept people as they are and don't try to change them. It doesn't matter what *other people* think."

Robert knew exactly what he meant by "other people" and wholeheartedly agreed.

"Thank you, Father."

Robert squeezed his hand. "I know you have questions," he said, meeting his family's eyes one by one. "Let's enjoy this meal, and one day soon, I will explain everything I'm able to."

"One question." Robert groaned at Hadley's teasing tone. "Do you have a pup suit?"

Henry's cheeks darkened, but he nodded. "I do."

"That's cute!" She clapped her hands together and smiled.

"Kill me now," Robert moaned, resting his head on Henry's shoulder.

Henry chuckled.

The lunch continued in a similar vein, embarrassing stories and questions interspersed with the usual getting to know you interrogation, but Henry seemed content to answer anything and everything he could. Henry's family wasn't as intrusive as Robert's was, but Robert returned the favour and answered as fully as possible. When the lunch finally ended, some two hours later, they saw Robert's family to their cars and said goodbye, promising to visit soon. Robert noticed a black car trailing after them as they left and frowned.

"It's a security team. There have been a few journalists hanging around your parents' house, and we wanted to make sure they were safe," Patrick Junior said.

"I didn't realise they were being hounded. I should've called them again this morning." Robert's shoulders tensed, hoping they wouldn't have too much trouble heaped on them because of the man their son loved. It was too much to wish for, he was sure. "Thank you."

"You're welcome. They're your family, which means they're now important to us. We'll ensure no harm comes to them." Henry wrapped his arm around Robert's waist.

Robert glanced up at him with a small smile until another thought came to him. "I need to visit the shop today. I have to get an idea of how much damage there is because I need to contact the insurance company."

"I'll come with you," Henry said.

"Thanks."

They turned to enter the house and wandered down the hallway when Henry paused and glanced over his shoulder. "Patrick, do you want to come with us?"

Robert faced Henry's brother, watching his expression lighten as he nodded. "Sure. What time are you going?"

Henry checked his watch and peered at Robert. "Is an hour okay with you?" Robert nodded, and Henry raised his voice, "An hour?"

"Sure. I'll meet you outside." Patrick waved and veered off in the opposite direction.

They continued their journey to Henry's room, and when he locked it behind them, Henry blew out his cheeks. "Wow, that was…"

"Yeah, it was." Robert chuckled. "I warned you my family was crazy."

Henry stepped closer. "But they're your family, and they're amazing."

Robert drifted backwards, pulling Henry along by his shirt until Robert's legs hit the bed, then he spun Henry around and pushed him down.

Henry laughed. "Oh, we have time for this, do we?"

Robert smiled. "I'm not fucking you. That will have to wait, Your Highness. I do, however, have a desperate need to feel your lips against mine."

Henry's eyes darkened, and his mouth dropped open when Robert crawled over the top of him and lowered his head. He paused an inch away, bracing himself above the man and taking every detail of his face into his memory. Henry swiped his tongue over his lips, leaving a sheen of wetness behind, and Robert bit his lip. When he could stand the separation no longer, he fused their mouths, and his eyelids fluttered closed.

Tilting his head, he opened his mouth a little, catching Henry's upper lip between his before releasing it straight away. He repeated the action on his bottom lip, alternating between them until Henry groaned and lifted his chin. Robert skated his tongue across the mounds, dipping into Henry's mouth to tease him with what was to come. Henry's hands gripped onto the back of Robert's shirt, putting pressure on him to drop down, but Robert kept his arms braced while he tormented Henry with his tongue.

When they were panting from the light touches, Robert deepened the kiss a little more, sliding his tongue deep and exploring the wet warmth, earning several shivers and moans from the man beneath him. As Robert's tongue retreated, Henry's followed, and Robert sucked on it as his fingernails scraped through Henry's hair. Henry's body trembled, and Robert pressed him deeper into the bed by resting down fully on top of him.

Henry's hands repositioned to where he held Robert with bruising force, but Robert just took Henry's mouth harder, their breath rushing through their noses. Robert didn't want to stop for breath, so he continued until he was lightheaded and pulled back with a gasp. He stared at Henry, watching as his lover's chest heaved, the colour in his cheeks darkened and his eyelids fluttered. His thin lips had plumped, bruised and used from Robert's mouth, and Robert took great satisfaction in that. As Henry panted, Robert attached his mouth to the neck that was temptingly arched towards him. He pressed kisses to the muscle running down the column, strained as it was, and sucked his collarbone after moving his shirt to the side. When he was content with the red circle at the base of his neck,

Robert licked a stripe up to Henry's jaw and ran his teeth along the bone until he reached his mouth once more.

This time, Robert took no prisoners. He held Henry's head in place as he devoured every inch of his mouth. Dizziness finally claimed him, and he lifted off, gulping in air.

Henry looked debauched, and Robert smirked. He could feel their hard cocks trapped between their bodies but did nothing to ease it. They could wait until later, but he slid off Henry with exaggerated slowness, ensuring he felt everything. Robert stood on shaky legs and grinned at Henry's splayed body. Any other day, he would've taken the invitation and climbed back on until they reached completion, but they needed to get ready to go. That amazing kiss had taken half of their time, but he didn't regret a minute.

"Henry?"

"Hmm."

Robert snorted at his barely audible hum. "We need to get ready."

"Hmm."

This time, he laughed out loud. "Come on, Your Highness." He grabbed Henry's hands and pulled, only to have Henry flop back down again. Robert chuckled and put his mouth to Henry's ear. "Henry dear, if you don't get ready to go, we can't come back afterwards and finish what we started."

Henry shot off the bed, almost smacking Robert in the face. "I'm ready." He glanced down at his groin. "Kind of."

He adjusted himself and glared at Robert. "That wasn't nice."

"I enjoyed every minute," Robert said. "Be careful, Henry. I could make you wait longer than absolutely necessary if I wanted to." His voice was low and authoritative.

A shiver went through Henry. "Yes, Sir."

They grabbed what they needed to take with them, and once they were ready, they strode to where they were meeting Patrick. With every step, the reminder of what awaited him at the shop fell around him.

"I thought you might like to be driven today," Patrick said, a solemn tone in his voice. "I wasn't sure how much of a toll this would take on you."

Robert gave a small smile. "Thank you."

He climbed into the backseat, telling Henry to sit in the front with Patrick, and stared at the scenery as they drove. He hoped the insurance came through for him. It covered him for a lot of things, and as it was arson, he assumed it would be fine. Depending on how much of the property had taken the brunt of the fire, it might not just be the shop he needed to think about. If the structural integrity of the building was a problem, his apartment would be off-limits until they secured the building. He was glad he'd arranged for the insurance to cover the wages of the staff in events like this as well. It meant he could keep Finn and Naomi on until they reopened the shop.

The closer they got, the more his heart pounded. He hoped they could rebuild it and not have to find somewhere else. That would be devastating. As they turned onto the road and the shop came into view, his heart skipped a beat at the blackened shell.

He climbed out of the car when it stopped and stood, staring at his livelihood. They had boarded the broken glass windows and the door. Police tape still surrounded the area, but he ignored it and ducked underneath. He wouldn't enter the shop from the front as he wasn't sure of how precarious it was; therefore, he wandered down the alleyway to the back entrance, letting himself in slowly, aware of the two shadows who were following, one of which pressed a torch into his hands.

The scent of smoke was the first thing he noticed. It lingered in the air like a curtain waiting to be pushed aside. He switched on the torch and took in the back room, realising most of the room had escaped the fire. Only the very front had a blackened soot line on it as if the fire had attempted but been refused entry. He shook his head at his wayward thoughts. Picking his way through the debris that littered the floor, he wandered down the hallway that housed the small office, toilets and kitchen area. All doors were open, and he could see black walls, burnt papers and overturned furniture as he went past.

Bracing himself, he entered the main shop and stopped still. Apart from the room itself and the counter, there was nothing but ash left. It reminded him of a wildfire that swept through the landscape and left the bare bones behind.

As his torchlight panned from side to side, his heart

dropped. This was more work than he'd first expected. He honestly didn't know if they could rebuild. Maybe he would be better off finding a new place, starting fresh.

A hand sliding around his waist made him jump and the light flicker.

"Sorry," Henry said. "Are you okay?"

Robert shook his head, not knowing if Henry could see. "This is worse than I imagined," he whispered.

"It's not an impossible feat. We can get this place up and running again soon."

"I need to contact the fire department or the police. I need to know whether I can get upstairs to get my belongings, but looking at the state of this place, it probably isn't stable enough."

"We can come back once we've spoken to them, or we can get someone else to get the stuff for you." Henry rested his chin on his shoulder. "I'm here to help in every way I can."

Robert inhaled. "Let's get out of here. I've seen enough."

Henry guided him back through the rubble and into the fresh air. Robert locked the door and stared at his home. He had hardly anything with him and could do with some clothes, although they were likely to smell of smoke for weeks, if not forever.

"If you want, you can stay with me for as long as you need. Or if you want to stay somewhere else, that's fine with me," Henry added in a rush. "I know that doesn't give you your belongings back, but you have somewhere to live while this place is sorted."

Robert tried for a smile and must've managed it because Henry returned the gesture. "Thank you. I'm glad you were both here." He glanced at Patrick, who had a frown on his face. "It's nothing that can't be fixed, I'm sure."

Patrick peered at him and nodded. "I might know some people who can help. I'll let you know if they can."

Robert took the offer with a grateful smile. "Now, to get the insurance claim sorted."

Henry pressed a kiss to his temple. "I'm here."

## 26

# HENRY

The shop had been almost unrecognisable. If Henry hadn't known what it had looked like before, he wouldn't have been able to guess from what remained. He could feel Robert's pain as if it was tangible, and he needed to help but had no idea how he could. At least until an idea popped into his head.

He spoke to Patrick, who suggested speaking to Freddie, which he did. When it was all arranged, he approached Robert while they were having dinner alone in Henry's room the following evening.

"I'd like you to come to the club tonight." Henry fidgeted with the napkin by his plate, awaiting Robert's response. He didn't know how he would react to Henry's request.

"Club Royal? Why?"

Henry glanced across the table at him, unsure of what

he expected to see. Robert had a crease between his eyes, though he didn't appear surprised by the words.

"I'd like you to see what it's like there. It's not all bad, although we seem to have a few bad seeds." Henry's mouth curled at one side. "I have to work tomorrow night, but I thought we could go together—as handler and pup." He rolled the napkin between his fingers, dropping his gaze again.

Robert placed his hand over Henry's, stopping his movements. "I'd love to come. Don't the memberships take weeks to arrange, though?"

Henry snorted. "Not when you're a prince." Heat invaded his cheeks. "I already asked Freddie to arrange it. Even if you said no, it wouldn't have mattered if they gave you membership. You can use it or not as you choose. Not every member attends the club, but it's given to them in case they want to."

Robert frowned. "Isn't that counterproductive? Surely you can't have every member attend on the same night. What if those people only wanted to attend when it was a busy night?"

"We have a sign-in system. You have to book ahead of time, mostly. If other people turn up, they might be turned away, but they know that because they have to read the rules."

Robert picked up his fork and moved the remains of his food around, seemingly deep in thought. Henry left him to it, trying to choke down the last bits of his meal as he waited. He'd love to share the club with Robert. Even though, as he said, it had its bad seeds, there was a lot of good that happened there. The people were friendly, the equipment was top quality, and the entertainment was amazing. He loved The Den because of the anonymity, and he knew going to the club would mean he would have to expose his secret, but if he wanted to share the club with Robert, he had to pluck up the courage to do it. His family would be there to support him—Christian and Douglas in an official capacity as they were working, but Freddie, George and Patrick said they'd be there for moral support.

"What about your pup? Will you be keeping that quiet while we're there?"

Henry shook his head. "No, they will know who, or rather what, I am. The club has rules that all members must show their face as they enter the club. It stops members from taking someone in who doesn't belong. It's fine. It's about time I did it. The others will be there for moral support."

Robert cocked his head and stared at him. "If you're sure, then all right. We can visit and see what all the fuss is about."

"Tonight?" Henry raised his eyes.

Robert wiped his mouth with his napkin, although Henry saw a hint of a smile. "Sure."

Butterflies took flight in Henry's stomach, but it was a mix of excitement and nerves. Only the other five of the Scandalous Six had seen him as a pup, so it was a strange idea that everyone who attended the club was going to see his preference. He wasn't the first to show up touting the new rules of royals having submissive status, but it was a big deal, nonetheless.

"We can do it another night if you'd prefer?"

"No, I'm happy to go tonight. It's a big thing, that's all."

Robert squeezed his hand. "I know, and I think you're brave to do it." He stared at Henry. "You have a lot of strength inside you; I don't think you even realise it."

Henry sighed. "No, I don't. If I did, I would've stuck up for myself and others against Aunt Charlotte and Charles sooner."

Robert scoffed. "Don't be silly. Anyone in their right mind would have paused at the possibility of what they could've done to you or others. It was self-preservation, and that was a good thing. I can't bear to think about what could've happened if you'd done something when you were younger." Robert visibly shivered.

Henry had the same thought, but he didn't believe he was strong. If Robert wanted to think that, though, he wouldn't dissuade him from the notion. His lover seemed to realise this and smiled.

"What time do we need to be ready?"

Henry glanced at him. "Whenever you want."

"How about we share a shower to get ready?"

"Sounds like a brilliant plan to me." Henry threw his napkin on his plate and stood, to the musical laughter of Robert.

"In a hurry?"

Henry smiled at him. "Of course. Who wouldn't be

eager to get you into a shower?" He wandered into the bedroom and through to the bathroom, ensuring the bathroom door was locked, then started the shower. He stripped down and stepped under the warm spray, brushing aside his nerves to deal with later. Arms came around him, and his eyelids fluttered closed.

Robert pressed a kiss to his shoulder blade. "If at any point you don't want to stay at the club, tell me. I don't want you feeling uncomfortable, especially in front of the people there. It should be a safe haven for you, not somewhere you feel you *should* go because your family owns it."

"Thank you. I know it may seem like I fear the people there, but I don't. If the few evil seeds were removed, I would be more than content to attend. Those few make it bad for the rest. I love the premise and what the club achieves. It's close to my heart and not just because I've been a part of it for so long."

Robert manoeuvred him around to face him. "I know the place is good. It wouldn't stay open if it wasn't. I don't want you being a part of something that makes you uncomfortable, that's all. If you're happy there, I'm happy to be part of it."

Henry watched several drops of water trail down Robert's face and neck, considering Robert's words. "I am happy there, and things are changing. Look at what Uncle Andrew has already achieved with the submissive family members. I believe in that club."

"That's all the reference I need."

Henry smiled and tucked his head into Robert's neck, licking a few drops of water from his skin. "Thank you."

They spent far too long in the shower, Robert coaxing a gentle orgasm from Henry, who dropped to his knees and returned the favour. It was for purely selfish reasons because he wanted the taste of Robert in his mouth when he arrived at the club. A sort of safety blanket for him.

When they entered the bedroom, Robert stopped.

"What's wrong?" Henry asked.

"I don't have my leathers."

Henry's heart skipped at the pain in Robert's voice, but he had a surprise for him. He strode over to his chest and opened it, pulling out a wrapped package and turning back to Robert.

"I don't know exactly if these are your style, but I tried to find something that looked similar to what I saw you wear at The Den. I won't be offended if you don't like them. We can return them and find something different. I don't know if they'll fit either. I had a quick look at the sizing on some of your clothes, but I know leathers are tighter and—"

Robert stepped closer and placed a hand over Henry's mouth. "Breathe, my love." Henry stopped and inhaled. "Good. Now, are you going to let me see the gift?" The corner of his mouth quirked up.

Henry held out the package with trembling hands and wrung them together when Robert sat on the bed to open it. It hadn't been difficult to find someone to get the gift for him, but he'd always preferred to buy his own things and didn't know if Robert was the same. He didn't want to commit some faux pas.

Robert's intake of breath caught his attention, and he

watched as the man skimmed his hand over the soft black leather. Placing the paper to one side, Robert lifted the leather all in one. Absolute silence reigned, and Henry was sure he hated it.

"Oh, my god, Henry. This is exquisite. Where did you find it? I've always wanted a catsuit-style outfit, but I could never find anything that suited me within my price range. It's beautiful."

Henry blew out his cheeks. "I'm glad you like it. I hoped you would because it's just your style. I thought it fit well with the clothes you wear daily, but I wasn't sure if you wanted to look different when you were a handler."

Robert laid the leather on the bed and darted across the space between them. "I love it! Thank you." He slid his arms around Henry's waist and kissed him. "You didn't have to do that, but I appreciate it."

Henry cupped the back of Robert's head. "I would do anything for you."

When they were ready to go, with Robert looking delicious in his new leathers, they met up with Patrick by the front door and rode to the club together. Parking in the underground car park, Robert took Henry's hand as they approached the lift, and he squeezed, gripping his pup mask in his other hand. He heard Robert's exhale when they exited the lift into the reception area, and Henry tried to see it as he had when *he'd* first experienced the club.

The earthy-coloured room with dark wooden floors and furniture, emerald-green walls and different shades of cream as accent colours appeared expensive, which was probably the whole point. It screamed extravagance and made the club feel more elite. To the side of them sat several armchairs, with a couple of small side tables. The room was large and across the opposite side sat a desk, behind which Clarice, the receptionist, sat.

Henry tugged Robert towards the desk. "Good evening, Clarice. How are you?"

Clarice bowed her head. "I'm good, Your Highness. I hear we have a new member tonight. Shall we get him into the system?"

"That would be great, thank you. Clarice, this is Robert. Robert, this is the woman who makes everything work around here. If you have any questions or anything you need, come and see Clarice, and she will work her magic."

Clarice's cheeks darkened under Henry's praise, more so when Patrick nodded enthusiastically.

"Nice to meet you, Clarice."

"And you, too, sir." She clicked a few buttons on the computer. "Right, Mr Martin, I have already added your details to the system. The only thing I need from you is a fingerprint. If you would place your thumb on the sensor here, we can get you set up."

Robert did, although glanced at Henry with a question in his eyes.

"Everything here works with fingerprints. It logs who is here and when they arrive and leave. It also enables you to order drinks at the bar, open doors within the club, and open the lockers in the changing room. Which reminds me. Clarice, could you add him to my locker and the Monitors' changing room, please?"

"Already in progress, Your Highness."

Henry smirked at Robert. "See? She's a magician."

Robert chuckled. "I can see that."

"There we go. All set up for you. Is there anything else I can help you with tonight, Prince Henry?"

"No, thank you."

"Prince Patrick?" Clarice asked.

"No, I'm all sorted. Thanks, Clarice."

"In that case, have a wonderful evening, Your Highnesses."

Her not adding on Robert's name at the end of the titles meant she had already accepted that Robert was part of the family. Henry didn't make a point of it because Robert probably hadn't even realised, but Henry had, and he smiled and nodded at her in thanks.

Henry guided Robert over to the changing rooms. "These rooms are open to everyone, but when we go in," he said as they entered, "we take a right here, and it takes us to the Monitors' room. The Monitors are always royal family members; therefore, we are given a separate room to ourselves. It's more for security than anything else. The family thought it would lessen the chances of something happening to them."

"I can understand that, and it seems like a good idea."

They entered the changing rooms, and Henry showed Robert where his locker was. "Try your fingerprint." Robert pressed his thumb to the locker, and it clicked. "Perfect."

"This is far more extensive than The Den," Robert said. "I understand the need for it, though."

"It helps us to feel secure, I think. Having a place where we know we can relax and be ourselves…" He tilted his head. "Hmm, where we should be able to be ourselves. I'll amend it to enables us to stay human, I guess is what I'm trying to say." Henry shrugged. "I can't explain it very well."

"I think you did a good job, brother," Patrick clapped him on the back. "I'll see you in there. Any problems, you know we're all here for you."

"Thanks." He touched Patrick's chin, and Patrick disappeared.

Robert smiled. "Why do you do that?"

"Do what?" Henry asked.

"The chin thing."

Henry wrinkled his nose. "I can't even remember when it started, but the six of us have always been close, as you know. It's a reminder to each of us we need to keep our chins up in this world. To remember, there are people there who care for and support us. That things can get better. It probably seems stupid—"

"No, it doesn't. Quite the contrary, to be honest. I love the idea behind it. I'm glad you have that support."

Henry grimaced. "I should've used it, though. All those years when I was hiding, I should've used their support instead."

Robert cupped his jaw. "You used it when you needed to. Just because a support system is in place doesn't mean you *have* to use it. When you need it, it's there."

Henry stared at Robert. "You have changed my life completely, and I can't thank you enough."

"Same goes for you." Robert pulled his head down for a gentle kiss and stepped away. "Let's get this show on the road. Are you putting your mask on?"

Henry shook his head. "I can't until we get into the main room. There are cameras on the entrance doors, but as soon as I enter, I can. Although I might wait until we get into the pet play area."

Robert paused. "Are you sure you want to do this?"

Henry nodded. "Definitely."

He slid his hand into Robert's and pulled him out of the room and towards the doors. His heart raced, his palms were undoubtedly sweaty, and his throat was dry, but he was determined. No one would stand in his way any longer, especially not Aunt Charlotte and Charles.

They entered the room, and the hum of conversation reached him.

"If you want to drink alcohol here, you can, but they won't allow you into the playrooms if you do. It's a safety precaution."

"And a good one," Robert said.

They drifted over to the bar and ordered two bottles of water from the bartender. "How are you doing, Oliver?"

"I'm good, thank you, sir. Busy as always," Oliver replied as he placed the bottles on the counter, the white of his cuffs shining starkly against the dark wood.

"It makes the time go quickly, though, doesn't it?"

"That it does. Have a good evening."

"You, too." Henry guided Robert through the crowds

towards another set of double doors. "This is what Douglas calls the conversation room. It's where members go to relax before and after scenes and where some members do their aftercare routine if they've been in the public area. Through here," he pointed at the doors, "is the public viewing area."

Robert nodded, and they scanned their thumbprints and pushed through the doors. Low playing music, louder conversation, and the slap of skin on skin and moaning reached his ears this time. He glanced at Robert to gauge his reaction, but the man had a fantastic poker face. Pausing to the side of the doors, he let Robert take in the scenes before him.

"Ready to see the pet play area?" he asked when Robert smiled at him.

"Absolutely."

Robert threaded his fingers through Henry's and allowed him to weave them through the masses. Henry waved to Christian and received a clap on the back from Freddie when he saw them but carried on to their destination. His nerves were getting the better of him again, but he refused to stop. He needed this. This was the last barrier—in his mind at least—to letting himself be free.

When they entered the large room, his tension slipped away, despite the butterflies still being there. There was something about this room that calmed him, even when he wasn't in pup form. Again, he stopped inside the room by the wall, waiting for Robert to inspect their surroundings. After all, Robert would oversee him here. Henry needed to make sure Robert felt confident in the space before he could relax and roam freely.

Robert's face was inscrutable, and Henry wanted to know what he saw. Afraid that Robert wouldn't like what he thought of as a sanctuary, he asked, "What do you think?"

## 27

# ROBERT

What did Robert think? It was the freaking Harrods of pet play areas. It was the Buckingham Palace of pup play. It put every other pet play destination Robert had visited to shame. It was understandable, considering the owners, but he was speechless.

There were the usual mats on the floor where the pups could rough and tumble, but there was much more. There was a climbing frame with a slide for the pups to scramble up and down; a built-in, shallow water pool; a ball pit, and a space for throwing a ball. It was heaven for pups.

"This is amazing," Robert said.

"I'm glad you like it. We keep adding things to it as members' requests change. The climbing frame is the newest addition."

"I would've never thought of bringing a climbing frame into the mix. It's fantastic that you add things if the members ask for them."

Henry's cheeks tinted. "We can't do it all the time, but if we believe it would work in the space we have, it's considered."

"I think it's great."

"Master Henry?"

Robert glanced over his shoulder to see an attractive man in a neoprene suit standing behind them. He was a sub, without a doubt.

"How can I help, Xan?"

"Are you a handler tonight, sir?"

"No, I'm afraid not." He glanced at Robert. "I'm a pup tonight."

Xan gasped, eyes widening, but the smile told of joy instead of derision. "That's wonderful, sir…um…"

Henry chuckled. "Henry is just fine, thank you."

"Oh, no, I can't call you that!"

Robert rolled his lips inwards to withhold his response at the exuberant denial.

"Okay. How about Dusty? That's my pup name."

Xan thought about it and nodded. "I can do that."

"Great. Do you need a handler, Xan?" Henry asked.

Xan waved his hand. "It's fine. I can just play around if no one's available. Thank you, though."

Robert watched Xan wander off to the mats, donning his mask and kneeling to the side for several seconds before another pup nudged him to join in. Once Xan was tumbling around with the others, Robert focused on Henry.

"Are you ready?"

Henry grinned, a lightness to his features that many

painful memories had once darkened. "Without a doubt." He slid the mask onto his head and buckled it into place.

"Present," Robert said, and Henry—no, Dusty—dropped to his knees. Robert crouched beside him, aware the eyes of several occupants of the room were on them. He gripped the back of Dusty's neck, his thumb rubbing at the side. "If at any point you are unsure, rest your head on my knee and look at me. Do you understand?"

Dusty yipped. Robert smiled. "Go play, Dusty."

Dusty scrambled across the floor to the ball pit and dived right in, sending balls flying in all directions. A ripple of laughter rounded the room, and Robert grinned. He hoped that was a positive response to Henry's newly disclosed pup persona. After checking to make sure Dusty was content for the moment, Robert wandered over to the opposite side of the room, where bowls, treats, cups, straws and anything else he could imagine he might need were housed. He grabbed a bowl, cup and straw, filled the cup with water and removed the packet of treats from his pocket. Ever since he'd found out Henry's weakness was fudge, he ensured he had plenty for Dusty time.

"How quaint," a voice close to his ear said, the sarcasm clear.

Robert raised his eyebrows and glanced to the side before returning his attention to what he'd been doing. If someone had something to say, they didn't need his permission to speak.

"A prince needing to be leashed was not something I was expecting to see this evening. It's rather unfortunate, really. Such a magnificent specimen of a man that will forever be tainted by his need to bow to others instead of the other way around."

Robert didn't know who this other man was, but he could tell from the accent that they were brought up amongst the upper echelons of society. He said nothing, finishing with his work, then turning away.

"Nothing to say? Well, that's disappointing."

Robert whirled back. "No, what's disappointing is that you feel the need to diminish what a prince wants from his life. That you feel the need to complain about someone being strong and reaching for what they need. That you feel the need to degrade what the entire community has tirelessly worked for. I don't give a damn who you are, but you have no say in how other people live their lives, so butt out."

He strode away, and only as he did, did he realise the rest of the room had heard every word. Quiet applause sounded, but he ignored it. As soon as he sat down, Dusty bounded over to him. The pup rested his head against Robert's thigh, panting. Robert squeezed Dusty's shoulder.

"Let's get you a drink." He reached for the cup and straw, holding the tube to Dusty's mouth. The drink disappeared within seconds, and Robert chuckled. "It's hard work being a pup, isn't it, Dusty?" he crooned.

Dusty yipped and scrambled off again. He stopped near a black and white pup and lowered to his chest, his tail wagging gently. The pup jumped closer, then backed away, and jumped closer, then backed away. Dusty yipped and pounced forward, startling the other pup. Robert laughed as Dusty chased the pup around the mats, both tumbling to the ground in a mass of limbs.

"I'm glad you told Arthur where to go. It's about time someone did."

Robert peered to his right to see Prince Frederick sitting beside him. He hadn't even realised someone had sat there. "I hope I didn't cross any invisible lines."

Frederick laughed. "Not at all. It's about time my cousin got his hide handed to him." At Robert's puzzled look, he closed the distance between them and continued in a lowered voice, "Arthur is Uncle John's son. The same Uncle John who Henry saw taking part in that...*activity* when Henry was younger."

"The apple hasn't fallen far from the tree?"

"Correct. He's sweet and innocent compared with Charles, but he's not completely in the light, that's for sure."

"I expected to get some push back from Henry's choices, but I'm more than happy to stick up for him."

Frederick smiled at him and rested his elbow on the back of the chair. "I'm glad to hear it because he'll need that support whether or not he realises it."

Dusty chose that moment to bound over and drop a ball on Frederick's lap. The heir laughed and threw the ball for him, Dusty scrambling after it.

The smile never left the prince's face as he watched his cousin. "I'm glad he has this...you. No one else would've been able to see him for what he is, but I know you do. It wasn't a surprise to me when he told us who he was, but it hurt that he hadn't felt like he could talk about it."

"He told you when he was ready to tell you. You can't ask for more."

"You're right." Frederick nodded as he watched Dusty. "No one can make anyone else talk when they're not ready to." He slid a glance to Robert from the corner of his eye, his mouth twitching. "You're good for him and for the rest of us. We like to think we're humble and well adjusted, but then someone like you and Maverick comes along, and we remember we're not as approachable as we thought."

"It's a learning curve," Robert said with a grin.

Frederick laughed, causing several eyes to look their way. "Isn't life?"

"Without a doubt."

Robert saw Damon hovering behind them and smiled at him, inviting him closer. He stepped behind Frederick and rested a hand on his shoulder. Frederick glanced up at him, his smile widening when he saw Damon. He stood.

"I didn't realise you were going to be here," Frederick said, hugging his best friend.

Damon slapped him on the back. "Moral support and all that." He glanced at Robert, and Robert saw something in his eyes that belied that comment, but he couldn't figure out why.

They pulled apart, and Frederick turned to Robert. "Thank you for this." He waved his hand around. "It means a lot to all of us."

Robert nodded his head, his answer interrupted by a mournful bark. His gaze skimmed the occupants until he landed on Dusty, who was being herded by two pups into the water pit, where Dusty obviously didn't want to go. Robert jogged over.

"Present!" he called as he approached, hoping the pups had been trained well.

All three pups, including Dusty, presented themselves immediately, and Robert sighed in relief. He crouched down in front of Dusty.

"Are you okay?" Dusty whimpered. Robert stared at the other two, taking in their suits and descriptions, so he could remember them. He pivoted around, still in a crouch. "Who are the handlers for these pups?"

A man stepped forward. He was shorter than Henry was but built like a tank. Robert didn't rise from his crouch. He didn't care whether the man was taller than he was. Dominance was not about height. "I am Tito's handler. Max doesn't have one."

"Why did you not step in before I did? You must've seen what was happening."

The man fidgeted. He was either a new handler or overwhelmed by the questioning. "I thought they were playing."

Robert tilted his head. "As soon as I saw Dusty's body language, I could tell he was unhappy. Surely, you saw the same thing. Did you think he deserved to be taken where he didn't want to go? Did you think he didn't need saving because he should be able to take care of himself?"

The man twitched, and Robert knew he'd hit the right reason. "A pup is in our care. In *all* of our care. Just because I didn't see what was happening when it started doesn't mean the rest of the handlers should let it slide.

This," he waved his hand at the pups, "was just as much in your control as it was in the pups. *This* shouldn't have continued. Just because Prince Henry is trained as a Dominant and handler does not mean he had to fulfil those roles and no other. Here, he is a pup and should be afforded the same compassion and care as every other pup in the room." Now, Robert did stand. "Today is my first visit to this club, and I have to say, I'm not feeling as welcome as I'd expected to. Throw all your beliefs out of the window, and for god's sake, do what is *right*."

He turned back to the pups. "Tito, go to your handler. I expect him to be retrained accordingly," he added to his handler. "Max, who is in charge of your care tonight?" Max shook his head. "Right, you will come with me. Dusty, follow me."

Robert strode to a sofa lining the wall and dropped into a seat, waiting until the pups sat at his feet. He leaned his elbows on his knees. "Max, I'm going to talk to you as a human for the moment. I understand you don't have a handler, but this behaviour is not acceptable. If a pup is showing body language that is upset, you need to stop what you're doing and think about it. Do you understand?"

Max nodded his head. "I do, sir."

It surprised Robert to hear his voice but acknowledged it with a nod. "Thank you. If you need or want someone to be your handler or to train you, I suggest speaking to a Monitor."

"I will, sir." Max faced Dusty. "I'm sorry. It won't happen again."

The response impressed Robert. There were no excuses made, just a sincere apology. "Glad to hear it. Go play."

Max turned and scampered off. Dusty stayed in position at Robert's feet, though Robert could see his arms were trembling.

"Dusty, do you want to stay as a pup?" There was a pause before he yipped his assent. "I'm sorry this happened, Dusty. I'll pay more attention in the future."

Dusty rested his head on Robert's thigh for several long minutes, and Robert stroked his back. Then he lifted and cocked his head. With a yip, he was off again, this time to the climbing frame. Robert leaned back on the sofa and watched his pup. A cup appeared before him.

"Thought you might need a drink," Frederick said.

"Thanks." Robert took the drink and downed the water in seconds. "I'll need to grab another one for Dusty."

"I've already sorted it. There is one on the table to your side, and the treats are there as well." Frederick paused. "You handled that well. I expected more push back from the audience."

"Me too, in all honesty."

"It will take some time before people see our family as anything but Dominants."

"But they will," Robert said with confidence, his eyes never leaving Dusty.

"They will," Frederick repeated, though his voice wasn't as sure as Robert expected it to be.

They sat in silence for several moments until Frederick rose. "I need to find Damon. Thank you for this. I know Henry appreciates it."

"I'd do anything for him."

"I know, but hopefully, you won't have to," Frederick murmured and strode out of the room.

Robert called Dusty over after several more minutes of play and gave him a drink and his treats. After a rest, Dusty leaned his head on Robert's knee and looked at him.

"Are you okay?" Dusty whined. "Have you had enough?" Dusty whined again. Robert chuckled. "You're worn out; you can't do anything else, can you?" He rubbed Dusty's head. "Come on. Let's get ready to go home." He leaned forward, lowering his voice. "Do you want to take your hood off now or when we get to the main doors?"

Dusty darted across the room to the door but waited before he exited. He wagged his tail, and Robert laughed again. Rising, he placed the used bowl and cup on the side and followed in Dusty's wake.

"Be careful of people's feet, Dusty," Robert warned as they exited the pet play area.

Dusty stayed by his side as they weaved their way through the crowds to the main doors. When they got there, Robert crouched. "Are you ready?"

There was a pause and Dusty rose to stand. Robert reached behind his head and unbuckled the mask, leaving Henry to pull it off. He ignored his flushed face and sweat-dampened hair in favour of the enormous smile he wore.

"Thank you," Henry said, leaning forward to steal a kiss.

"You're more than welcome."

They exited to the conversation room and strode to the bar. Both were thirsty, so they ordered a couple of drinks and chose a seat away from everyone else. Once Robert sat, Henry sat beside him but curled his legs up and to the side to rest his head on Robert's lap. Robert stroked his fingers through Henry's hair as they sat in silence. By the time their drinks had gone, Freddie, Damon, Patrick, Christian and George had joined them, none saying anything. If anyone thought it was strange that there were six men sitting in silence, they could go shout their opinions to the wind as far as Robert was concerned.

When Henry moved to an upright position, though resting his head on Robert's shoulder, Patrick put his drink on the coffee table. "Are you okay?" he asked Henry.

Henry smiled, the kind of lazy smile he did when he was content. "I'm good."

"What about you, Robert?" Patrick asked.

Robert considered his answer, not wanting to offend but also wanting to ensure he got his point across. "All in all, I'm impressed with the place. A few of the members leave a lot to be desired, but I think I spoke up enough for them to realise they can't walk over us."

"I agree. You did a phenomenal job of putting people in their places." Frederick grinned.

"I wish you hadn't needed to," Henry said.

Robert gripped him tighter. "I know, but there will always be people who don't like what we have. Most of the time, it will have nothing to do with our sexual orientation or our status. It will be purely because they want what our relationship gives us."

Henry glanced up at him. "And what's that?"

"Each other. Support. Guidance. Camaraderie. Friendship. Love. Who wouldn't want that?"

"Me," Christian said. "I'm happy as I am, thanks. No one to tell me what to do—except my family—no one to expect me to be somewhere, no one to think about when I want to do something. I'm staying single forever."

The grins the others shared had Robert fighting one himself, but he said, "That's your choice, and if that's what you truly want, go for it."

The conversation continued, and Robert heard some interesting stories from when Henry was a child. Most of them involved the group in some way or another, and by the end, he agreed with George that their group name was a perfect fit. George threw his arms in the air in victory.

"We'll never hear the end of this now. We're stuck with the name Scandalous Six until we're old and grey," Henry said with a grimace.

"And you'll probably be continuing your games then, won't you?" Robert asked.

Henry grinned. "Maybe."

Seeing Henry so content, so free, shifted something inside of Robert. When he'd first met the prince, it had surprised him by how quiet and highly strung he was, but the more he got to know him, the more he understood what he hid beneath the facade. Only when they were with the people they trusted most could Henry be himself.

He hoped that continued throughout their life because

it was one of the best support networks Robert had ever seen. His family was great, but the royals? Well, if he ignored the evil people, they were loyal, supportive and caring of every member, no matter who they were. There were still changes that could be made to make things better, but slow and steady wins the race, as his mother always said.

They had a lifetime to fight for the changes, and Robert would be with him every step of the way.

## 28

## DOUGLAS

Douglas popped his head into the pet play area, wanting to see his cousin in action. When he caught Dusty rolling on the floor with the other pups, he grinned and sought out Robert. He was talking to Freddie. Instead of interrupting them, he went to stand in the corner and do his monitoring. It was a shame he'd needed to work tonight because he would've loved to interact more with them. Nothing was stopping him except his own reasoning that he couldn't concentrate on everyone when he was talking with his family because they often got carried away.

Luckily for him, he was in place when the pups began tormenting Dusty. He was about to go over and break it up when Robert shot out of his seat. Watching the handler in action was impressive. He kept the peace, sent one pup to his handler, who he gave a dressing down to, and dealt with the other pup, too. They could do with the likes of him working here, maybe even training handlers. That was something he could speak to his father about.

He braced himself for an issue with the members, but no one spoke up. If anything, they were looking at Robert with something akin to pride. Douglas made a note of that to tell his father, too.

Dusty dashed over to the entrance at one point, and Robert followed, laughing. When they exited, Douglas smiled, glad they had found each other.

"Master Douglas?"

He smiled at the man who approached him, wondering what Tito's handler wanted. "How can I help?"

"I wanted to apologise for my behaviour earlier. Dusty's handler suitably chastised me, and I would like to request some extra training."

Douglas raised his eyebrows. "May I ask why?"

The man fidgeted, as Douglas had seen him do earlier. "I want to be confident in my ability to deal with potential problems. I know I wouldn't have reacted to the pups playing earlier because I didn't think there was anything wrong with it. I honestly thought Dusty could protect himself, and when his handler told me he shouldn't have had to, it made me realise I was doing something wrong."

The monologue impressed Douglas, and he agreed. "I'm glad you can accept constructive criticism. You work well as a handler from what I've seen, but maybe some additional training would be beneficial, even if it's to remind you of what you need to do. Ask Clarice at reception, and she will ensure you get on the right course for your needs, and if there isn't one, let me know, and I'll see what I can do."

"Thank you, Master Douglas. Please send my regards and apologies to Dusty's handler."

"I will."

The handler called Tito over, and they left. He wasn't the last member to approach him that night. Several members asked if Robert did training sessions, some asked if he and Dusty were looking for packmates, and some asked if they were together romantically. The pair of them had certainly caused a stir.

As he finished his shift in the pet play area, he found the Scandalous Six resting in the conversation room. He wandered over to Robert and leaned against the back of the chair, watching as Robert spoke to Freddie as he stroked a hand through Henry's hair. His cousin was laying on the sofa with his head on Robert's lap, fast asleep, if Douglas wasn't mistaken. When their conversation paused, he gained Robert's attention.

"I've had many comments about your behaviour tonight."

"Oh, really? Do tell." Robert tilted his head.

"Well, first, Tito's handler approached me asking for additional training to become like you. Then, I had someone ask if you wanted some pack mates. Someone else asked if you were in a relationship. I could go on, but we'd be here for a while. On that note, I was thinking… what do you think about providing training for the handlers here?"

Robert raised his eyebrows. "Um…maybe?"

Douglas waved his hand. "You don't have to answer now. I would need to speak with Father anyway, but it came across from many members that they would like to be as good as you are."

Robert's cheeks flushed, and he cleared his throat. "Thanks, I guess."

Douglas chuckled, careful to keep the noise low so he didn't wake Henry. "You did well. Keep it up."

"Douglas!" Freddie said, shaking his head.

"What? I complimented him."

The rest of them laughed, and Henry slept on.

## 29

## HENRY

"Well, if it isn't little Henry and his big bad bodyguard."

Henry froze as fear wormed its way through his limbs, stopping him in his tracks. The voice had come from behind him, and he couldn't turn around. He thought he'd recovered from the impulse to give Charles more power, but obviously, he was still a work in progress. Robert tightened his grip on Henry's hand, whether it was in support or fear of his own, he didn't know, but it gave him courage.

Inhaling, he spun on his heel. "What do you want, Charles?"

They were at a royal event—a charity fundraiser that had merged with Douglas's birthday celebration. Uncle Andrew couldn't keep them away without the media wondering why because Aunt Charlotte and Charles often supported these types of events. If they wanted to keep their true colours from being dragged through the spot-light, they needed to let it play out.

Charles sneered. "I want all *you* people to go back under the rocks you came from."

Henry snorted. "Not going to happen. Anything else?"

Charles narrowed his eyes and flexed his jaw. "What about your little boyfriend there? How can you even put up with someone who looks like that but bosses you around? Or is it because he looks more like a girl that you can take it?" Charles laughed. "I bet that's it, isn't it? Dear Robert looks enough like a girl that you can pretend you're gay just to get some."

Henry glanced at Robert, seeing the strain on his face. He knew the words would be knives carving into the wall he'd put up between them and the bullies, but it would take its toll. Saying stuff about him was one thing. Focusing on Robert was entirely another. Henry raged, "If you think Robert looks like a girl, you need your eyes tested. Or maybe you're projecting, and you're aroused by him and need something to focus on to stop you from thinking you're gay yourself."

Charles stepped closer, but not enough for either to touch, which Henry was grateful for. "I'm not gay, asshole. That curse word is just for the likes of you." Charles pulled himself straighter after a glance behind Henry.

Henry peered over his shoulder to see his Scandalous Six comrades closing in behind him. He faced Charles again, his fear receding now that more support was behind him.

"It's a word I will happily wear, Charles. Shame you can't say the same."

"I'm *not* gay!"

Henry shrugged. "Doesn't matter if you are or not. The LGBTQ+ community will not disappear. You can rant and rave about us as much as you want; we're here to stay."

Charles hummed. "We'll see about that." He glared at each person. "You'd do well to align with better allies. Things are going to change." He stepped back as if he didn't want to turn his back on them.

Henry took a small amount of pleasure in that thought. No one said anything until Charles was gone, then he closed his eyes and breathed, calming his racing heart. Robert pulled him into his chest, and Henry wrapped his arms around him, inhaling his comforting scent.

"We need to talk to Father. Something is in the works, and I don't think we're going to like what it is," Frederick said.

Henry lifted his head. "How are we going to find out what their plans are?"

Freddie shook his head. "We won't be able to. They'll keep everything close to their chests now. I doubt we'll find anything out until it's too late unless we can find a defector from their group."

"A defector?" Henry frowned and tried to follow his train of thought. He didn't know everyone who worked with Aunt Charlotte or Charles, but he knew some. Who might help them? He shook his head. "I can't think of anyone who might do it from those I know of."

"It's fine. If you think of someone, though, let me

know, and I can get someone to work on them. Same goes for any of you. If you see them interacting with anyone, make a list, and we can look into each one. We might be able to speak to Albert, too, but I don't want to push him too hard at the moment."

"Henry?"

Henry spun around at the familiar voice. His eyes focused on Kean, and his heart pounded. What did he want?

"Do you want to speak with him?" Patrick whispered in his ear.

Henry cleared his throat, his focus never wavering from his ex-best friend. "I suppose it's about time. It has been over a year."

Someone squeezed his hand, and he transferred his gaze to Robert. "I'll let you speak with him. You need to clear the air."

"No," Henry said. "Stay."

Robert curled the corner of his mouth. "No. Speak to him alone. Explain things. If he's anything like the man you told me he was, he'll understand. Maybe you can repair your friendship."

Henry swallowed hard. "And if I can't?"

Robert cupped his cheek. "Then he wasn't worthy of you, anyway." He lifted onto his toes and pecked Henry on the lips. "Either way, you'll have closure."

George squeezed his shoulder. "I'll stay with Robert. We'll find Mother or Aunt Victoria and stay close by. You don't need to worry about him."

"Thanks." He turned back to Robert. "Are you sure you don't want to stay? I have nothing to hide from you."

Robert smiled. "I know you don't. That's why I'm happy letting you deal with him. I trust you. I love you."

Henry ducked his head and smiled. "I love you."

Robert kissed his cheek and wandered off with his family. Henry watched them go and, when they disappeared around a corner, focused on Kean.

"I don't want to make you uncomfortable," Kean said, staying several feet away.

With those words, Henry exhaled and relaxed, remembering what it was like to be in his best friend's presence. "You never made me feel uncomfortable."

"Except that night."

Henry shook his head. "Even that night. I wasn't uncomfortable—except for the obvious reason." He grinned, then sighed. "I was scared, Kean. No, not scared. Petrified. If anyone but Freddie had walked in on us, I might have ended up dead."

Kean's eyes widened. "What? Why?"

"Before we get into that, and I *will* tell you the reason behind it, I want to say something. I'm sorry I walked away from our friendship and what we could have been. I believe we could've made a go of things if circumstances had been different, but," Henry licked his lips and winced, "I never felt for you what I feel for Robert. I'm sorry if that's callous of me to say, but it's the truth. I had feelings for you for years, but it pales in comparison."

Kean blinked and looked away, then studied him. "I know. It hurts, but I know. I can see a light in you that was never there, even when it was only the two of us. I've wanted to approach you for a while, but I didn't want to make you more uneasy. When you started seeing Robert and things escaped into the media, I was jealous. You still hold a piece of my heart, Henry, but I understand it will never happen. I will never, ever try to split you up. Please believe that."

"I do. You forget I know you, Kean. Almost thirty years of friendship will do that." He smirked.

"What made you run?"

Henry blew out his cheeks and paced to a seat along the edge of the hallway. Dropping into the chair, he rested his elbows on his knees and threaded his fingers together. Kean sat beside him.

"Do you remember when we were twelve and had sex education at school?" Kean nodded. "That was when I realised I was gay. My crush on you made me all kinds of nervous that year." Henry leaned back and stared across the hallway, not seeing the decorative sconces or highly polished mirrors. "The following year, I saw three men tortured for being gay."

"What?" Kean whispered.

The images still hurt him as they whipped past in his head. "From that moment forth, I hid who I was."

"I wondered why we seemed on the same page, then you changed. You'd flinch whenever I touched you or was too close. I thought it was just me."

Henry shook his head. "They got into my head. It's taken Robert and my family to help me claw my way out of the darkness."

They were silent for a few minutes. "Did anything ever happen to you?" Kean asked.

"No. There were threats, but nothing actually happened. The threats were enough, though."

Kean rubbed his hands over his face. "I can't believe it. Have they stopped?"

Henry shook his head. "They're just more discreet now."

"Fuck."

Henry snorted. "That's one way to put it." It was nice to talk about things again with Kean. He'd missed it, but he hadn't realised how much he'd missed it until it was right in front of him again. His heart lightened, and hope flowed through him. "Would you like to join the party?"

Kean bit his lip, visibly unsure. "I don't want to make Robert uncomfortable."

"He'll be fine. I want to introduce you."

"All right. Douglas will be pissed. I didn't bring a gift."

Henry chuckled. "I'm sure you can make it up to him."

They stood and wandered towards the noisy ballroom. "Does he still like cheesy crisps and dip?"

Henry laughed out loud. "Yes, he does. You'll be his best friend forever if you get him some of that."

"I'd like to think that position might have been refilled?" Kean said, a question in his tone.

Henry smiled across at him. "I don't know. I'll have to consider what I get from it." More seriously, he said, "I'll speak to Robert."

Kean nudged his shoulder and grinned. "One step at a time. I get it."

They found Robert chatting with Henry's mother and Aunt Louisa. Henry slid in beside his boyfriend and kissed his cheek.

"Everything okay?" Robert asked, glancing at Kean.

Henry smiled. "Yeah, they're good."

"Kean! It's nice to see you again. How have you been?" Victoria embraced his best friend. "You must come over for dinner soon." She turned to Robert. "Have you met Henry's friend?"

Henry chuckled. "I was coming to do just that, Mother, but you almost beat me to it. Robert, this is Kean. Kean, Robert."

They shook hands.

"You should definitely come over for dinner, Kean. You have plenty of information I'm sure this family is hiding from me," Robert said, and with those words, Henry knew they would get along well. He made a mental note to thank Robert later.

Victoria waved a finger at Robert. "Some things you need to figure out yourself." She focused on Henry. "Henry, would you take your dear mother on a whirl around the dance floor?"

"Of course." He kissed Robert's cheek. "I'll be back in a few minutes."

"Have fun."

He held out his arm for his mother and guided her through the guests to the small dance floor in the centre of the room. The layout reminded him of those scenes in historical films or programmes where the guests waited around the perimeter, and the main characters were dancing in the middle of them. He would've preferred not to be the centre of the attention, but it was unavoidable.

As soon as he took his mother into his arms, she said, "I'm glad you've found your way back to Kean. He's a lovely boy, and I know he's struggled for the past year."

Henry frowned. "What do you mean?"

Victoria gave a sad smile. "He loves you, Henry. He always has."

Henry swallowed hard, blinking back tears. "I loved him for a long time."

"You were never meant to be together, but it was painful for him. I've spoken to him several times over the past year. Things with his father are difficult, and I'm glad you've found your way back to each other. The support you have given him over the years has been what's kept Kean going when you weren't there."

Henry frowned. He didn't know what his mother was talking about. "Why has it been difficult?"

Victoria narrowed her eyes at him. "His brother died six months ago. Did you not know?"

Henry missed a step as memories of ignoring phone calls and walking the other way when Kean approached bombarded him. "Oh, my god. How can he ever forgive me?"

Victoria stopped, cupping his face. "You're here now. That's all that matters."

"But I ignored him when he needed me!"

"I didn't realise you didn't know; otherwise, I would've told you. I thought you were dealing with it in your own way."

Kean's brother, Simon, was five years younger than they were and often tried to tag along with them. Henry would've been happy to include him, but Kean wanted him gone. Henry didn't persuade Kean otherwise. Now, he wished they'd included him.

"How?"

Victoria's expression closed down. "Overdose."

Henry shut his eyes and lowered his head. He wished he could rewind the past year and know what he knew now. He'd never start a relationship with Kean, he'd wait for Robert, but maybe they could've saved his brother.

"Come on. Let's go back. I'm sure you want to spend more time with Kean."

His mother held the crook of his elbow as they weaved through the crowd back to the table where Aunt Louisa, Robert and Kean were waiting. When they arrived, they found more people sitting with them. Several of his cousins were there, as were Uncle Andrew, Uncle William and Aunt Lou. The conversation was loud and upbeat, and Henry momentarily forgot his turmoil. Robert and Kean were in the middle of a discussion about Floresco, which reminded him of Kean's father's job. Mr Seymour owned a large company that dealt with the construction of office buildings, large apartment complexes and high rises. Although Floresco would be below his higher-paying jobs, they might be able to gather some information from Kean about the best way to rebuild, as he worked alongside his father.

His mother patted his arm as she disentangled herself and drifted over to her husband. They shared a kiss, then his father rose, offering his mother his chair. Henry smiled at the move, done easily and many times over the years.

Henry grabbed a chair from a table beside them and wedged it between Robert and Patrick before sitting down and kissing the back of Robert's neck. He wouldn't interrupt their conversation. He had no idea how to fix the wrong he'd done Kean. Leaving him to grieve alone was one of the worst things he could've done.

An arm slid around his shoulder, and he glanced at Robert, not having realised they'd stopped talking. "Are you okay?"

Henry gazed at Kean. "I'm sorry about Simon. I never knew. I should've answered your calls."

Kean dropped his eyes but not before Henry saw the sheen of tears. "Thank you. You had every right not to. I understood."

"You shouldn't have had to deal with that alone. I'm sorry."

Kean nodded his head but said nothing.

Robert cleared his throat. "We were discussing the plans for Floresco. Kean has some good ideas about how to make the layout easier for me."

"That's great." Henry smiled. "He's got his father's head for business and design. He's a good man to get information from." He squinted at Robert. "I wish you would allow me to help, though."

Robert shook his head before Henry had even finished talking. "No. I appreciate the offer, as you know, but I want to do this the way I would've had to do it if I wasn't with a rich boy."

Kean snorted his drink, banging his chest when he coughed.

"Serves you right," he told Kean. "But you are with a rich boy, sweetheart. Why not take advantage."

Robert narrowed his eyes. "You know why."

Henry sighed. "All right."

Kean smirked. "You can tell who's the boss of your relationship."

They laughed, and Henry was once again reminded of how things could've been if he'd never missed that year with Kean. He could've had this escape from reality instead of dealing with the shit Charles and Aunt Charlotte had been throwing his way. His mother believed in Fate and that things happened for a reason. He needed to believe that, too, because otherwise, they'd wasted many months.

He caught Kean's twinkling eyes before the man said, "When's the wedding?"

## 30

## ROBERT

Robert choked on his drink. "I'm not sure we're ready for that just yet, Kean. We've only known each other for two months. I think we can put that on the back burner for now."

Although Robert said the words, he'd love nothing more than to propose to Henry. The man was everything he had ever hoped for in a life partner, and he couldn't imagine not being with him. There were many things he loved about him, but it was the ability to let Robert deal with Floresco on his own that hit hardest at the moment. Taking Henry's help would make the process easier, but he didn't want to be known as taking the prince's money this early in their relationship. Maybe, when they'd been together for years, Robert might be more agreeable to Henry's generosity, but for now, he was content doing things the long way around. Even if that meant waiting several months or even a year before he could open the flower shop again.

The idea of spending his life with Henry was not as scary as it had been when they'd first begun the uncertain journey, but as time passed, he realised just how right they were for each other, which brought him back to the subject at hand. He'd love to marry Henry, but not yet.

"I want to visit The Den again," Henry whispered in his ear.

Robert squinted at him. "Why? If I come with you, everyone will know who you are."

"I know. We'll have security, but I enjoyed it there."

Robert narrowed his eyes. "Why do you really want to go?"

Henry sighed. "I want to check in with the brown and white pup. He seemed…unhappy."

His heart ached. This man beside him had everlasting compassion and love to give. "All right. When?"

"Tomorrow?"

"Sure. I'll speak to Elton."

They spent the rest of the evening celebrating with Douglas, Maverick and the rest of Henry's family. Douglas had invited Robert's family, but they had declined. Robert had been surprised Ophelia hadn't wanted to come, but when she'd explained that she didn't want to be in a room with so many posh people, he'd laughed. He'd tried to reassure her, telling her most were just like Henry's family, but she wouldn't have it. Instead, they had decided to throw a separate party in a few days just for the Scandalous Six and their immediate family and friends.

Merging their families had been easier than they had expected, and Robert, for one, was happy for that.

"Can I come with you to The Den this time?"

George put his head between Henry's and Robert's faces with a grin. "I want to see how the other half lives."

Henry raised an eyebrow at Robert. "I don't see why not. Maybe check with security first. It's a different matter for me to be out in public than you being there. You're more important than I am."

Robert slapped his chest. "That's not true."

Henry smiled. "I meant in relation to the royal family, not anything else. He's higher up the line than I am. Hence, he needs more protection."

"But I want to chill out without having my every move watched," George whined.

Robert laughed. "Ask your security; otherwise, my answer is no."

George pouted and turned away. "Ruining all my fun," he muttered.

Henry snorted, resting his forehead on Robert's shoulder. "He's a menace. I pity the man or woman who snags him."

"They'll certainly have their hands full." He kissed Henry's temple, noticing his droopy eyelids. "Are you ready to leave?"

Henry nodded.

They said goodbye and exited into the balmy night. A valet brought their car around to them, and Robert took the wheel, nodding at the security guard he knew would follow them home. He smiled over at Henry, seeing him asleep with his head against the window. He'd been working hard the past month, trying to research the royal family's history. There were many other people doing the same thing, but Henry was in the unique position of being able to pick the brains of those around him who were more likely to spill secrets. He wouldn't disclose those secrets, but it would give some credence to his findings. What he wanted to know was the history of the club. They knew the initial bits of information about how it first came about, but since then, records were spotty.

Henry was working on getting together something based on stories from generations past. Stories that descendants may have forgotten about. Stories that were based more on fact than fiction. It might not help in the grand scheme of things, but Henry hoped getting this information together would give them something to fight Charlotte, Charles, John and Miranda. Robert wasn't sure, but all Henry's family agreed that it wouldn't hurt, whether or not it helped.

"Come on, sleepyhead. Let's get you into bed," Robert sang the rhyme his mother used to say to him as a child.

Henry roused himself enough to walk to his rooms, but Robert knew he wouldn't stay awake for long. He crooned and spoke in whispers as he encouraged Henry to undress and tucked him under the covers while he went for a shower. It was strange how quickly he'd become accustomed to living in the same room or house as Henry. He didn't feel out of place at all.

As soon as he dried off, he slid beneath the covers, wrapping his boyfriend in his arms and followed him in to sleep with a hope and a prayer that tomorrow would work out okay.

They entered The Den and darted up the stairs to Elton's office. Some people had already seen Robert, and one had assumed the pup walking next to him was someone other than Henry and threw curse words at Robert for cheating on the prince. Another had assumed, correctly, that it was Henry and wanted an autograph.

By the time they entered the office, Robert was rethinking this plan.

"I don't know if this is a good idea, Henry." He stood with his hands on his hips, staring at the prince.

"It'll be fine," Henry said after he removed his mask.

Robert inhaled and stared at the floor. "The security guards are coming onto the same floor as us. We're not leaving them downstairs this time."

"Okay."

Elton cleared his throat. "Everything okay?"

"I have a feeling we'll be inundated with people wanting to see the prince once they realise he's here," Robert said. "We have two security guards waiting downstairs and two more in a car outside. People will text their friends soon, and more people will show up. I never thought I'd have to think about a security risk by being your boyfriend." He smiled to lessen the sting of his words.

Henry rolled his eyes. "You don't need to think about

security. That's what the security guards are for. You just look after me, or rather Dusty."

"It's easier said than done, Henry."

Henry stepped closer. "Look, if it gets to be too much, we'll leave. I don't even know if that pup is here. We'll look and stay for a short time, but if there's any trouble, we're gone. All right?"

Robert gazed at the man who was so caring about other people that he'd put his own safety at risk. "When I say it's time to leave, we leave. No arguments."

"Okay."

Robert glanced at Elton. "This is a bad idea. George's security team had the right idea saying he couldn't come."

Elton grinned. "Maybe. Maybe not."

"You're no bloody help." Robert threw his hands up in the air. "Come on. Let's get this over with."

Henry smiled and kissed Robert before sliding his mask back into place. They exited the office with a last farewell to Elton and made their way to the upper bowels of The Den, with the security team following behind. Robert checked where the men situated themselves—one in each diagonal corner—and told Dusty to present.

The noise of the room gradually lowered until there was barely any sound apart from the music, but Robert ignored it. He strode to the mats and sat down where he usually did. He inhaled and smiled at Dusty. "Go on, Dusty. Go play."

Dusty yipped and ran off. Robert leaned back and glanced around the room, noticing most people were looking and pointing their way. Again, he ignored it and focused on seeing if he could find the brown and white pup Henry was concerned about. He couldn't see the pup, but he'd give Dusty time to play, then call him back to leave. He didn't want them to be swamped as they tried to leave the club.

"Excuse me?" Robert turned to the voice. "Is that Prince Henry?"

Robert inhaled and stared at the woman steadily. "That is Dusty, my pup."

"I know he's a pup but is it Prince Henry underneath?"

"Why do you think you can ask that question? If he wanted to announce who he was, he wouldn't have worn the mask, would he? Let him be the pup he's come here to be. It doesn't matter who he is when he's outside of these walls. That's none of your concern."

He turned away. He heard the woman muttering, something unkind, he was sure, but he didn't care. He'd say the same thing to anyone who dared approach him.

"I'm surprised you got up the nerve to come back here."

Robert widened his eyes as he heard a voice he'd never expected to hear again. He stood and whirled around. "You need to get out of here. You know you're not allowed within five hundred feet of me, Vincent."

"Yeah, well. Who's going to tell? You?" Vincent sneered. "I doubt it. Not when you're busy ensuring your pup is safe."

Robert glanced over his shoulder to find the pup in question waiting behind him. "I can do both."

"We were here first. If anyone should leave, it's you."

Robert narrowed his eyes. "Who are you here with, Vincent?"

The man smirked. "I have my own pup. Barney! Heel."

Robert winced at the tone of voice used, but a pup came bounding up and presented beside Vincent. The brown and white pup they'd been looking for. Robert sighed. This was going to get ugly.

"Barney, you need to come over to me. It's okay. You'll be safe with me, I promise," Robert said.

Barney stayed still, and it surprised Robert that Vincent hadn't argued until he said, "I've trained him well, Robert. There's no need for him to go anywhere but with me."

Robert stared into the pup's eyes, seeing the tears brimming even through the neoprene suit. "Barney." He lowered his voice and crouched. "You don't need to stay with him. I know he's not looking after you. You'll be safe with us."

"Barney, do not move." Vincent's voice was like a whip through the air.

Robert could see Barney was wavering. Dusty came and pressed against Robert's side, yipping quietly. Robert rested his hand on his head. Barney's paws moved, and Robert's heart pounded.

"Barney, stay."

Robert stared at Barney, never breaking his gaze, and lowered his head in a slow nod. He saw the moment Barney was going to move, but Vincent must've too because as Barney stepped away, Vincent's foot flew out and caught Barney in the side, shoving him several feet away from them.

"You despicable animal! You dare to defy me!" Vincent stepped closer, but within seconds, the police were cuffing his arms behind his back.

"Vincent Dwyer, you are under arrest for assault and for ignoring your restraining order. You have the right to remain silent. Anything you do say can and will be used against you in a court of law."

The two police officers dragged Vincent away as he screamed his displeasure. Robert had rushed over to Barney when Vincent had been grabbed, and the pup was okay. He'd be extremely bruised the following day, but he'd be fine. Robert raised his hand as Dusty went to remove his mask.

"Not yet." Dusty whined. "Let's get him to Elton's office."

They each took one of Barney's arms and helped him to the smaller room. When Elton saw Barney, he called down for some ice and the first aid kit. Once it had arrived, the door closed, and Henry removed his mask.

"Are you okay?" he asked Barney, holding the ice to his ribs for him.

Barney hesitated, then pulled his hood from his head. His sweaty brown hair fell in waves down to his ears, and his flushed, tanned face showed deep lines from not only the hood but possibly years of being outside in the sun.

"Thank you. Both of you. I wasn't sure I'd ever be able to get away from him." Barney's accent was a strong East End one.

Robert crouched beside his seat. "You're welcome. I wish you hadn't had to go through that. I didn't realise you were with Vincent; otherwise, we would've done something earlier."

"It's okay."

"Well, I'm Robert, and this is Henry, and that is Elton. What's your name?"

"Liam."

"Nice to meet you, Liam," Henry said. "How long have you been a pup?"

Liam's eyes widened a bit when Henry spoke. "Um… around two years. I've been moving around a lot and haven't found somewhere to settle down."

"I'm sorry you ended up here, but I'm not sorry we met you." Henry smiled, and Liam relaxed.

"I can't believe the freaking prince is coming to the club." Liam glanced at Elton and grimaced. "Sorry, no offence."

Elton waved his hand. "None taken. I was surprised, too." He glanced at Robert. "Vincent is gone, but there are a few people milling around outside waiting for you. I would recommend leaving sooner rather than later."

Robert nodded. "We'll head out now." He shared a look with Elton, who nodded. "Liam, Elton will look after you now, but if you ever need anything. Even if just a handler for a night, get Elton to contact me. We can get it arranged with someone who will look after you better than that asshole did."

"Thank you."

Robert and Henry shook Elton's hand, and they

escaped down the stairs after Henry donned his mask. The security guards were waiting for them at the bottom and ushered them into the chilly night air as soon as they joined them. They climbed into the waiting car while approximately thirty people tried to get photos of them. Their shouts and screams followed them until they turned out of the car park. When they were five minutes away, Henry removed his mask.

"That went better than I thought it would," Henry said with a smile. Robert stared at him and raised his eyebrows, not saying a word. "What? It did!"

Robert shook his head and snorted. "I suppose it could've been worse, but I wish I didn't have a run-in with Vincent. I could've done without that."

"I should've known Liam could've been with Vincent. It never occurred to me he'd been present every time Liam had been there."

"It's sorted now. That's the main thing. Let's not go through that again, eh?" Robert said.

"Deal." Henry laid his head on Robert's shoulder and closed his eyes. "I didn't play much, but I'm still tired."

Robert chuckled. "You're always tired after being Dusty, even if it's just for half an hour." He kissed his head. "You can rest at home."

"Hmm."

Robert smiled, knowing Henry would be asleep within seconds. His phone buzzed in his pocket, and he removed it, trying not to jostle Henry.

. . .

*GEORGE: I'm pouting because you're there, and I'm not. It's not fair.*

*ROBERT: Well, if you're around when we get back in ten minutes, you'll get to hear what we got up to. It was a riot.*

*GEORGE: I'm there.*

Robert smiled and relaxed back. He knew George wanted to go, but after tonight, he'd be siding with all the other people who said it was a bad idea, but he knew that wouldn't dissuade George.

By the time they arrived, there were three cars in the driveway. The traffic had held them up, and it had taken longer than the ten minutes he'd told George. Robert woke Henry, and they stumbled through the hallways to Henry's wing. They found George, Douglas, Maverick, Freddie, Damon, Patrick and Christian waiting for them.

Robert raised his eyebrows. "I thought the party was tomorrow."

George smiled. "I thought they might want to hear what went down tonight. We can all have a sleepover like we used to when we were younger. What do you think?"

Henry groaned and rubbed his face. "I'm going to shower before I deal with him."

Robert hid his smile behind his hand and nodded. "See you in a few minutes."

He watched Henry traipse to his bedroom and close the door behind him.

"How did it go?" Freddie asked.

"Well, we found the pup. Turns out he was Vincent's," Robert said, dropping into a seat.

"What the hell?" Patrick said, standing to pace.

"Was Vincent there?" Maverick asked.

Robert nodded. "Yeah. We had an altercation, but the police took him away. We don't need to worry about him for a while. They took him in for ignoring the restraining order but also assault because, in plain view of many witnesses, he kicked his pup. We helped the pup afterwards, and Elton is now taking care of him."

"I'm glad Vincent's being dealt with. I was tempted to find some way to make him disappear," Douglas said.

"You're not the only one," Damon agreed.

Everyone grabbed drinks, and Robert answered the door when someone knocked. He opened it to several household staff.

"Princess Victoria asked us to bring you some food, sir."

Robert smiled and let them in. After filling the large side table with the various plates, they disappeared again. Henry stepped up beside him, and Robert slid his arm around his waist.

"Your mother is awesome."

Henry smiled. "I know."

"So is your family." He gestured around the room.

Henry grinned. "I know."

"So are you."

"I know. You tell me enough."

Robert kissed him.

## 31

# FREDERICK

Freddie slipped out of Henry's room and into the hallway, closing the door firmly behind him. He pulled his phone from his pocket and dialled, resting it against his ear.

"Commissioner, it's Frederick Sutcliffe. I wondered if I could speak with you for a moment."

"Of course, Your Highness. How can I help?"

Henry's door opened, and Damon exited, coming to stand in front of him.

Freddie met his gaze. "I believe one Vincent Dwyer was taken into custody today. I would like more information, if possible, please." Freddie leaned back against the wall and locked eyes with Damon.

Silence met his request until the Commissioner cleared his throat. "Bear with me, Your Highness."

"Thank you, sir."

The phone went silent, and Freddie assumed he had

put him on hold, but he wouldn't take the risk by saying something incriminating. The corner of Damon's mouth quirked up as he crossed his arms over his chest and leaned against the opposite wall.

"Prince Frederick?"

"Yes, sir."

"We arrested Vincent Dwyer for ignoring a restraining order and assault. Apparently, he was in the same club as someone he shouldn't be near, a Robert Martin, and assaulted a fellow clubgoer by kicking him in the ribs. The officers on the case are speaking with Vincent and his lawyer as we speak."

"May I be frank, Commissioner?"

"By all means."

"I would like to see Vincent Dwyer on the inside of a prison with no hope of parole. Is that possible?"

The Commissioner sniffed, and Freddie heard a tapping on the other end of the line. "There has to be some evidence to make this possible, Your Highness. I can't make the request without it being justified."

"Oh, trust me, Commissioner, it's justified, but I will see the evidence on your desk first thing in the morning. If you would be so kind as to keep me updated, I would appreciate it."

"Will do."

Freddie closed his phone.

"Are you pushing your title again, Freddie?" Damon said with a smile.

Freddie winked. "Maybe."

Damon chuckled, the sound dark and deep. "Sometimes, I wonder if you have more sway than your father does."

"No chance. No one would say no to him. There are plenty of people who would say and have said no to me."

Damon stared at him. "Hmm."

Freddie lifted his phone again. "One more call to make."

"Who this time?"

He held up his hand. "Good evening, Mr Franks. I believe we have some acquaintances."

"And who might they be?"

"One Robert Martin and Georgie Cliff." Damon raised an eyebrow.

"I can see you're right. Might I ask who I'm speaking with?"

"Someone who is working in their best interests. I hear there was an altercation tonight between Vincent Dwyer and a pup named Liam. I would like to inquire how Liam is doing."

The owner of The Den sighed. "He's fine. A little bruised, but his ego more than anything. He should've known better than to deal with Vincent, but..." The man didn't need to finish his sentence.

"I wondered whether you could ask Liam if there would be any chance we could talk. He might have information that would help us keep Vincent Dwyer from the public. He may not even realise he has such information."

Mr Franks chuckled. "I can certainly ask the question. How can I reach you...?"

"Call me Fred."

Damon snorted and held a hand over his mouth.

"Okay…Fred. Can I use this number?"

"Please do, and thank you." He ended the call and slid his phone back into his pocket. "What were you laughing at?"

"You are so not a Fred," Damon said, barely holding in his laughter as he stood from his lean.

Freddie stepped closer. "Why not? It could be my business name."

Damon shook his head. "No way. You are not a Fred. At all. Ever."

Freddie shouldered Damon, pushing him into the wall, and rested his hands on either side of his best friend's head. "You'd be surprised who I could be. I have many aliases, some you don't know about."

Damon swallowed but said nothing. Freddie grinned and pushed away from the wall, sliding his hands into his pockets and curling them into fists. He entered Henry's room and ignored the need to be close to Damon. What the hell had that been about?

## 32

## HENRY

*Eight months later*

"Thank you all for coming," Robert said as he stood in front of his newly rebuilt shop. "I won't keep you too long, as I know you probably have a million errands to run, but I wanted to take a few minutes to thank those who have helped make this happen. Some of you have donated your time to help refurbish the interior. Some of you have donated some money towards the costs of strengthening the walls so the apartment above the shop could still be used. Something the insurance didn't cover. Some of you have donated furniture to replace that which was smoke-damaged. I appreciate every one of you. Although I will not be living in the apartment any longer," he glanced at Henry with a smile,

"I will rent it out to someone who needs it more than I do. Without further ado, I deem Floresco—take two—officially open."

Henry waited until Robert joined him at the door, then held out the ceremonial scissors for him to cut the ribbon. As he did, cheers and applause rose from the onlookers, and lights flashed from the photographers.

"And as a surprise, I will serve the first customer!"

Henry glanced over his shoulder at George, who was standing at the microphone with a huge grin on his face. He shook his head and waved for Robert and George to precede him into the shop. He wedged the door open to let customers come in as they pleased.

"Really, George? Do you even know how to work the till?" Robert asked, trying to hide his smirk when George faltered.

"It can't be that hard."

His cousin rounded the counter and stared at the till as if it was a puzzle he needed to finish. Henry studied the shop, remembering what it had looked like in its first incarnation. All down one side of the shop, they had coated the entire wall with the different varieties of flowers Robert now sold. He had set them up, in colour order, and it looked like a rainbow had thrown up in there —Robert had smacked him when he'd made that comment earlier—but the effect was stunning. The counter now sat at the rear of the shop on the right, with a door to the side, which led to the back rooms. In front of the counter were shelves full of different vases, boxes and containers that customers could choose for arrangements.

Running along the opposite wall to the flowers were shelves with ready-made arrangements, both fake and real, accessories, greeting cards, ribbons and small gift ideas like candles.

Henry loved every bit of the shop. The displays Robert had created for the windows were a work of art, even if he might be a little biased.

"I'm sure I can figure it out," George muttered.

Robert chuckled. "I'll be right here to help if there are any problems."

"Prince George?" Henry peered at the photographer who'd approached the counter. "Could I take a photo of you serving the first customer?"

George glanced at Robert, who nodded. "Sure. You'll need to ask the customer for their permission first, of course."

The photographer smiled. "Of course. Thank you."

Henry felt a little out of his depth as he knew nothing about running a flower shop, even after being with Robert for so long. He knew about flowers though, that was it.

"I'll head into the back to get everyone a drink if you don't need me here," he told Robert.

"No, that's great. Thank you, dear." Robert winked. He knew how uncomfortable he was.

"George, do you want tea?"

George cocked his head. "Do you have coffee?"

"Yes."

"That will go nicely with some fudge," George teased.

"Leave my fudge alone." Henry narrowed his eyes at his cousin.

That was the other thing Robert had insisted upon for the opening. A fridge full of fudge for the customers. They'd bought some large chunks from a local and had it cut into small bite-sized pieces, then Robert had placed a couple of small bowls on the counter for customers to help themselves. Robert thought it highly amusing to watch Henry give evil looks to anyone who took a piece.

"There is plenty left," Robert said.

Henry huffed. "Call me when George makes the sale. I want to watch."

"Will do," Robert said and turned his attention to a customer. "How can I help?"

"I'd like to order some bouquets for a funeral, please."

The request saddened Henry, but he knew it was part of life. He wandered down the corridor to the backroom, which was a lot chillier than the front of the shop. Robert had told him it was to keep the flowers from wilting, making it like a fridge, just not as cold. It was *colder*, though, because Finn and Naomi wore jumpers and gilets, and goosebumps rose on Henry's skin.

"How's it going out there?" Finn asked.

"Good. No sales yet, but plenty of people are looking around. George is serving the first customer, so that should be interesting. I'm making drinks. Would either of you like one?"

"Yes, please!" Naomi shouted. "I need something to warm me up. I'm sure this area is colder than it was in the first shop."

Henry laughed and headed back down the corridor to the small kitchen area. He filled the kettle and switched it on before Robert called him. He hurried back to the front area to see the photographer hovering over George and a customer.

"Okay, sir. Let's get that put in for you." George bit his lip, his hand hovering over the keys before pressing several, then pausing again. "Robert, which is the subtotal button?" he murmured.

"The blue one."

George pressed it. "That will be fourteen ninety-nine, please."

The man held up a card and smiled. George froze, then smiled, strained as it was. He grabbed the card machine, pressed some buttons and held the machine out to the man. The man held the card over the machine, it beeped, and George took it back before hesitating again.

Robert leaned closer and whispered, "The green one."

George pressed the green button on the till, and it made some noises before producing a receipt. "There we go, sir. All done. Have a wonderful day."

"Thank you, Your Highness."

Henry watched George as his cousin stared after the man with a small frown on his face. When the customer disappeared out of the shop, George shook himself and smiled. "That wasn't too difficult."

"Good job."

Henry grinned and went to finish the drinks, handing them out once ready. The day went by quickly. George left after an hour of being a nuisance, and Robert told Henry he could go if he wanted to, but Henry wanted to show his support. If all he could do was make sure everyone had plenty to drink, then he could do that. Although he took a trip to the nearby bakery to buy some lunch for the staff, including some treats. He had an underlying reason, though. If he brought them treats, they might leave his fudge alone.

By the time the shop closed at six o'clock, all of them were wiped out. Robert had let Finn and Naomi leave at five, so the last hour, which was usually the quietest, was just him and Robert. It was nice to work side by side for the few customers who came, and Henry became a dab hand at working the till. He could preach to George about that later.

"Are you ready for dinner?" he asked.

Robert groaned. "So ready. I'm starving."

Henry drove them back home, and he remembered the conversation they'd had about Robert moving in with him. Robert's mother had wanted him to live back at home while the renovations on the flower shop were taking place, but Robert had told Henry that he'd prefer not to because he'd never be able to leave again. Henry had jumped at the chance to invite Robert to stay indefinitely, but initially, Robert had been hesitant. It had taken a conversation with Henry's mother for Robert to agree. He didn't know what his mother had discussed with Robert, but he would be forever grateful.

Although Robert had refused help with the funding for the shop's refurbishment, he had allowed Henry to help him replace the clothes he'd lost in the fire. They'd reclaimed some items from the apartment above the shop, but a lot of it had been extremely smoke-damaged, and no amount of washing had taken the smell away. Robert had agreed that Henry could pay for some new items.

Henry being Henry, he went a little overboard, and it had been their first huge argument. Since then, he'd been less extravagant, only buying one or two small things here or there. Robert had been completely right, but Henry had been excited and hadn't been able to stop himself.

"What are you thinking about over there?" Robert's sleepy voice made him smile.

"About how far we've come since we first met ten months ago."

"Do all you princes work quickly in your relationships?" Henry frowned at him. "I mean, I was talking to Maverick, and he mentioned how quickly Douglas persuaded him to have a relationship and move in. I wondered if this was a genetic disorder."

A grin accompanied Robert's words, and Henry shook his head and rolled his eyes. "We just know when to grab hold of a good thing and never let it go, I suppose."

"I'll have to warn any suitors for the rest of the family. Fair warning would've been nice."

"You don't regret a minute, stop moaning," Henry said.

"True."

They both jumped into the shower as soon as they returned and, unable to delay any longer, which upset Henry, headed for dinner with the family. His mother had made him promise they would celebrate with them that night.

Dressed in suit trousers and a shirt, Henry grasped Robert's hand and smiled. "You look gorgeous."

"Thank you, kind sir."

Robert wore red, skin-tight jeans, a white shirt secured with a red belt and several layers of necklaces over the top, and ankle boots with a small heel; his makeup, flawless as always, shimmered on his skin.

Henry squeezed his hand and led him down the hallways to the guest dining area. Why his mother had insisted on this room, he didn't know, but he followed his orders.

"I love you," Henry said before they entered.

"And I love you."

He opened the door to a cacophony of shouts and drumming. His eyes widened as he took in the room. Decorated with a multitude of banners, streamers and balloons, the room was full enough without the crowd of people waiting to greet them. Henry pulled Robert in front of him to allow him to receive the well-wishes.

"Congratulations!" Douglas shouted above the music that someone had started. "Did you have a good first day?"

Robert nodded. "Brilliant, thank you." He gestured around the room. "Was this your idea?"

Douglas frowned. "I don't know what you mean," he said in mock grumpiness, then he smiled. "No, actually, it was Patrick's idea. We just went along with it because, hello, party!"

They laughed, and Robert continued around the room, speaking with whomever he could while dragging Henry behind him. At one point, Henry had left to get them a drink and returned dutifully to his boyfriend's side. He had a plan, but he had only expected to have maybe a dozen witnesses, but this was more like three dozen. Swallowing hard, he decided to go ahead as planned and nodded at his mother, who had been looking at him in question. She beamed in reply and spoke to someone beside her.

A ding of a glass being gently tapped brought the noise level to a minimum, and someone lowered the music. Patrick Senior stood at the head of the room.

"I would like to say a few things before we carry on with the celebration. Robert, you have been a joy to add to the family, and I'm exceedingly glad you're here with us. Congratulations on the re-opening of Floresco. It's been a journey, but it will be remembered, in both incarnations, for many years to come. Henry, I will admit to being concerned about you at the beginning of the year, but that has changed. I can see a different person when I look at you now. Some of it is because you found love. Some because you found your strength. Some because you realised you could rely on your family to have your back. Regardless of where it came from, you deserve every bit of happiness."

Everyone cheered, and Henry caught his mother's eye, and she nodded.

Henry cleared his throat. "Thank you, Father. It's true that I am a different person than a year ago. Despite what my father said, all of it is because of Robert. If I hadn't met him, I don't think I would be where I am today. I'd still be the shell of a man." He stepped in front of Robert, cupping his jaw. "Thank you for taking a chance on me. I know it was difficult, but I will forever make it worth your while."

He dropped to one knee, hearing a gasp going through the guests. Glancing up at Robert, he saw tears glistening in his eyes, which overflowed when Henry pulled a small, black, velvet box from his pocket.

"I love you, Robert. Will you marry me?" His heart pounded as he waited for Robert's answer. It felt like it took years, not seconds, but when Robert nodded, an enormous sigh of relief left him. He pulled the ring from the box and slid it on Robert's finger before Robert yanked him to his feet and kissed him.

"I love you, Henry."

"Cake! Cake! Cake! Cake!"

A chant started behind them, and they turned to see a huge white and red cake sat on the table waiting for them. They stepped closer.

"Congratulations on your re-opening and engagement," Robert read. He gazed at Henry's mother. "How did you know I'd say yes?"

Victoria smiled. "I didn't, but I had Winnie leave a gap at the bottom in case you did. If you hadn't, she would've added some flowers instead."

Robert chuckled. "Mother! You knew I'd say yes," he said, hugging her.

"I know, but Victoria wanted to be sure." She grinned. "Congratulations, my dear." She hugged Robert, then Henry. "Thank you for making an honest man of him."

"Hey!" Robert said.

Henry laughed. "I think it's the other way around, Winnie."

They received well wishes from the other guests,

and Robert's mother cut the cake and doled it out to everyone. Henry nudged Robert towards a corner of the room, away from most of the guests, and stole a kiss.

"I can't believe you kept that a secret," Robert said, twining his arms around Henry's waist.

"Well, I know we said no more secrets, but this was one I couldn't tell you."

Robert smiled. "It was a lovely surprise. Thank you. The ring is gorgeous."

Henry smiled, glad he'd spoken with Winnie, Hadley and Ophelia to get their advice on which ring Robert would like best. The one he'd chosen was a white gold slim band with a rainbow of gems around it. He dropped his head, pecking kisses against Robert's mouth, and held him closely. "I wish we were alone right now," he murmured.

"Well, you're not. Get your head out of the gutter, Prince Charming."

"Get lost, George," Henry said, resuming kissing his fiance.

"No can do. Some guests need to leave, and you have a duty to say goodbye."

Henry dropped his head to Robert's shoulder and growled.

"Now, now, pup. Get back in your cage," George said.

Henry glared at him, but George grinned and left unrepentant.

"Why do I put up with him?"

"Because he's your cousin, and you love him."

"You might have to keep reminding me of that," Henry said.

Robert laughed. "Understood. Come on, let's say goodbye."

Around half the guests left after an hour of socialising, and the rest were mainly family. They cranked up the music, much to the older generation's groans, and pushed seats to the side to make a small dance area. Robert tugged on Henry's hands, ignoring his pleas, and dragged him to the floor, gripping him.

"One dance won't kill you," Robert said.

"It might."

Robert smiled. "Thank you for tonight and for every night and day before and after."

"You're welcome, my prince."

Robert chuckled. "I think you have that the wrong way around."

Henry raised his eyebrows. "You're engaged to a prince, Robert. What did you think your title would be?"

Robert froze, and his eyes widened. "Fuck."

Henry couldn't help it. He burst out laughing, tears leaking from his eyes. He had no idea how long it had been when he finally calmed down, but Robert had his hands on his hips and a frown on his face.

"Sorry," Henry said. "You could choose a different title if you don't want to be a prince, I'm sure, but you'll always be *my* prince." Henry held Robert, staring into his eyes. "Whatever you decide, I'll be with you every step of the way."

Did you enjoy this book? Pre-order Grieving Royal to see how losing someone close affects George's ability to live his life the way he would've before and who helps him through it. It will be delivered to your kindle on Feb 3, 2022.

Sign up to my newsletter to get a free prequel from Club Royal called Royal Firsts.

# ABOUT ELOUISE EAST

I am Elouise East but feel free to call me Elli. I write sweet and steamy connections in gay romance. I also touch on taboo stories under the name Elouise R East.

Books that tell the stories where friendship and family are the focal point - be it blood family or chosen - is very important to me. That's why I include a variety of personalities, talents, ages, situations and abilities as I believe a story needs, or a character needs. I want my characters to be real, to be relatable, to be free to have whatever views they tell me they have. And trust me, most of the time, I do not have *any* say in the matter!

My characters come to life on the page for me as well as my readers. Their stories unfold in front of me, and I have very little input into how they want to be shown. Just like real life, the lives of my characters change with every choice, every interaction and every conversation. And I wouldn't have it any other way.

I write books that are emotionally realistic, even if liberties are taken with other aspects of my stories. I don't know any other way to write. It comes from deep inside.

Who am I? A single parent to two children who make life worth living. An avid reader who still devours every book she can get her hands on. A student of learning about any subject that takes her fancy. An author of books she would read herself. And a romantic at heart who loves anything cheesy.

Who's in?

**<u>Stalk me here... ;-)</u>**
Website
https://elouiseeast.com/

Newsletter
https://elouiseeast.com/newsletter

All links
https://linktr.ee/elouiseeastauthor

BOOKS BY ELOUISE EAST

## CRUSH

First Kiss

Instant Desire

Primary Seduction

Deep Down

A Crush for Christmas

Life Support

Covert Strength

Love Scene

Lawful Attraction

## CLUB ROYAL

Rogue Royal

Secretive Royal

Grieving Royal, coming Feb 3, 2022

## LOVE IN FLAMES

Out of the Frying Pan

Smokescreen, coming December 2, 2021

## JUST A LITTLE CRUSH

He's Behind You

A Special Love

Three Thirds

## DADDY

Love Me, Daddy

Soothe Me, Daddy

Spoil Me, Daddy

## DARK & DIVERGENT

Forbidden Temptation

Too Many Secrets

When Fantasies Collide

## STANDALONE

Treehouse Whispers

Star-Crossed

Protecting the Thief

Sizzling Chauffeur